Population 3000

Lay Dee

First Edition
First Revision
ISBN: 978-90-829109-0-2

DEDICATION

To all my childhood bullies that made me stay inside and read,
instead of going outside and play.

CONTENTS

ACKNOWLEDGMENTS

Joris, I want to thank you for making it possible for me to write this book. Without you telling me to go for it, I probably never would have done it.

Jessie, thank you for being a great daughter and my first beta reader. I know I've hounded you to read my chapters and you did it with great dedication. I'm genuinely sorry that you now have a phobia of lawnmowers.

Elena and Logan, thank you for being the loveable little distractions you are.

Pidgie, my friend whom I have never met in person, thank you for reading my book and having it be the first book you ever read since you don't like reading books.

Hubert, thank you for creating this amazing cover free of charge for I'm just a poor person who can't afford to pay. You truly delivered!

You, the reader, for picking up this book by an unknown author and giving it a chance.

CHAPTER ONE

I live in a quiet town; it's not too big with a population of almost 3000. 2998 to be exact. Number 3000 wasn't far away though, with both Mrs. Kelly and my Mom expecting a baby. Their due dates were close together as well, which led to the townsfolks holding wagers on which of them would deliver number 3000. It would be the highest population count to date, a population of 3000 citizens was never reached before! The town was in preparation of celebrating their 3000th citizen. Not Mom and Mrs. Kelly, they were just busy doing Mom stuff, cleaning the baby's room over and over even though there was no one making it dirty. Constantly checking if they had everything in order, for when the baby arrived. It was quite the ritual to witness. Any day now, Mom kept telling me, but enough already I wanted to meet my new baby... ehm... brother? Sister? We didn't know. Mom always said that it's no fun knowing in advance. "It would be like telling you what you're getting for your birthday nine months in advance." Well, to be honest, I wouldn't mind knowing my presents nine months ahead. I figured it must be a hormone thing. Mrs. Kelly was having a baby girl and wanted the world to know. If it were up to her, she would have painted their whole house pink. Thankfully Mr. Kelly would have none of that.

He worked at the factory, a very down to earth kind of man. Tall, his shoulders covered in tattoos. He looked like a badass, but he was sweet as a kitten. I remember this one day when I fell off my bike and scraped my knee as he drove by. He instantly stopped his truck and came running over. He had a bigger scare than I did. Of course, I was screaming at the top of my lungs as if I fell into a knife, but what'd you expect, I was 4 and just scraped my knee after falling off my bicycle. He was ready to pick me up and take me to the hospital if not for Mrs. Mitchell. Mrs. Mitchell lived a few doors down, and she was my elementary school teacher at the time and has since retired... A sweet little old lady, gray curly hair, glasses, a firm stare, and a lovely warm smile. She came over with a first aid kit, cleaned my scrape, and gave me a nice band-aid with a cartoon figure on it. Like magic, my tears dried up, and I was able to ride my bicycle again. I gave them both a hug and went on my merry way home. I smiled at this thought and figured Mr. Kelly would make a great father to his daughter. He might look tough, but he had a big caring heart.

Even though our town wasn't that big, it did have a huge town square where our town hall was located. Our town hall looked like a castle that came straight out of a Disney movie, at least, from the outside. On the inside, its magnificent structure was hidden behind what the people at the time considered art, and pots filled with plants, places to sit, and office spaces with desks and filing cabinets. The grandeur from the outside definitely did not translate to the inside. The town square was surrounded by lots of bars and restaurants, an ATM machine and the odd little shop. Most shops were in the center of the town and not aligned with the square. In the center of the square was a magnificent fountain. Most days of the year the square wasn't used for much, but if there were an event, it would be held in the town square.

Old Mrs. McHenry would spend most of her days at the town square. Feeding the pigeons, watching the people go by. She used to be a seamstress but had retired long ago. Mr. McHenry died years before I was born, so there isn't much I can tell about him. He used to work at the bank as a teller, that's all I know. Mrs. McHenry was a bit unconventional; she still made all her clothing herself, the only thing she would ever buy was fabric from the weekly market at the town square. She made the most colorful pieces of clothing. She once made a jumpsuit with a bright parrot pattern. I swear, if you'd turn off the lights, it would probably still light the room, that's how bright the colors were. Usually, she was just sitting there mumbling to herself or to the birds she was feeding. Scaring away the odd cat that came to close for her liking. But this particular day she sat there, staring into the distance, repeating the same thing over and over again. "It's coming; you can't run, you can't hide, it's coming." We, Roger and I, just figured the old bint finally lost it, shrugged and continued on our way to Mr. Tyler's antique shop.

Mr. Tyler, or Adam I should say for he doesn't like to be called mister, owns a big antique and oddities shop that is aligned to the town square. Despite him selling weird and old stuff, Adam wasn't weird or old at all. Well, maybe he was a bit strange. He could tell you some odd stories about the items in his store. There are shrunken heads with certificates of authenticity! He could tell you everything about where they came from up until details on the tribesman that actually shrunk them. He was a great storyteller. His crown piece, standing in the center of his shop was a dining set. A large square table with oval edges, it had four chairs on each side and one chair at each head. It could seat ten people for dinner easily. The seats looked as if they were the most comfortable seats ever made. They had the most beautiful pattern. I wouldn't know though; he wouldn't let anyone sit on them. "Sitting on it is buying it," he yelled out if you even looked in their direction. I wouldn't dare sit on them, knowing the nifty price he put on it. The table was set with the most exquisite tableware, cutlery, and glasses and let's not forget the gold and silver napkin rings, with satin napkins being held. It looked fit for a king!

Where it truly came from, no one knew, but that never stopped Adam. He would make up the story as he went along. This one time it was a stonemasons table, another time it was the round table for the Knights of the Round Table, and of course "the knights didn't have a real round table, no one at that time would have made a round table!" When he was telling you a story, he could tell you the biggest lies and yet, you'd still believe him. This brief moment in time, it all appeared true. He knew how to draw you into what he was making you believe. We all loved listening to his stories. Unfortunately, we weren't here for his stories. Mom had made it abundantly clear that she wants an antique pram for the baby, so off to the antique shop, we went. Just Roger and I. Mom wasn't lying when she said any day now; she looked ready to explode.

When we entered the antique shop, Adam was engaged in conversation with a man. I had never seen this man before, he was dressed in a smart suit and looked really slick, but there was something off-putting about him. It appeared they were wrapping up their conversation as we entered. As the man left the shop, I gave Adam a look that said nothing other than "who was that man," Adam greeted us with a warm smile. He apologized and said that the man was selling his collection of antique books, and Adam was interested in buying them. Adam turned to Roger and said that he had found the perfect antique pram for only $100 and motioned for us to follow him into the shop. It was the cutest pram I've ever seen. It was Ivory in color, looked completely handmade, and had these huge wheels with a beautiful little Moses basket on top. "Fit for a little prince or princess," Adam said. Roger wasn't too pleased with the price, but then again, nothing ever seemed to please Roger. Roger wasn't my father, nor my father figure. To me, he was merely my mom's boyfriend, and later, my mom's husband.

They met two years ago at some new age festival, and within six months they were married. Now two years later, they were expecting their first child together.

Roger never took an interest in me, and I was completely fine with that. I didn't care much for him either. Always trying to solve everything with homeopathic nonsense and homemade ointments. In medieval times they would probably have burned him at the stake for being a witch! I sometimes long for those medieval times. The way he appears to care about nature, I am surprised by his occupation. He's a delivery truck driver, and his excuse is that he always takes the shortest routes which might not be the most convenient or obvious, but do the least harm to nature. He could get a cargo bike and deliver his goods that way, guess that would be too much of an effort. At least Mom appeared to be happy with him, and that's all that matters to me. Roger was trying to get something off the price, but Adam wouldn't budge. He never lowered his prices. At the entrance to the store, there was a sign stating that all prices are fixed, but you are always welcome to pay more. Roger wouldn't dare to come home to Mom without the pram. As soon as Mom found out she was pregnant, she expressed her wish of having an antique pram for the baby. She gave Adam the order to look for one straight away. Now Adam had finally found one, and it was beautiful, there was no way Roger could come home without it. Reluctantly he paid the $100, and we left the store with the pram.

On our way home, Roger kept on complaining about how the price was too high and how he could have bought a state of the art brand new one for that price. I just started listening to music and put on my headphones. Picturing myself pushing the pram with my new baby brother or sister in it. Have all my friends come and take a look, the oohs and aahs on how cute the baby would be. I didn't care if the baby would be citizen 2999 or citizen 3000. I just wanted it to be here already so I could hold it, hug it, play with it, and teach it things. But no, the little bugger was still happy where it was. Besides Mom looking ready to explode any minute, there were no signs of the baby actually making any attempts to come out yet. Mom's due date was 4 days away, and Mrs. Kelly's due date was only a day before moms. Mom really couldn't care less who went into labor first and who had their child last; all she wanted was for it to be over. She was fed up with looking like a baby elephant, being unable to bend over to pick something off the floor or do a simple task like tying her shoelaces. All she wanted was to have her newborn happy and healthy in her arms and have her mobility back!

She didn't have the easiest of pregnancies. She was in a lot of pain with every movement, so I definitely could understand she wanted it to be over for obvious reasons. I just wanted it to be over, so I was no longer alone. I've been an only child for so long, and I was looking forward to having a sibling. Even though my friends who had one or more siblings kept telling me it wasn't as fun as it seemed, I still wanted my sibling to be here already. I already loved the little worm and couldn't wait to teach it about boys or girls, or both. Take it to the park, hold picnics, teach it to walk, run, swim, dance, love, everything! Unfortunately, we still had to wait for the little bugger to decide it was time to come out. Mrs. Kelly's due date arrived. The town was waiting in anticipation... as if a baby would meet an appointment set by a doctor based on a good guesstimate. Mrs. Kelly's due date also went, and none of the babies announced themselves yet. Mom's due date came and went in the same matter.

It was the heart of summer, School had ended a few weeks ago and was close to starting again. All my friends were away on holiday. I was stuck in our old town. With Mom being pregnant, we couldn't go on holiday. One day she would make it up to me, at least that's what she kept on saying. It was almost as if she felt guilty that we couldn't go away on holiday. I didn't blame her though. I was just excited to meet my new baby brother or sister. I have been an only child all my life. I couldn't wait to meet the little worm. I wondered if our lives would change a lot. It probably would with a little infant. I just hoped it wouldn't turn out to be a cry baby. I know that babies cry, but you have those that never seem to stop crying. Please don't let it be one of those. Just let it be a happy, healthy baby.

My friends were scheduled to return in a few weeks. The babies would have been born by then. They would probably have the wildest stories of the things they did on holiday whereas I could tell them about the babies and the party in town. Who won the bet and what they won. At least I would be here for our town's new milestone. I would be a witness to this moment of history in the making. I kept trying to convince myself that this too was a nice thing to witness. It didn't beat long walks at the beach, having fun in water parks, staying up late, and swimming at the hotel swimming pool, falling in love with someone from another country only for the few weeks on holiday. I was jealous, I didn't mind staying home to help Mom around the house awaiting the arrival of the baby, but I sure wouldn't have minded going on holiday either. I just had to live vicariously through my friends to enjoy their holidays this year. I couldn't wait for their return.

Now my days were filled with listening to Mom and Mrs. Kelly complaining about swollen ankles. Listen to Roger, complain about the price of things. I helped around the house as much as I could, but I loved to escape and go to the antique shop. Not to buy anything, but to listen to Adam's stories. If I wasn't there, you could most likely find me at home in my room, reading a book. I loved to read. Using my own imagination to create the world as someone else had described it, escape my own reality for a few moments, and live in this fantasy world of make-believe. I could be a knight, fighting dragons, or a warrior fighting for freedom. In this world, anything could happen. I could be described as a dreamer. Always dreaming of a better place.

In her younger years, Mrs. Kelly, Diane, was the head cheerleader for the high school basketball team cheerleaders. She was fit and had straight, long blonde hair. She and Mom were like sisters all through high school and remained close up until now, even though Mom could be described as a nerd in high school. They had been friends since they were little girls. Never did they have a big falling out, just the little arguments that friends have and at their age would describe as big fights but in hindsight, were just a squabble over nothing. Now, even though quite a bit older than her cheerleading days, Mrs. Kelly still had long blonde hair. Her athletic body was traded for a bit more firm figure over the years, and now being pregnant and all, she looked pretty bloated. But like Mom, she never complained. Unless you put the two together, oh boy. Not only were they pregnant at the same time, but their due dates were also only a day apart.

They were sitting at the back porch, complaining about their little worms taking their time, how their due dates had passed, and how long it would take before doctors would induce the labor. Both were pretty fed up with being pregnant. When I came outside, they changed the subject, knowing full well, I did not care to hear about labor, induced labor, or anything that comes with going into labor. Mrs. Kelly started to fantasize out loud about how great it would be if Mom had a baby boy and how the children would grow up to be lovers and get married eventually. A few seconds later, she was romanticizing Mom having a baby girl and them growing up to be the same good friends as she and Mom have always been. Ha, hormones, they make you do and say funny things I guess. I joined into the conversation and added how I could be a great babysitter and teacher to both the little ones. I could teach them how to get on their mom's nerves without getting punished. They both gave me an evil stare, and we all chuckled. I went back inside when the topic went back to backaches, swollen ankles, looking like a baby elephant, feeling like a surprise egg and whatnot. I didn't mind fantasizing about the babies and what they would look like or grow up to be, but this pregnancy talk about all the pain and agony and dislikes, that was no subject I was interested in. As I was fixing myself something to drink, a lot of commotion came from the back porch!

Mom came running in at full speed, looking for her phone, the same phone that she was already holding in her hand. She opened her purse and tossed everything out, lifted up every book and magazine to look under it. There was a look of sheer panic in her eyes. This panic made her totally forget she was already holding her phone. Before I could tell her it was in her hand, she yelled "quick, call a doctor, call 911, call the hospital, call fucking anyone, Diane's water just broke. Her baby is on its way now! Mom's statement was accompanied by loud screams of pain and agony coming from the back porch. They sure as hell made me not want to go out there, so I took on the responsibility of calling an ambulance to pick up Mrs. Kelly and drive her to the hospital. After I called for the ambulance, I wanted to get away from Mrs. Kelly as far as possible. I liked her a lot, but there are some things you do not want to witness. Mom told me to go upstairs and grab some towels. I did as I was told. Mom grabbed the towels and went back outside to Mrs. Kelly.

The ambulance took 7 or 8 minutes to get here. Those 7 or 8 minutes were the longest of my life. Hearing Mrs. Kelly screams as if, well, as if something was killing her slowly from the inside out, was pure torture to my ears. Poor Mrs. Kelly, she seemed to be in a lot of pain. Things were set in Motion so fast. She was in instant pain after her water broke. The paramedics came in and strapped her on to a gurney. As she was put on the gurney and wheeled into the ambulance she said, "Well, looks like you are going to have number 3000 for 2999 is currently on its way." Mom smiled and told her not to worry about the stupid population count and focus on delivering a healthy, happy baby. They gave each other a hug, and Mrs. Kelly was wheeled out, loaded into the ambulance and on her way to the hospital. Mom had called Mr. Kelly to let him know he needed to go to the hospital as well. No one knew it at the time, but this was a day that would remain in all our memories for a long, long time. The events that unfolded during the remainder of the day, should have been a warning to all of us for things to come. But no one recognized them as such.

Mom and I began cleaning up the back porch. I opted to throw away the chair that Mrs. Kelly was sitting on, but Mom would have none of that. She gave me a bucket with a sponge and a towel. "Here, wash it off and dry it, it'll be fine" Yeah, thanks Mom, that was the chore I was hoping to get, NOT! As I bend over to clean the chair, I was expecting it to emit a foul smell, to my surprise it didn't. If I had to describe what it smelled like, I would have to say it smelled fruity. I started with the chair, and after the porch was cleaned and mostly back to its original state, Mom walked up to me and said: "Don't panic sweetie, but I think my water just broke as well." Oh, okay, don't panic. Don't panic? Who are you kidding? I am panicking! My Mom just told me my baby brother or sister is on its way, the ambulance left like half an hour ago, and now I am going to have to call them again to pick up yet another pregnant lady? And Roger, ugh I am going to have to call Roger and let him know his child is on the verge of arriving. Where is the baby bag, the overnight hospital bag, where is everything! Don't panic, sure... "See you in a few," I heard Mom say as she ended a phone call. I was too busy stressing myself out to realize she just called the hospital and Roger. It was nothing like the screams of pain and agony I heard from Mrs. Kelly. Mom was calm, paid attention to her breathing, and just awaited the arrival of the next ambulance. She even asked me if I thought there was enough time to have a cup of coffee.

I had no idea what was going on. How could Mom be so calm and collected, and Mrs. Kelly be screaming as if she was being torn open from the inside out? Within a few minutes, the ambulance arrived. Mom laid down on the gurney and was wheeled away. I saw none of the panic on her face that was present when Mrs. Kelly's water broke. I was allowed to go with her to the hospital in the ambulance but chose not to. I had to call grandma and let her know the news and all my friends. Update my Facebook, my Instagram, and my Twitter. I needed to clean the house, the mess that Mom made. I would use any excuse I could find to not hold the hand of a woman going into labor. I am quite fond of my ligaments and have no desire for them being crushed by the painful squeeze of a woman going into labor. No, thank you. I was pretty content staying home, tidy up a bit here and there and go to the hospital after the baby was born. As I was attempting to tidy up the kitchen, the doorbell rang. It was our nosy neighbor Ms. Belle. She lived a few doors down from us.

Even though her name meant beautiful in French, she was far from. She was the old spinster, the cat lady, and the local tabloid all rolled into one. If anything happened around town, she would know about it. She had never been married; I don't even think she was interested in that kind of relationship. She was happy being on her own. If she would've been a religious person she'd probably joined a convent. She had wild curly hair; it looked as if it hadn't seen a brush in years. I suppose at one time or another, it had color, but as long as I knew her, it was gray and greasy. I am not implying she didn't take care of herself or her hygiene. She always smelled like flowers, but her hair... it just seemed to live a life on its own. She was a whole lot of woman if you catch my drift, she had to buy her clothes at the plus plus size stores. Yet she still had this natural charm that made her being nosy never feel intrusive. She would just strike up a conversation with you, and it would be a pleasant conversation, yet she'd still manage to get all details about anything she wanted to know out of you.

I opened the door and said hello, she stated that she saw two ambulances come and go and wanted to know if everyone was alright. After assuring her that everything was fine and informing her that both Mom and Mrs. Kelly went off to the hospital to have their babies, she insisted on helping me tidy up. She wasn't an annoying person to have around, and she always meant well, so I let her in. Together we tidied the house. It was now ready for Mom to return and so spotless a president, minister or king could come in for a visit, and we'd have nothing to be ashamed of. I was ready to sit down and await a phone call from the hospital. Ms. Belle would have none of that. She insisted on taking me to the hospital and no matter the excuses I came up with, she wouldn't budge. "You don't want to miss that first moment, dear. The first cries of a newborn have something magical. Come, let me drive you to the hospital." She accepted none of the excuses that I came up with to stay home, and that's how I ended up, reluctantly, being driven to the hospital.

It was just a small-town hospital; the building wasn't too big. We had to venture into the nearest big city for specialist care. The hospital was equipped for basic examinations, basic surgery, and only consisted of 2 floors for patient housing. Most beds were empty as there was no long-stay care. People only went for day treatment and hardly ever had to stay overnight. Last time I was here, was to have my tonsils removed, not a pleasant memory. I did like the amount of ice cream I had to eat afterward though. I think I pretended to be in pain longer than I actually was.

My dad is a doctor here, and I use the term dad very loosely. He never was a father figure either; he was too busy trying to be my friend. He was in my life that's not it, but he never acted as a parent. He was too young to have a child my age. He preferred it if I called him by his name. Calling him dad could get him truly riled up. He was the head of the dermatology department. I never cared to learn too much about it. Skin diseases just freaked me out, unexplained lesions on people's skin. Having to look at the ugliest pustules or cutting them open and be greeted with this foul-smelling infected liquid. No, that was not for me, thank you. I never even went to visit him at his work. As I walked into the hospital, I thought it was rather funny that I've never gone there for my dad. Sure, we did meet up outside the hospital from time to time, but I never went into his office. My thoughts were interrupted when Mr. Kelly almost bumped into me on my way to the delivery rooms.

Roger and he were pacing back and forth in the hallway. I was wondering what was going on, this wasn't in the 1960s, men were allowed inside the delivery room, so why weren't they in there? Was something wrong? "Roger? Are Mom and the baby okay?" He assured me they were fine; the doctors just wanted to run a few more tests. After a little while, Mom was being wheeled back into the delivery room by a nurse. Roger went in there with them. The nurse asked me if I wanted to join, as well. I loved my Mom dearly, and I was anxious to meet my new sibling, but there are things one does not wish to see of their Mom. Her giving birth to my new sibling is one of those things. Everything was fine with Mom, the last tests they did all came out positive, and she was ready to deliver. Her face gave away that she was in a lot of pain, but she remained calm, unlike Mrs. Kelly, whose screams could be heard throughout the hospital. Mr. Kelly said they took her down to give her an epidural.

Mrs. Kelly looked bewildered when they wheeled her back into the delivery room, even though she stopped screaming in agony, it was pretty obvious she was still in excruciating pain. Mr. Kelly joined her into the delivery room. Soon two more babies would grace this world. I couldn't help but wonder which of them would be delivered first. Mrs. Kelly went into labor first, but I knew that this meant nothing. I've heard of women going into labor for well over 48hrs before their baby arrived. I certainly hoped it wouldn't take that long. Mrs. Kelly was in so much pain; she wouldn't survive a 48hr labor. Mom could probably take on 48hrs, but for her sake, I hoped it would be over a lot sooner than that. A bit selfish as well, as I wanted to hold my baby brother or sister. I was curious as to what he or she would look like, smell like, and what his or her name was going to be. But most of all I wanted it to be a healthy, happy baby.

CHAPTER TWO

Meanwhile, Ms. Belle lived up to her reputation of being the town's tabloid. After she dropped me off at the hospital, she went off to spread the news to anyone who was willing to listen. She went to the local supermarket, told the cashier, who told it to her boss and the news spread like wildfire. In no time, everyone knew that Mom and Mrs. Kelly were both in the hospital delivering their babies. Outside the hospital, there was a gathering of townsfolk. It felt as if a royal baby was being delivered inside. Even the local press was there.

Patrick, their star reporter, made his way into the hospital. He spotted me, sitting on a bench, waiting for the news that the babies had arrived. "How is your Mom doing?" he asked. I shrugged, "She seemed to be in a lot of pain, she's currently trying to deliver a baby, how do you think she's doing? I bet she's fine and dandy," I replied with some sarcasm. "Who do you think will deliver their baby first?" Does that really matter? It's not like they get a ton of money or presents for delivering citizen number 3000. I was in no mood for this. I just shrugged. Patrick was starting to annoy me, I was just sitting there awaiting the arrival of my brother or sister, and now I had this sleazy reporter asking me all kinds of silly questions. As Patrick was getting ready to ask yet another question, Roger ran out of the delivery room.

"IT'S A BOY! IT'S A BOY! WE GOT A SON! IT'S A BOY!" I looked at Patrick and said, "Well, there you have your answer!" Patrick tried to get Roger to answer a few questions, but Roger was beside himself. He was in no state to answer silly questions like, "You almost had citizen number 3000, don't you feel a bit disappointed that it's number 2999?" Roger didn't even hear the question and went back into the delivery room, where Mom and my newborn baby brother were being tended to by the nurses. The soft cries of a newborn could be heard in the background. I looked at Patrick, "really dude, the man is ecstatic with his newborn son, and you ask him if he isn't disappointed about missing citizen number 3000? You really have some wires crossed up there," Patrick heard what I said, realized the stupidity of his question and quickly looked down to the floor. This brief moment of shame didn't last very long as his attention was drawn to the other delivery room. Citizen 3000 would be delivered in there, which was where the news was.

I was waiting for Mom and my new baby brother to be transferred to a maternity ward room, not a single part of me would even consider walking into that delivery room. If they were still patching and cleaning things up, that would be stuff I did not want to see. Roger came out into the hall again; he sat down next to me. He looked tired; it must have been a big ordeal for him as well. Even though I didn't care much for Roger, I have to hand it to him, he stayed with her through all of it, holding her hand and everything. "So, what's his name?" I broke the silence. Roger looked up with a puzzled look on his face. "He does have a name, right?" Roger stuttered "I... I..." He let out a deep sigh. "Your Mom and I talked about names a lot, but, we never finalized one, I guess we still have to truly name him." I couldn't help but laugh at this point. Living up to this very moment for so long, and the key part, naming the baby, just kind of slipped their minds.

Mom was being wheeled out in a wheelchair, hospital policy, I reckon, by one of the nurses. In her arm, this little mini human, with tiny arms, legs, hands, and feet, with tiny fingers and toes.

He was the cutest thing on the planet. She motioned for me to come closer and get a good look at him. His eyes were the bluest in the world. His hair was black as the night. I was puzzled, neither Mom nor Roger had black hair. Mom saw the confusion in my eyes and smiled. "Almost all babies are born with blue eyes and black hair sweetie." As we were making our way to the maternity ward, we heard a lot of commotion coming out of the other delivery room.

Patrick, who went outside to let the people know it would be Mrs. Kelly to bring citizen number 3000 into this world, entered the hospital again. Right as the commotion started. Mrs. Kelly was screaming at the top of her lungs. Mom didn't seem to have such a hard time delivering my brother as she did delivering her daughter. Mom guessed it had something to do with this being her second child, made some comment about the road already being paved. I wasn't going to ask her if she was in as much pain and agony as Mrs. Kelly clearly was in, during my delivery. I would feel guilty if the answer was yes. Not knowing, surely was the route to take here. Mom and the baby got settled into their new room for the day, and I made my way to the hospital gift shop. The delivery rooms were in sight of the gift shop.

I could see Patrick pacing up and down the hall in anticipation of his story when Mr. Kelly stormed out of the delivery room, white as a sheet. Patrick tried to ask him a question, but all he muttered was "Blood, blood, there is so much blood." I walked up to Mr. Kelly, who instead of a badass factory worker, now looked like a broken man. I shielded him away from Patrick and his stupid questions and escorted him to the vending machine.

Clearly, he was in no state for an interview or answering silly questions. I got him a cup of coffee and watched some color re-enter his skin. He started to describe the horrors that went on in the delivery room. Apparently, the baby was in breach, so it couldn't find its way out. The doctors first tried to turn the baby from the outside, but that didn't work out. Eventually, the doctor managed to turn the baby internally. Mrs. Kelly was ruptured badly, and there was blood everywhere. On the bed, on the floor, on the walls, on the nurses on the doctors, "Here, look," he held up his arms, and both his sleeves were drenched in blood. "I can't do this alone," he muttered, "I can't lose her, but, there was so much blood." One of the nurses came running down the hall, looking for Mr. Kelly. "The baby is almost here, Diane is asking for you," she told him. Reluctantly he followed the nurse. Poor man, scared for the life of his wife and baby.

Mrs. Kelly had an easy pregnancy, not a care in the world, never even had the morning sickness. Seems like she's repaying for that with one hell of a delivery. Mrs. Kelly's screams got louder and louder; this urged the nurse and Mr. Kelly to step up their pace and start sprinting back into the delivery room. As Mr. Kelly ran into the delivery room, he slipped on one of the bloody spots on the floor before he could reach his wife. He slipped and fell backward, hitting his head on the point of the metal counter from the sink that was in there. He hit his head so hard, his skull fractured. Blood sprayed everywhere. He was dead before he even hit the floor. The baby was born the exact second Mr. Kelly's head hit the counter. Mrs. Kelly was left screaming hysterically at the sight of her husband's lifeless body in an ever-growing pool of blood. Doctors and nurses put him on a gurney and wheeled him out of the delivery room. Not informing Mrs. Kelly of the death of her husband just yet. She lost so much blood they needed to get her stable again. One of the nurses cut the umbilical cord and tended to the baby while another nurse was trying to suture Mrs. Kelly's wounds. A doctor was adding medicine to her I.V. to stabilize her blood pressure. Patrick and I, still out in the hallway, saw Mr. Kelly being wheeled by on the gurney. Doctors were frantically checking his vital signs. We looked at each other confused; we had no idea what had transpired in there. After the gurney passed, we could hear the cries of a baby.

Patrick rushed outside to let everyone know citizen 3000 was born; the baby was born! People outside the hospital all started cheering. They had no clue of the drama that unfolded inside the hospital. They started decorating the town square. A big pink banner, welcoming our 3000th citizen, was put on top of the entrance to the square. The mayor was informed. The local bakery put out all pink pastries in the window. He spelled out 3000 in the window of the shop with pink cupcakes. The elementary school teacher instructed all her students to make a nice drawing for the new babies. The supermarket replaced their worn-out welcome mat with a bright pink one. Someone made their own sign spelling out: Population 3000 in bright red paint and put it up under the name sign of our town. They should have let the paint dry before putting the sign up though. Now the red paint started running and dripping, making it have the eerie look of smeared out blood.

Ms. Belle was at the antique shop talking to Adam about finding the perfect gift for number 3000. Perhaps something that's 3000 years old, or something only 3000 were made of, or a book with 3000 words or letters? Adam didn't go for this 3000 craze. To him, it was just a number like any other. He did own a book called 3000. But this was no book to give as a gift for a newborn. The cover of this book showed a desolate land and incited a feeling of dread. The story in this book was about protecting the gates of hell from being opened, not exactly kids friendly. He browsed through his shop to search for something else that could be to Ms. Belle's liking. He found a nice antique rattler, perhaps that could be a good gift, even though it wasn't 3000 years old. It was a cute little rattler; it even had a silver bow with a pink lining to its end. "It can be yours for the solid price of $25," Adam told Ms. Belle. She looked around the shop for a few more minutes but agreed on buying the rattler. When she entered town square, she noticed Mrs. McHenry feeding the pigeons. She walked over to Mrs. McHenry and asked, "Haven't you heard? Number 3000 is born, we reached a population of 3000!" She looked up at Ms. Belle and said, "Yes, I've heard the babies are born, but the town is calm and quiet. 3000 citizens, we have not," she turned back to her pigeons as she tossed some bread crumbs their way. Ms. Belle was puzzled by what Mrs. McHenry said. The town, calm and quiet? It was far from! Everywhere people were decorating, putting up signs, rushing off to buy gifts and whatnot. Eventually, she just shrugged and moved along.

She bumped into Patrick on her way to the hospital. "Hello Patrick, any news about the babies? Are they doing fine? And the mothers?" Patrick answered that he had no idea. Patrick didn't care much for Ms. Belle. He liked to report his news in the paper and not through the towns' tabloid. She could get her gossip anywhere, but not from him. The town remained in a state of celebration. Besides Patrick and me, no one saw Mr. Kelly being wheeled out of the delivery room on a gurney. And nor Patrick or I knew what the state of him was or what happened. All we saw was a lot of blood, and all we heard were the hysterical screams of Mrs. Kelly, followed by the soft cries of a little newborn baby.

I made my way back to the maternity ward, with a little blue teddy bear in my hands. Mom and Roger finally decided on a name for my baby brother. "May we introduce you to Sean?" they said as I entered the room. Perfect, a perfect name for a perfect little baby. I tickled his cute little face with the small teddy I just got him. There wasn't a care in the world in this room. Mom was sitting on the bed, holding baby Sean close to her chest, Roger on one side of the bed and me on the other. It was blissfully quiet, the only sounds breaking the silence were the chirring sounds little Sean made. Mom asked what I thought of him. I told her he was perfect. 10 cute little fingers and 10 cute little toes, the way he rested on mom's chest, he seemed to be very content. Mom used this opportunity to stress out I had to be a good role model for the little one, how it would be good for me to start straight away. Start cleaning your room, doing your homework on time, be home at the set time, walk the dog without whining, etc. Wow, he's not even an hour old, he has no perception of what's happening around him at all, yet Mom already found a way to try and get me to behave the way she'd like me to behave for his sake. Good one Mom, good one.

"I wonder how Diane is doing," Mom broke the silence again. I didn't know what to tell her. Should I let her know what happened? That I saw them wheel out Mr. Kelly? That I heard Mrs. Kelly scream hysterically, that I could hear the cries of a baby coming from the delivery room? Roger noticed a change in my demeanor. He suggested to let Mom and the baby get some rest. I was happy to leave the room without answering mom's question. Mostly because I had no idea how Mr. and Mrs. Kelly and the little Kelly baby were doing. Over a cup of coffee, I told Roger all I had witnessed. We decided it was best not to worry Mom with all this and Roger would see if he could inquire about the wellbeing of the Kelly family.

I went back to the maternity ward to see Mom and Sean. He was so cute, and I could barely take my eyes off of him. I kept stroking his head; he already had lots of hair. A nurse came in to check on Mom and the baby. "Isn't he the cutest?" she said as she was giving him a quick exam. "Would you like to hold him?" Her question was directed toward me. I looked in mom's direction; I never held a baby before. "Go ahead, you'll be fine," Mom whispered to me. The nurse told me to sit up straight and fold my arm a bit, so his head could rest on my arm. She gave me the baby, making sure I had one arm under his tiny body holding his side and his head resting firmly on the other. Here I was, holding my baby brother for the first time. I was so proud, and he was so beautiful, so small, and so perfect. "No matter what happens in the world, little one, I will always be here for you," I whispered into his little ears. This was my promise to this perfect little tiny human that was falling asleep in my arms. I was afraid to move, holding this fragile little baby, but his head started to feel heavier and heavier. Luckily the nurse took him from me before I made a complaint about it. "Here, let me take this little one to his own bed."

She told Mom it would be wise for her to try and get some sleep as well. Mom was filled up with happiness and adrenaline, there was no way she could fall asleep right now, but she said she would give it a try. She told me to go home and have some lunch; there was no point for me being in the hospital watching her trying to sleep. I kissed her and little Sean, who was now chirring in his own little crib next to mom's bed, goodbye and made my way out of the room. Just as I was about to go through the doors, they opened, and they wheeled in Mrs. Kelly. She was heavily sedated and unconscious. They wheeled her in without her baby. I wondered what happened, but Mom urged me to go home. So I left the maternity ward.

As I made my way to the hospital's main entrance, I found Roger and Dennis, my dad, engaged in conversation. Dennis saw me coming up and gave me the fakest smile I've ever seen. Before I could ask what they were talking about, Dennis gave me a hug and congratulated me with my little brother. I stated that Mrs. Kelly was just transferred to the maternity ward, alone and unconscious and asked Dennis if he knew more. He couldn't tell us anything, and only the direct family was allowed to inquire at this time. He wasn't at liberty to discuss the health of Mrs. Kelly, Mr. Kelly, or the newborn baby Kelly. Besides that, he said, he knew nothing anyway. He was a dermatologist, not a pediatrician or obstetrician. Yeah, I guess that made sense. Roger excused himself and made his way back to the maternity ward. Dennis invited me to have lunch with him. I accepted the invitation, seeing the other option would be going home and making my own lunch.

I regretted my decision almost instantly. Dennis wasn't interested in me or what I had to say. All he talked about was how good he was doing, how much money he made, how my Mom should never have left him, she could have the life of a doctor's wife, a queen, how he was the best in the world, God's gift to women! I didn't care for any of those subjects. I am glad Mom left him many moons ago. I can't remember nor imagine them being together; they broke up when I was still a little baby. They never told me the details of their break up, but it seemed to have been an amicable breakup since they always had a friendly chat if they ran into each other. Once every two weeks, I spend my weekend with a babysitter instead of Dennis.

Dennis always seemed to have some kind of emergency, making him only home for dinner and a small part of the evening on most weekends. Not until I got older, I realized that Dennis just didn't want to be there for he had no clue how to take care of a child. Unless someone with the bubonic plague showed up at the hospital, there wouldn't be an emergency call for a dermatologist. But as a small child, it made sense for a doctor to leave for an emergency.

Dennis had plenty of girlfriends over the years. I guess that has to be a perk that comes with being a doctor because no girl would go for him just for his looks. He looked average, maybe even a little below average. He wasn't as ugly that you wouldn't talk to him, but he wouldn't pique your interest either. He had short brown hair, average build, and missing a part of one of his fingers. How that came about, I don't know. He kept telling me a different story about losing it. First, it was a hiking accident, then he lost it while sanding a door. Eventually, he wrestled a bear during a camping trip, and the bear bit it off.

His current girlfriend, Linda, was nothing more than a doormat to him. She wasn't much to look at either. She wasn't his typical blonde gold-digging bimbo; I guess he stepped off that concept. The bimbos never lasted that long anyway. They liked the money he brought in but surprise surprise, had too much dignity to be treated like a doormat. Linda apparently didn't mind. She was short, had very short dark hair, her face was that of a woman who had been scarred by life more than once. She appeared to be wise, at first glance, but obviously wasn't. Ha, how looks can be deceiving. I couldn't tell if she was happy with Dennis or just settled for a life with him as her master. Yes, master, for I wouldn't be surprised if he'd ask her to jump she would reply with "how high?" According to Dennis, she lived to serve him, and that's how it should be. He brought in the paycheck, so she could spend it like a queen. Therefore she'd better treat him like a king and clean their home like a castle. Not once during lunch, he asked me how I was doing, how school was going, if I had any dates, how Mom was doing, what I thought of having a baby brother, it was all about Dennis, as always. I thanked him for the lunch and excused myself. I wanted to get back to moms' room for some more baby cuddles.

Roger put his index finger over his lips, motioning me to be quiet as I entered the maternity ward. "They are asleep," he whispered. The room was quiet; the only noises you heard where the beeps and whirring machinery sounds coming from the bed of Mrs. Kelly. They closed the curtains around her bed, but they weren't fully aligned, granting us a peek inside. I could see Mrs. Kelly being hooked up to all kinds of monitors and some I.V. lines. Her delivery sure as hell wasn't as easy as her pregnancy was. Poor Mrs. Kelly. I glanced at Mom before looking back at the curtains and was thinking about how different their pregnancies had been. Mom had it rough, heavy morning sickness, bleeding gums, pelvic instability, feeling overly tired, hot, and always itching all over. She probably had many more complications, but those were the ones I observed. Mrs. Kelly, on the other hand, had none of those. She made being pregnant look easy. But their deliveries were the exact opposite. Of course, I had no idea what went on in the delivery room at moms end, but she was awake and cuddling the baby when they transferred her to the Maternity ward, Roger looked very proud, tired but not worried in the slightest. Never will I forget the look on Mr. Kelly's face when he ran out of the delivery room, pale as a ghost. He didn't look proud or tired; he looked worried, scared, and drained. Come to think of it, where was Mr. Kelly? I figured he was with the baby as the little girl hadn't been brought in yet either. I couldn't imagine what Mrs. Kelly had to go through to deliver her little girl.

"Ro... Rob...? Robert...? ROBERT! WHERE IS ROBERT?"
Mrs. Kelly had woken up and was screaming at the top of her
lungs for her husband! Her screams woke up Mom and little
Sean. Sean instantaneously started crying. Mom instinctively
took him out of his crib and started shushing him. Nurses
rushed in towards the bed of Mrs. Kelly. "WHERE'S MY
HUSBAND? WHERE'S ROB?" She yelled at them. The nurses
spoke to her softly, trying to calm her down. The doctor would
come in later to talk to her; she had a rough delivery and needed
to rest. They assured her the baby was doing fine. She asked the
nurses to open the curtains. I was taken aback by the way Mrs.
Kelly looked. Her face looked as if she'd taken a severe beating;
it looked as if every single vein in her face had popped. I quickly
looked away, back at Mom and Sean. Mom looked perfect as
ever. "It's from pushing, pushing the baby out," she whispered
at me. Mrs. Kelly could have been the picture face of the
battered wife campaigns the way she looked right now. I
immediately felt ashamed for having that thought.

"Are you okay, Diane?" Mom asked her. She replied that she
wasn't, she had the delivery from hell, was still in a lot of pain,
and on top of that, she had no idea where her husband and baby
were. Nurses didn't tell her shit, only kept drugging her up. She
started crying. "I just want my husband to comfort me, and my
baby to love," Mom asked Roger if he could look around to see
if he could find where Robert was. Roger left the maternity ward,
leaving me in this rather strange situation. On one side of the
room, there was happiness on the other side of the room; there
was pain and worry. I had no idea how to cope with this
situation. I didn't know what to say, what to do, or how to act.
I wanted to congratulate Mrs. Kelly with her new baby girl, but
she was alone in the room. There was no baby in the room with
her, no proud husband looking over them. Instead, she looked

like a makeshift robot, hooked onto I.V. drips and monitors and whatnot.

"What's her name?" Mom broke the silence. Mrs. Kelly looked a bit confused at first, but then answered, "Nora, we named her Nora," Another beautiful name for a little baby. Mom and Mrs. Kelly started talking about the babies. I bet Mrs. Kelly couldn't wait to hold her, cuddle her, kiss her, and do all the things Mom already did with Sean. Mrs. Kelly stated that her husband probably didn't even see Nora get born, she told us he slipped on the floor when running back into the delivery room at the exact moment the little worm finally came out. "He probably fainted at the sight of all the blood. Doctors had to wheel him out on a gurney." I could see the expression on moms face change from attentively listening to worried. She told Mrs. Kelly to get a rest, she needed it after such a hellish delivery. Roger entered the room again; he went all over the hospital but couldn't find Mr. Kelly anywhere. Mom asked if Roger checked patient rooms as well, which, of course, he did not. Why would he check patient rooms, not like patients are going to be happy with a nosy Roger peaking in. Mom expressed her concerns to us in a soft, whispering voice. "I am afraid something serious might have happened to Robert. Hospital policy is to let husband and wife recover in the same room if they are patients at the same time, and Robert isn't in here."

At this moment, a doctor and 3 nurses entered the room and headed over to Mrs. Kelly's bed. One of the nurses closed the curtains again, as we saw the doctor gently trying to wake Mrs. Kelly. They kept their voices down so we couldn't hear what was said. Sean made his little baby noises again, drawing all our attention back on him. He was the cutest little baby I've ever seen. "No...! No..! NOOOOOOO...!" Mrs. Kelly was screaming. "LIES, YOU ARE FEEDING ME LIES! ROBERT GET ME MY ROBERT!" She started crying, hysterically. The nurse gave her a glass of water and asked if she wanted something to calm down. "No, I don't want anything to calm me down, I want my Robert!" She took a sip of water, curled up in a ball and asked to be left alone. With the curtains still closed, the doctor and nurses left the room. We all sat in silence; even baby Sean didn't make a single noise.

What had just happened? Was something wrong with the baby? Where was Mr. Kelly? All the questions going through my mind, all our minds probably, were soon to be answered. "He... he's gone," she sobbed from behind the curtains. "My... my Robert... he's gone. Dead they said, he's... he's... dead. When he... he lost his balance, in the... in the delivery room" She took a pause, a deep breath and continued. "He hit his head, really ehm really hard, on the... on the counter and ehm... ehm... apparently the blow to his head was so hard it caused a fractured skull and brain hemorrhage. The doctor said his death was instantaneous and he didn't suffer. But he's still FUCKING DEAD."

Mom immediately gave Sean to Roger and motioned for me to get out. I was shocked, stunned. I saw them wheel Mr. Kelly out of the delivery room, but to think he would die? Or actually, already be dead? I left the maternity ward without saying a word, as Mom made her way over to Mrs. Kelly to console her, offer support, and talk with her about what happened.

I probably walked here on autopilot and blind to the world around, but I found myself standing at our front door. All I really wanted now, was a nice hot shower. After my shower, I threw in a microwave dinner and settled in front of the television. Ms. Belle came over, but I was in no mood to talk to her, so I told her I was tired and asked her to come by another time. All in all, it was a pretty uneventful evening. I went to bed early, hoping to forget the events of the day. I am happy with my baby brother and want to be happy for Mrs. Kelly for having a baby, but it feels bad to do so. She also suffered a huge loss this day, and Mr. Kelly? Gone? Just like that? A big man like Mr. Kelly, built like a truck, no man could take him down if they tried. This man... was gone? He slipped, fell, bumped his head and died? Inside a hospital of all places! Eventually, I managed to fall asleep while all these thoughts kept going through my mind.

I had a terrible nights rest. Roger stayed in the hospital with Mom and Sean. It was still dark outside; I looked at the clock, 5 am. Ugh, way too early to be awake already. I got out of bed and stumbled to the kitchen. Coffee, yes, let's make a big pot of coffee first. I heard the newspaper fall on the mat as I was enjoying my first sip of freshly made coffee. I got up to go and get it when my eye fell on the headline. It read "Population 3000!" Oh, bloody hell, they didn't know, none of them knew what happened in the hospital. I rushed outside to catch up with the paperboy. Luckily he was a little chubby fellow that could be accused of many things, but being fast was not one of them. I caught up with Oliver and asked him to not deliver the rest of the newspapers, I asked for contact details of the newspaper's office, and if he could get in touch with the other delivery boys, these papers had to be stopped.

The town was still in a state of celebration, but in all honesty, there was no reason to celebrate. Yes, both babies have been born, but with the passing of Mr. Kelly, our population count was still 2999. Mrs. Kelly probably would be hurt if she saw this newspaper. Oh, bloody hell... the hospital will be getting lots of newspapers. I asked Oliver to pick up the newspapers he already had delivered and weren't picked up and brought in yet. When he argued he would get in trouble, I told him I would take the blame for it, and even pay his salary for this day if the newspaper wouldn't. He agreed. At no point yesterday did it come to mind that the entire town was in preparation of celebrations. When I walked home, none of it caught my attention. When Ms. Belle came over, perhaps I should have let her in, told her what had happened, the entire town would've known by now. I couldn't have done that anyway, who am I to inform everyone of Mr. Kelly's passing? That's a very private family matter. But the celebrations had to be stopped!

Oliver didn't have any contact details; I scoured the newspaper for them. At the very bottom in really tiny print, there were the contact details. I made out a phone number and called it, no answer. Well, shit, I phoned the hospital, luckily Becky was at the reception desk. She volunteered at the hospital most weekends. I told her about the newspaper, its headline and that she had to snatch up all copies before they were handed out to patients and Mrs. Kelly in particular. She didn't even ask why she just said that she would take care of it and we ended the phone call. I left messages on the answering machines of all the stores that sold or might sell newspapers, urging them to not offer today's issue. I called the head office of the newspaper again and was greeted with their answering machine this time. I left a message with my mobile phone number and asked them to get in touch for more details. Patrick, the sleazy reporter, I knew where he lived, he could probably get in touch with his boss faster than my message could reach him.

I ran over to Patrick's house. On my way I passed by the population sign, the bright red population count 3000 was crossed out, and the number 2999 was added below it. It took me a little while to realize that was very strange, besides the doctors, nurses, Mrs. Kelly, Mom, Roger and I, no one knew or could know what had happened, but I paid it no mind. I made my way to Patrick's house, probably a quarter to 6 in the morning and started ringing his doorbell. No answer, I pushed the button again... still no answer. I started pressing it repeatedly and pounding the door while yelling out his name. "All right, all right, there better be a fire or something," he yelled out from the inside. I ran inside after he opened the door, rambling on that today's newspaper should be recalled immediately and that I needed the contact details for his boss. Patrick wasn't very inclined to share those with me; he first wanted me to tell him what was going on. I wasn't going to give this news to a sleazy reporter for it was not mine to share. I bluffed that it would cost him his job if he didn't get me in touch with his boss straight away because this was huge. Reluctantly he dialed his boss' number and handed me the phone.

Mr. Stevens owned the newspaper. He was a short and chubby man, always had a cigar clinched to his lips, a dark mustache which was in contrast with his light hair. He came to the phone, and I stressed that I needed to speak to him in person, right now, that it was of the utmost importance that we should meet right away. He could tell by the tone of my voice that this wasn't a prank and told me to give him my address and go home; he would come over straight away. I thanked him and thanked Patrick for calling him and headed home. 15 minutes after I got home, the doorbell rang, it was Mr. Stevens. I invited him in and told him, in confidence and not for printing purposes, what happened at the hospital. He agreed that the paper should be revoked and assured me he would take care of it.

Meanwhile, Oliver did his part and contacted as many paper boys as he could and told them to contact others as well. All delivered newspapers, bar a few that subscribers already brought in, were picked up again and returned to the head office. I expressed my anger, how could they just run a story and not even verify how their subjects are doing? How dare they cause an extra amount of grief! Mr. Stevens agreed with me and said he would have a word with his reporters. The mayor, the town, they all need to be informed that celebrations are canceled. I... I don't know how to do all this. I started crying; I was slowly losing it. Mr. Stevens walked up to me and put his arm around me. "Chin up kid, you just go back to your Mom in the hospital, I'll do my part and inform the mayor and the town that there are no celebrations. You just worry about your Mom and baby brother now." It literally felt as if the weight of the world was lifted off my shoulders. I thanked Mr. Stevens as he went back to the office.

I made myself some cereal with milk and tried to eat it. I wasn't hungry, but apparently, according to Roger, breakfast is the most important meal of the day and shall not be skipped. Halfway through my bowl of cereal, I truly couldn't eat another bite. I washed the dishes, cleaned myself up, got dressed, and made my way back to the hospital. At the reception, Becky greeted me and said, "Mission accomplished" with a big smile while pointing at a big pile of newspapers. I let out a sigh of relief and thanked Becky for her swift action. As I entered the maternity ward, I was greeted with a big silence. Everyone was still asleep. I heard the chirring of a baby, but wait... that wasn't Sean. I looked over to Mrs. Kelly's bed and noticed her baby girl was now in a little crib next to her. I took a quick peek at the baby; she was perfect as well. As quiet as I could be, I settled in a chair next to Roger at the side of mom's bed.

CHAPTER THREE

Little Nora started crying at the side of Mrs. Kelly's bed, Sean decided to join in and thus waking up Mom and Roger as well as Mrs. Kelly. Mom got up and took Sean out of his crib and started to gently rock him back and forth to make him stop crying. It worked, but little Nora was still crying at the top of her little baby lungs. Mrs. Kelly made no attempt to get her from her crib. She turned to one side, facing away from the baby. I couldn't imagine the pain she was going through, physically, but most of all, mentally. Mom motioned for me to come and sit on her bed and told me to get comfortable, then she handed baby Sean to me and walked over to Mrs. Kelly.

"Diane, it's not the babies fault, she needs you now!" Mrs. Kelly started crying. "How can I take care of that baby after all that happened? It might not be her fault, but if it weren't for that delivery from hell, Robert would still be alive, and by my side! How am I supposed to love that which caused what I loved most, to die?" Mom got Nora from her crib and sat down next to Mrs. Kelly's bed. "Look at her Diane, yes, Robert is dead, but she is very much alive, and she is a part of him! He lives on through her. She definitely got his nose, his eyes, and even his curly hair. Do you think Robert would want you to give up on her because of a freak accident?" Mrs. Kelly just shrugged and didn't even glance at Nora. Mom got Nora to stop crying and put her down in her little crib again. Mrs. Kelly's attitude towards little Nora was shocking, terrible, but also completely understandable. How could she be happy with her little girl when she lost her husband the same day, in the same room she gave life, she lost one. Mom told Mrs. Kelly that even though it hurts now, the hurting will become less and less with time and that she would always be there to help. I heard her say, "You know Diane, everything in this world comes into it small and needs to grow big, everything, except grief, grief comes in huge and needs to grow small. We'll get you through this." Mrs. Kelly was trying to fight her tears but lost the battle. Mom grabbed her in a tight hug and told her to let it all out, cry over the loss of her husband, be angry over it, scream and do whatever she needs to do, but to also remember that her little girl was the part she didn't lose and the part she needed to hold onto. That it was okay to be proud of her beautiful baby, proud of herself for enduring that labor even to be happy that the baby was healthy and strong. It's okay to be in pain, to be suffering, it's okay to be angry at the world for what has happened. But it was not okay to take that out on an innocent little baby; it was not okay to blame her baby girl. She reminded her of how much she and Robert looked forward to this moment, the moment their daughter had arrived, the moment they could take her home, how much they already loved her. Mrs. Kelly just listened to what Mom had to say. She even looked at little Nora a few times, first her glances looked as if she was scared, but they changed into more of an endearing glance. Nora was peacefully asleep in her little crib.

The doctors came in for the routine morning check. Mom came back over to our side and retrieved Sean from my arms. I was going to teach that little worm everything. I was going to teach him to walk, to talk, to swim, about girls, about sports, about life, about everything! Later that day, Mom and Sean were released from the hospital and allowed to go home. Mom asked if she could stay with Mrs. Kelly at least until tomorrow. She asked Roger to take Sean home. I freaked out. She wanted us to take the baby? Dude, I know nothing of taking care of a little baby and neither does Roger. Mom definitely saw the panic on my face. She smiled and assured me we would do fine. Due to all the medication Mom had to take during the pregnancy, she had to bottle feed little Sean and reminded us that we needed to go to the store and get some formula. The doctor agreed to let her stay, and Roger agreed to take Sean home. Mom kissed us all goodbye and moved her things over to the bed next to Mrs. Kelly with Nora's Crib right in between them. "You know Diane, she's absolutely gorgeous, and you did very well." I heard Mom say as we left the room.

When we arrived back home, we realized we forgot to go and buy formula, so Roger went to the supermarket alone while I stayed home with Sean. Roger was nearly out the door when Sean started crying. I went over and gently took him out of the pram. Upon picking him up, I immediately knew what the problem was. Sean didn't weigh this much when he was put into the pram. Really, little dude, you wait until your daddy leaves and present me with a full diaper? I had no idea how diapers worked but still took him to the changing table. I stared at the instructions on the box of diapers. That couldn't really be too hard, now could it? I was hoping he only peed in it. It didn't really smell like poop anyway. Oh boy, did I wish someone told me, at some point in my life, someone should have taken me aside and told me. I undressed my baby brother and thought to myself, wow that little baby pee sure smells sour.

Nothing in the world prepared me for what I found when I opened that diaper. It was filled with little foul syrupy bright yellow poop; it was poop, it looked like yellow mustard, the smell, oh bloody hell, I hated that smell. I started gagging, trying to contain myself not to throw up. As I was still gagging, I lifted his little baby legs and removed the diaper from underneath him and folded it; I forgot to realize that this mustard poop was also on his baby buns. Luckily the baby wipes were on the changing table, I started to clean Sean, while trying to wipe his buns my hand touched the cover of the changing pillow and landed right in a transferred bit of baby poop. Now it seemed as if I couldn't stop gagging, oh boy, I don't want to throw up, I have no desire to regurgitate, none what so ever. I quickly wiped my hand off and covered the spot on the pillow with a baby wipe. I managed to clean Sean and, after a few failed attempts, I even managed to put a diaper on him. Getting this tiny little human dressed was quite a challenge. Everything is so small and flexible, you get one leg into the little romper, and the other is out again. I managed to get him fully dressed eventually, with quite some effort.

Roger returned home from the store; he started unloading the shopping bag. I saw a few items come by that I didn't think we needed and was missing one item we did need. "Roger? Where is the formula?" Without saying a word, he took a carton of soy milk out of the shopping bag. I looked at him in disbelieve. "Please tell me you are joking, there is no way in hell you are giving this to Sean! He needs formula and not frikkin soy milk!" Roger tried to argue that soy milk was just as good. It sure as hell wasn't, I might know nothing about babies, but I do know that soy milk isn't good enough for a small baby! I asked Roger for money and got on my bicycle and went to the store myself, reluctantly leaving Sean with Roger. That man is not fit to feed anyone, not even himself. What an idiot. How can he even think that you can feed a baby with soy milk, that's beyond ridiculous! I arrived at the store, grabbed the newborn formula and a carton of normal milk, and went back home.

When I arrived at the house again, I could already hear Sean crying at the top of his lungs. I rushed inside the house. Roger was sitting on the couch watching some television while he put

Sean on his back on the cold tile floor. Sean was crying as loud as he could, that floor was way too cold, and Roger didn't even bother to put a baby blanket on the floor. His excuse was that he had no idea where Mom had put them. "God Roger, you are such an idiot." He looked at me as if he wanted to hit me, but that was the one thing he was smart enough to realize he would never get away with, if I wouldn't kill him after he did that, Mom sure would!

I got Sean off the floor and started gently rocking him while also making a bottle for him. Like an expert caretaker I checked if the formula wasn't too hot or too cold and after I decided the formula was just right, I started feeding him. He didn't seem that hungry, and it took a while, but he finally finished the bottle. After he burped, I put him to bed. I went to ask Roger what he knew about babies, if he took any parenting classes, ever looked at other parents in public. How can you think it is okay to feed a newborn soy milk? Maybe if he tried really hard, he could find some healthy crackers to dip in the milk and then feed them to Sean, idiot. I left him alone with little Sean for only 15 minutes, and the little one was crying his little lungs out with Roger being unfazed, watching sports.

How on earth could Mom have fallen for someone like him? Yes, he adored Mom, there was no question there, but... he couldn't care less about me, moms' friends, her family, and now it even seems his own son meant nothing to him. Roger just shrugged and went on watching television, further ignoring me.

Roger sure as hell wasn't going to step up to the plate. What a waste of space. I went to take a quick shower and a quick nap, figuring I had to be the one taking care of Sean for as long as Mom was staying at the hospital with Mrs. Kelly. Every single fiber of my body wanted to wake Sean, get him dressed, put him in his pram, and go to the hospital. I would beg Mom to come back, tell her Roger did absolutely nothing and had no idea how to take care of Sean. But she would probably smile and tell me he still has to learn and probably suggest that it's a great way to form a bond, caring for Sean together, and I would end up taking Sean home again. I decided to not go and do that; I was going to need my energy, taking care of a little demanding newborn was going to require a lot of energy. I wasn't wrong, on schedule little Sean had to have a bottle every 3 hours. Mom better not stay in that hospital too long, there was no way I could take care of a baby, besides, on Monday school would start again.

Luckily the very next day Mrs. Kelly got released from the hospital as well, so Mom came home again. She had no idea how happy I was that she returned home. I decided not to tell her about the soy milk, about Roger being an idiot, about Sean crying his lungs out on the cold tile floor. She just had a baby, lost a good friend, and had a best friend with a near mental breakdown; she had enough on her plate already. She asked how it went; I just stated that changing a diaper and undressing and redressing a baby was hard! He's a fuzzy eater, he only gets like 30cc of formula but likes to drink only 1cc a minute. There was one thing I could not let slide, though. I asked her why on earth she never told me about baby poop! About its horrible color and it's foul sour smell! I will never ever eat yellow mustard ever again! She started laughing and just said she never even thought about bringing that up. Poop is always disgusting; it's poop. Yeah, poop may be poop, but baby poop is on a whole new level. With Mom back home, I no longer had to worry about Sean's well-being. I was free to leave the house again.

The next few days were quite uneventful, Mom took care of Sean, and I helped where I could, Mrs. Kelly was with us all the time, she practically moved in. She arrived early in the morning and left late at night. Nora's carrycot had a permanent spot next to Sean's crib. I don't know what else Mom said to her at the hospital, but it seemed to have worked. Mrs. Kelly seemed happy and very loving with little Nora. A few days later, I ran into Mr. Stevens. I asked him how the mayor and the town took the news of there not being a celebration. He told me that he only informed the mayor and that the mayor came up with the plan to inform the people that there was a miscalculation and that neither of the babies would be citizen 3000. The paper did not report on the freak accident in the hospital at all. The only notice of Mr. Kelly's passing in the newspaper were the ads placed by Mrs. Kelly to inform everyone of his unfortunate, untimely, and unforeseen demise. It had information about when the service would be held, and that he left behind his wife and baby girl. I thanked Mr. Stevens for keeping it out of publicity and asked him to thank the mayor for me the next time he would see him. Miscalculations... genius. The town went on as normal, no big celebration and no big fuzz as to why not.

Mr. Kelly's passing wasn't even noticed by the majority of its citizens. Only the people that truly knew the Kellys were shocked to hear of his demise. Mrs. Kelly didn't tell anyone how it happened; she just stated it was an accident and that he was killed on impact. Most people just assumed it must have been a traffic accident, maybe he hit his car into a tree or got hit by a car, and it didn't really matter anyway. They were there for their friend and to support her in this difficult time.

The day of the funeral arrived, and I know people say this all the time, but it truly was a beautiful service. There were loads of flowers surrounding the coffin and a lot of people at the church. Some of their good friends stepped forward and said some nice words about Mr. Kelly. In the end, it was Mrs. Kelly, who went to the front. She held a speech stating that we should cherish the ones we love and show them every day how much, it only takes a split second, and your loved one can be gone. She stated, that even though her husband was gone now, his legacy lived on in little Nora. That little Nora was the only piece she had left of her husband, and she would cherish every day she had with her. A few times, she had to pause her speech to catch her breath again. Tears were rolling down her cheeks, but she became a very strong woman. She fought through her tears and finished her speech. When we were on our way back to our house after the ceremony, we noticed a "for sale" sign in the garden of Mrs. Mitchell. I was trying to think if I saw her at the church or at the cemetery. I thought I did, but I wasn't sure. I asked Mom if she had seen Mrs. Mitchell at the funeral. Mom said no, she didn't see anyone for that matter. Her eyes watered up with all the beautiful words people spoke of Mr. Kelly, and she was too focused on Mrs. Kelly and how she was doing to even notice anything or anyone else. Maybe she died too, I thought.

Just as I was about to voice that thought, Mrs. Mitchell came walking up from behind us. "That was a very nice service, just like he deserved!" she said to us. Indeed it was, but I wanted to know about the "for sale" sign in her garden. Mom shushed me before I could even produce a single sound. Mrs. Mitchell had a keen eye, though, and she knew exactly what I wanted to ask. "Oh... the sign," she said. "Yes, I am trying to sell the place before I move to Ever Shades." Ever Shades was the retirement home in the next city. Our town didn't have a retirement home yet.

She said she was getting too old, the house was getting too big and daily chores were getting too hard. One morning she could barely get out of bed and therefore now sleeps with a ton of pillows on her bed, if need be she can stack them into a tower and help her get out of bed. She realized that she couldn't go on like this forever and applied for a room at the retirement home, last week she received a letter stating that she was next on the waiting list. Next time one of the old-timers would trade the temporary for the eternal, and a room opened up, she would get it. Mom and Mrs. Mitchell took a little stroll down memory lane together. She was Moms' elementary teacher as well, and then, years later, she was mine. I actually felt a bit sad she was leaving. I couldn't imagine Mrs. Mitchell no longer living down the road. She was always very friendly, in for a chat, willing to help if needed. She was pure gold, and now, she was about to leave our town.

Mom and I returned to our house. It was strange; I was so used to seeing Mrs. Kelly at our house that I actually wondered where she was. Of course, she was at her house, with her and her husband's family sharing a private moment of grief and support. I decided to just take a little walk around town, and take the dog with me. Poor thing, she barely got any attention lately. So many things happened in such a short while. She was deserving of a nice walk since all she had the last few days were short trips for her to do her business and return back home. I put the lead on her, and out the door we went. First, I took her to the doggy field; its purpose was very clear; it was a doggy toilet. There were poopy bag dispensers, and there were quite a lot of rubbish bins, stickered with big red letters that read "poopy bin," all around the field where you could drop the filled and sealed bags. After she did what needed to be done, we left the doggy field and went on for a walk through town. We ended up at the town square.

I looked at the people, all doing their things. I saw Ms. Belle ordering some food at a table at one of the restaurants, Patrick was eavesdropping here and there with a little voice recorder for dictating purposes I am sure. Adam was outside his antique shop, cleaning the windows. I greeted him as I walked by, but didn't stay for a chat; I just wanted to walk and listen to the sounds around me without having to speak, just look around at what everyone is doing, and how life goes on as it always does. "It's very worried... came to close... it won't stop now until it feels safe again" That voice appeared to come out of nowhere and scared the hell out of me. I turned around to find Mrs. McHenry standing behind me. Before I could tell her she just really scared me, or even reply to what she had said, she turned away from me and started to feed the pigeons some more breadcrumbs. I tried to not pay any more attention to her and started to walk away. "Until it feels safe again!" She repeated with her frail but still very clear voice. She was starting to freak me out, and I decided my dog, and I had been gone long enough.

When I got home, I looked for Sean and Mom. Both were peacefully asleep, little Sean in his crib and Mom beside him in a comfortable recliner. I found Roger in the living room, on the couch, watching television. I sighed, it figured. I went up to my room, laid down on my bed, and kept repeating the words of Mrs. McHenry. "Until it feels safe again." until what feels safe again, what is this "it," why doesn't it feel safe, when will it feel safe, and what exactly is it doing that isn't going to stop? So many questions but not a single answer. I didn't mean to, but I fell asleep and actually managed to sleep till the next morning.

Today was Saturday, most of my friends were finally returning from holiday this weekend. School starts again on Monday; it's our senior year. Somewhere today, Chris, Emma, Paul, and

Nicolle are coming back home. Tomorrow, Nigel, Marcy, and Amy were scheduled to arrive back home. They all went away for the holidays. We didn't, with Mom being pregnant and all, we kind of were forced to stay home. With all my friends leaving town, I actually was not looking forward to being bored all the time. I spend most of my time listening to Adam's stories in the antique shop. With the events happening in the last few weeks, I can't quite say it's been very boring.

Chris and Emma lived next door to us. Chris to our left with his parents and 3 little sisters, he kept telling me having a younger sibling wasn't fun at all. He could know, he had 3 of the little brats. Emma lived to our right with an older brother and her Mom, her dad lived in another part of the country. We kept an eye on their houses and watered their plants while they were away. Paul and Nicolle, or Nikki, were twins. They were like a package deal, buy one, and get one free. We all liked Paul a lot, but Nikki could be quite a drag. Some days she was cool; on others, she just had to claim all the attention possible and was more of a nuisance than a friend. The most stupid question I ever heard was someone asking them was, if they were identical twins... people's stupidity never ceases to amaze me. They lived with their Mom and dad in the house on the corner. Nigel moved in with his Aunt and uncle a few years ago. His Mom was a drug addict and went to rehab; she didn't finish the course and never came back for Nigel. Nigel was quite happy living there with them and his cousins. Marcy was an only child and lived with her Mom and dad a few blocks away from me. Amy lived close to Nigel near the edge of the town with her dad and younger brother, on paper her Mom lived there too but she was never there, always out on business trips, yet once in a while, she would come home for a weekend and then she went off again. She was a foreign reporter for a news station and therefore practically lived abroad. Amy had a face like an angel and always came across as shy to other people, but she was quite the rascal. Whenever we got in trouble, it was usually due to an idea Amy came up with. She wanted to be an actress when she grew up, and we all thought she'd make a fine actress indeed. She had this innocent look over her, she would be the last one you'd blame for setting off the fire alarm while she'd actually be the first to do so.

I went to kindergarten with Chris, Emma, Paul, and Nicolle. We instantly became friends and have been ever since. Marcy and Amy moved to our town in 5th grade, and we all became friends after a while, the last person to be added to our pack was Nigel in our freshman year. He was instantly enrolled on our friends list. He was quite the charismatic fella. He looked a bit rough the first time we met. No one knew his backstory, but we could all tell his life hadn't been easy with the way he looked. He wanted to keep to himself; he never had any real friends. His Mom never stayed in one place long enough for him to make any, but I guess we kind of forced ourselves upon him. In the end, he was glad we did. Now he had friends to fall back on, and he was quite the addition to our group.

I couldn't wait for all of them to return home. What was I to tell them about the last few weeks? So much had happened. My little brother was born, little Nora arrived, Mr. Kelly died due to a freak accident, thanks to our sleazy reporter all the news got out before it was meant to come out, the newspaper was recalled, the town was covered with streamers and balloons for exactly one day, celebrations were canceled and all this in the last two weeks. Of course, I was going to respect Mrs. Kelly and not tell them how Mr. Kelly died or that she didn't care for little Nora at all in the beginning. I was just going to relate the sad events, the beautiful service, the pushy reporter in the hospital, and how I heroically stopped that newspaper from spreading. They would probably tell me all about their holiday adventures first, and I'd be green of jealousy, I am sure. A truck pulled up to Chris' house; he got back home first. Even though I wanted to run out to say hi, I thought it would probably be best to let them get home first and unpack their stuff, get some rest. Half an hour later, a car pulled up to Emma's house.

I sent a welcome home message to our group app. They both started typing a reply. Chris wrote he had a horrible holiday and was glad to be home again and that we should meet up later. Emma, on the other hand, wrote that she had a great holiday met loads of interesting people and was quite sad she had to leave again. Paul and Nikki wrote to the app that they were only about an hour from home then their holiday was over as well. Paul described it as great fun where Nikki said it was just okay. Nigel, Marcy, and Amy all said they were in preparation for returning home, packing their suitcases and whatnot. I jokingly wrote that they all better had brought me a souvenir, no one replied to that message.

Later that afternoon, Paul, Nikki, Emma and I went over to Chris' house. Mr. Nelson, who lived across the street from Chris, was mowing his front lawn on his riding lawnmower. It made quite the noise, but we stayed out on Chris' lawn anyway because we didn't want to bother his parents or be bothered by his little sisters. As everyone was talking about their experiences during this holiday, the sound of the lawnmower seemed to get louder. Everyone was engaged in conversation when I looked up and saw it coming straight towards us. Mr. Nelson was still sitting in its seat, but his hands were just hanging limp to his side and no longer on its steering wheel. His eyes were slanted and his face drooping to one side, kind of looked like a melted waxed candle face. I jumped up and yelled for everyone to move. For a split second, they all froze into place, which was the exact opposite of moving! Then they realized there was a big lawn tractor heading our way and they started to move out of its way. I grabbed Emma and managed to pull her out of its way just before... just before it ran over Nicolle. It shredded her clothes, her flesh. I can't even describe the fear, the panic, and the terror in her screams as she was being cut by the blades of the lawnmower.

Paul grabbed one of Nikki's arms and tried to pull her out from underneath the tractor. All the neighbors came running out of their houses to see what the screams were about. They were greeted with a horrific sight of a lawnmower still on top of Nikki. Her body was shaking as its blades were still shredding her. She was no longer screaming; she wasn't making any sound at all. The tractor had come to a full stop against Chris' house but was still running and mowing. Paul was still trying to get his sister out from underneath it, and everyone was yelling at Mr. Nelson to stop its engine and turn it off. Mr. Nelson was unresponsive and didn't turn the tractor off. At some point, Paul thought he was successful in getting his sister out from underneath the tractor because he fell back still holding her arm. Unfortunately, that was all he was holding, her arm. The lawnmower cut through her flesh and bone and severed her arm. He looked at the severed arm in shock and disbelief before he dropped it to the ground. We all stood there and looked in horror at the scene that was unfolding, Emma fainted and Chris was staring with a devastated look on his face after falling to his knees. Some of the neighbors called the emergency services, and in no time, the police, fire department, and ambulances had arrived. Everyone was told to leave the scene, everyone except eyewitnesses that saw it all happen. Chris and Paul couldn't speak, they were truly traumatized by the events that just happened, and Emma was still out cold.

The paramedics got Mr. Nelson from the tractor and killed the engine. It would appear Mr. Nelson had suffered a stroke and died while mowing his lawn; this caused the tractor to just keep going in the direction it was going. Amy, Paul, and Chris were taken to the hospital for checkups. I refused to go and stayed to talk to the police. As the fire department removed the tractor, I had a clear view of what was left of Nikki. Her arm was severed, and everything else was like a big gooey mess of cut flesh and lots of blood. Her face was unrecognizable; it was one big mess of blood and hair and a little flap of skin hanging here and there, her skull was visible and had some clear cuts from the blades as well. I tried to fathom what just happened. After talking to the police, Mom took me home. Like the other neighbors, she too came outside to see what the fuzz was about.

She didn't know what to say, and I didn't speak a word. I was in a state of shock. One of my friends just died, in a horribly painful way, and there was nothing I could do to save her. I kept replaying it in my mind. A lot of what-ifs went through my mind. What if I grabbed Nikki instead of Emma, what if we were all facing the other way in the first place and could see the tractor coming our way, what if we went to Emma's house instead of Chris' house? None of it mattered. Nikki was dead, and none of the what-ifs in this world would bring her back. Later that day I tried to call Paul, but he didn't answer his phone. I did get a hold of Chris and Emma; they still couldn't believe what had happened. We decided to go over to Paul's house, offer our condolences to his parents and our support to our friend. Not only did he lose his best friend, but he also lost his sister, his twin sister. Paul's dad answered the door and let us in. His Mom was at the kitchen table, crying her eyes out. We all gave her a big hug, and we all started crying together. Paul hadn't returned home after he left the hospital. They had no idea where he went but figured he needed some time alone. After talking with his parents for a while about Nikki and all she did and was, we all went to our own houses again to at least try and get some sleep.

The next day after Nigel, Marcy, and Amy returned from their holidays and learned about the news, we went back to Paul's house. He still hadn't returned home, and by now his parents were getting quite worried. We decided to go look for him around town, but we couldn't find him. We decided to split up so we could cover more ground. I was going to the outer edge of the town to look for him while the others covered all the other areas. As I passed the population sign, I noticed that the number 2999 was crossed out and replaced with the number 2997. I wondered who was so cruel to change that sign so soon but didn't pay it much attention. I found Paul near the forest entrance, staring at a tree.

He planted that tree with Nicolle when they were about 5 years old. It was a save the forest project where everyone could buy and plant a tree at the edge of the forest. I planted the tree right next to it. The tree they planted was about twice the size of my tree. I called his name, but he didn't respond. I walked over to where he was sitting and sat down next to him. I put my arm around his shoulders. Without speaking a word, he started crying. We sat there like that for a little while and then I told him to get up and to come home, his parents were worried sick about him. He looked at me as if he just realized he still had parents. He got up, and we started to walk towards his house. He still hadn't said a single word. When we were close to his house, he finally spoke. Do you... do you think they are angry with me because I didn't save her?" he said. "No of course not, why would they be, there was nothing any of us could have done, and the only one that could have prevented these events was Mr. Nelson by not mowing his lawn that day at that time!

"Paul, they love you and are worried about you, why on earth would they blame you for an accident that none of us could have stopped?" I replied to his question. He shrugged, straightened his back, and went into the house. His parents sprinted towards him, crying and hugging him, asking if he was okay, where he had been and that they were glad he came home. They hugged him in a warm embrace, and they all cried together. I let our friends know he had been found and was back home, safe and sound. That's when I headed back to my house, still defeated by all that happened. As I walked out the door, I was greeted by Patrick on their front lawn. I told him to go away, there was a grieving family behind that door, and they were in no mood to talk to a reporter. This time Patrick had a little sidekick who he introduced as his intern. Well isn't that great, someone aspiring to be a cheap ass dirtbag sleazy reporter like Patrick. The future is saved now. I once again made it clear that no one in the house was willing to speak with him at this time and it would attest to some matter of dignity if he would leave them alone in this time of grief. He wanted to ask me some questions. Instead, I just told him to go away and went home.

Next day the newspaper headline read "Young girl killed in freak accident" and described most of what happened and featured a picture of the exact make and model of the lawnmower tractor that killed Nicolle. I scouted the article to see if there were any quotes in it. There was only one quote, and it apparently came from me. "A close friend of the family stated that they were dealing with their grief and morning over the loss of their daughter and sister and therefore would not speak to yours truly." Even though that wasn't quite what I said, it was close enough. I was just content that he decided not to bother anyone else for his article.

As our school learned about the traumatic events, they decided to start classes a week later. I didn't like school, but if going to school this Monday would have meant that Nikki would still be alive, we all gladly would have gone to school this Monday. We all tried our best to help Paul and his parents to get through this difficult time. 3 days later, the funeral for both Nicolle and Mr. Nelson took place. The church was packed with people for Nikki's service. So many people showed up that the church doors had to stay open so the crowd that couldn't enter the church could also follow the sermon. I can't describe it as a beautiful service, how could I. A young girl had lost her life, my friend. No flowers, gold and silver letterings, white casket with gold accents, or people saying the nicest things about her could make this a beautiful service. It was sad from start to end.

Two hours later, the service for Mr. Nelson started. I can't tell you how that one went. I couldn't go there, I blamed him for her death even though he was dead before he killed her, and in my mind, it was still his fault! In a month's time, I now had witnessed two burials for people I cared about. It felt horrible. The only thing I even knew or ever experienced about death before was the loss of two goldfish a hamster and a canary. But this was painful on a whole new level. Our group of friends was together every day since the accident trying to cheer each other up and pull Paul through it all. I don't know how successful we were in cheering Paul up, all I know is that ever since that day he became more and more of an introvert.

CHAPTER FOUR

Monday came, and school started. None of us were in the mood for school. Going to classes where there would be an empty seat, or even worse, another unknowing student, sitting on her seat. We all missed Nicolle dearly. Sure, she had her days of claiming all the attention, at times claiming to be better than us all combined, truth be told, she could be a stuck up little... whatever. But even those qualities were missed. I noticed that if I made an obvious mistake, she wasn't there to point it out... to the entire classroom. Something I used to hate when she did it, turned into something I missed now she was no longer there to do it.

Our teachers all tried to be understanding, but they had a job to do. They had to get us ready for our final exams and hopefully stimulate us to find a college and offer help with applying to one or more. They all wanted to tell us to pay attention to class and drop all personal problems until after class, but none of them did. They missed her too. During history class, Amy lost it. History was Nicolle's favorite subject. Amy and Nikki always sat next to each other in history class. Amy didn't care much for history, live in the now, not in the past, she always proclaimed. Having Nikki next to her during that class was a great help. If the teacher asked her a question she didn't know the answer to, she only had to glance over to Nikki's desk and find she had written the answer on a piece of paper for her to read out loud. Today the teacher asked her a question, and she glanced over at Nikki's desk, she realized it was empty. There was no piece of paper with an answer for her to read out loud; there was no Nicolle sitting there with a smirk on her face. Amy burst into tears and ran out of the classroom. Marcy ran after her. The rest wanted to go after her as well, but the teacher stopped us. Not in a harsh authoritarian way, but he told us that it's better if only one of us goes after her instead of the entire classroom. Let her deal with her grief without it becoming group therapy. He fully understood the pain we all felt, but there was no point in drowning in sorrow.

During lunchtime, we all sat at our regular table in the cafeteria with two empty seats in the middle. Nobody would dare sit on Nikki's seat, almost as if we were hoping she would still come over and sit down to have lunch with us. The seat across was empty as well, that was where Paul always sat. Paul hadn't come to class today, and we didn't blame him. How could he go over to the order of the day? Go to school as if everything was fine. We mostly missed her on times we normally would be together, for Paul that was close to always. They always been together, had the same hobbies, liked the same sports, shared the same bedroom until they were 10 years old. For Paul, it felt like a part of him went missing, died when she did.

We all discussed the classes so far over lunch. How strange it was to be back in school after what happened. How Nicolle would have reacted to some of the things that were said by teachers and students. How she would have hated being back in class. Nikki didn't have a goal for the future; there was no profession she wanted to do. Her plan was always to find a man, preferably a rich man, settle down, get married, have kids, and be a housewife and she sure as hell didn't need school for that!

That is where Nikki and Paul differed. He wanted to be somebody, leave his mark on the world, and be remembered as a great man. He wanted to become a scientist and find a cure for the common cold. People tended to laugh if he said that, and asked why not find the cure for something serious, like cancer.

Paul scoffed at them and usually replied that the common cold kills more people than cancer does. The weak, the elderly, and people with aids are more likely to die of a common cold than anything else, besides that, more people were suffering from the common cold than there were people diagnosed with cancer, and fairly often had it more than once a year. We decided to go to Pauls' after school. When lunchtime was over, we all went back to class and tried to pay attention.

Our last class of the day was sociology. We all liked our sociology teacher, but not today. He decided to turn the transpired events into a class. He made a case stating in a global description that a student died in a horrible accident, witnessed by 5 other students and asked the class to describe what could be the impact of that on the students and their environment. He asked for a worst-case and a best-case scenario. Nigel was the first to pack up his books and leave. He didn't say a word, he just left the classroom, and Chris was soon to follow. I wanted to get up and leave too, but not without addressing the teacher first. I got up and told him how tasteless this assignment was, and that it was uncalled for, there was no need to rub it in our faces. If he wanted the answer to his case, he could just look around in his classroom and notice that there now are 4 students missing. One because she died, the other because he still can't quite cope with her loss and two because they felt this assignment was so tasteless a pig wouldn't eat it. As I closed my books and was about to put them in my bookbag, I noticed the entire class was doing the same. We all marched out of sociology class, leaving the teacher behind in an empty classroom.

Chris, Emma, Nigel, Marcy, Amy, and I met up outside of the school. None of us could believe that teacher and his stupid assignment. How could he be such a blunt idiot? Surely as a sociology teacher, he should have known better. We kept discussing it for a little while and then decided to make our way to Paul's house. His mother opened the door when we rang the bell. She apologized and told us that Paul wasn't home and wouldn't be home for a while. She answered our puzzled looks with a warm smile and invited us in. She explained to us that Paul went to a mental in-house patient treatment facility. Ever since the day that Nikki died, he would wake up screaming her name in the middle of the night. He blamed himself for her death. He blamed himself for not being able to save her, for not noticing the tractor heading their way and for ripping off her arm. The void that the loss of his twin left was too big to be filled with kind words of others. She told us she was afraid he would end up seriously hurting himself or worse. She begged and pleaded for him to go see a doctor, a psychiatrist to help him get through this. At first, Paul refused, stating that he was far from crazy. One night she came home, and Paul was in the bathroom, cutting his arm with a razor blade. Small horizontal cuts all over his left arm. Little blood drops all over the floor, some on the edge of the bath and in the sink. She yelled out his name in fear and horror. Paul just told her not to worry; he would clean the bathroom before he was done. At that point, she fell to her knees and started crying and told Paul she couldn't lose him too! She wouldn't be able to live with herself if she was to survive both her children. She needed him, now more than ever, she loved him, and it wasn't his fault! I guess the sight of his mother, broken, down to her knees, and crying her eyes out, brought back some sanity to Paul. He agreed to talk to a doctor and made an appointment for today.

He went to a psychiatrist, and they discussed in-house treatment. With the image of his Mom still on his mind, he agreed to an in-house patient program. The last thing he wanted to do was cause his parents more pain. He was to stay there for at least six weeks. At first, there would be no contact with the outside world at all; later, he would be allowed to write and call people. We all looked at each other. None of us saw this in Paul over the last week, and we met up daily. We only noticed him being quieter, suffering in silence, closing himself off a bit for what was happening around him. We all gave his Mom a hug and told her to let us know if there was anything she needed, and we left the house. We went to the park and discussed the events of the day some more. Paul, being gone for a few weeks, our dumb sociology teacher, empty seats in class and during lunch before we all went back to our homes.

Our sociology teacher did apologize the next time we had his class. He wanted to help us, find insights on how we felt and why we felt what we felt. He forgot to realize how fresh and hurtful it still was and promised to no longer touch the subject. After that, everything went on as normal. The sun came up in the morning and went in the evening, classes went on, homework was given, shops opened and closed at set hours, and the newspaper was still outside every morning. Nothing changed; the world was still the same. Today was Saturday, and I woke up way too early for a Saturday. Mom was up as well, Sean woke her up, and she was at the kitchen table feeding him his bottle. "Be a dear and grab the newspaper, would you?" She asked. I grabbed the newspaper and put it on the table. I went to go and make myself a cup of coffee. Mom yelled out for me to listen up. She read one of the articles in the newspaper out loud.

"Reporter accused of lewd acts with a minor. After parents made a complaint to the newspaper, a thorough internal investigation followed. Even though the reporter maintained his innocence, the newspaper felt his integrity was deeply compromised. Both parties agreed to cancel the contract between them. Patrick S. will no longer report for our newspaper" Well I'll be damned, no longer will we have Patrick the sleazy reporter crouching around for a story, I guess. Or maybe he'll try to go freelance and find a big story that can go nationwide. I wondered who the minor in question was. The poor girl, traumatized by dirty Patrick with his greasy dark gray hair and his white gums and unbrushed teeth. He should be happy the parents only launched a complaint. If someone would do that to my child, if I were to ever have any, I wouldn't launch a complaint, I'd lynch the bastard. Hang him from the highest tree I could find.

The story spread around town like a wildfire. Everyone was guessing on who the minor could be, how old she was. The story changed from each person telling it to another. Patrick, who already wasn't a much-loved member of the community, now truly had become a pariah. A few days later, the reporter made the headlines. Patrick S. indicted for sexual harassment, abuse of power, lewd acts with a minor and sexual misconduct. Apparently, the minors' parents weren't satisfied with him losing his job, they decided to report him to the police, and the district attorney felt there was enough evidence to present a case to the court. On arraignment, a trial date and his bond were set. It was clear Patrick had to stay in jail at least until his trial date, for his million-dollar bond, he could not cough up. With Patrick removed from the population and people returning to their normal business, the news around him died down.

Extracurricular activities always looked good on college applications. Last year I volunteered at an animal shelter, the year before that I volunteered at the local library. This year, however, I wanted to earn some money, so I went out to find a job. I wanted to become a journalist. A well-respected journalist, not a sleazy dirtbag reporter. I tried the local bookstore to see if they had any openings. The bookstore was owned by the Mitchell family. It has been there for years, and I was a regular customer. I loved to read and study the books. Unfortunately, the time we were living in, was not a great time for bookstores. With the internet and the arrival of E-books, bookstores found themselves in a struggle to remain open in a physical shop. The Mitchell's were smart and opened a webshop where people could order their books online as well as an E-book catalog. Due to the business in the shop being half of what it used to be, they didn't need any help. I was bummed out; I would have loved to work for the Mitchell family, with my nose in the books all day.

I passed by the antique shop, Adam was outside smoking a cigarette. "You do know that those will kill you, right?" I said as I was about to walk by. Adam smiled and said there were too many things in life that could potentially kill you to not endow a few. He asked why I carried the look of disappointment, and I told him about the bookstore. "You're looking for a job, huh?" He said and paused for a little while. "I could use some help around the shop," he said. There were many new items he still needed to price and add to the catalog before he could put them up on the shelves to be sold. On top of that, most of the antique items that hadn't sold in some time were gathering dust and could use a cleaning. Adam loved his shop and the items in it, but cleaning the shelves... no, he didn't like doing that. He cleaned out the shelves and items only once a year, other than that he felt sweeping the floor and keeping the windows clean was enough. I immediately said I would take the job. I forgot how bummed out I was over the bookstore and realized I hadn't even considered asking Adam for a job. I would start the next Saturday. I went home feeling pretty content with myself, dreaming about working in the antique shop and wondering what kind of items I would run into.

When I got home and told Mom about my new job, she was happy for me but also fast to point out that School should remain my main focus. She had nothing to worry about, though; school was always the main focus. I might not like going to school and listening to the most boring lectures, sit through classes that didn't interest me at all, I did know and realize I needed all that to graduate and go to college, get a degree and stand a fair chance at becoming a well-respected journalist. Unlike my friends, I already had my college application letters ready, all I needed were my final exam scores, and out the door, they would go. It is our senior year we were buried under a mountain of homework and study assignments. I would make sure to finish all of it within the set time. I was sure I could combine it with a job. I went up to my room to go and do my homework assignments. As I walked by Sean's room and found him asleep in his little crib, I couldn't help but feel a bit jealous. Little Sean, peacefully asleep with not a care in the world. No worries about school, homework, a job, bills, death. He wasn't even aware that there was a whole world out there. My jealousy faded when I realized that all the horrors of the world would still bestow upon him. He wouldn't remain oblivious to the world around him and experience the pain and cruelties of life. My grim thoughts became a bit less grim when thinking about all the beauty that is still out there. He would still experience taking his first step, riding a bicycle for the first time, and falling in love, it wasn't all bad.

Instead of working on my assignments, I decided to sit next to Sean's crib for a little while and just watch him sleep. I would guard him against all the bad things in this world for as long as possible. I heard Mom walk up the stairs. She came to get Sean for another bottle, and I went to my room. I worked on my homework assignments and managed to finish them before dinner. After dinner, I would have to go over to my dad's house because it was his birthday. I would rather spend the evening with my friends, tell them about my new job and have some fun. Instead of that, I had to go and celebrate my dad's birthday. We all would probably sit in the living room, talk about how great he is and how much wiser now he's got another year under his belt. Sure seemed like a fun-filled evening. I'd rather go to the dentist and have some teeth pulled. As I crossed the town square on the way to my dad's house, I passed by Mrs. McHenry. I was hoping she wouldn't notice me and would just carry on feeding the pigeons. She was always feeding those pigeons. I was surprised those pigeons didn't weigh a ton by now. "It trembles in fear... not safe... not safe..." she mumbled. She didn't notice me; she just kept mumbling that sentence. I kept walking toward Dennis' house.

Linda opened the door when I rang the bell. As she greeted me, I noticed she always looked so tired and worn down. They hadn't been together that long, Linda only moved in last month. If I'd had to guess I'd say they hadn't been together for more than a year. As I entered the living room, I noticed that I wasn't wrong. Some of his friends were sitting on the couch, talking about their younger days. "Hey kiddo, come join us," he said as he pointed to an empty spot on one of his couches. I listened to the stories, none of them very interesting. A lot of stories about drinking during their college years. Pranks they pulled and got away with. The punishments they received for the ones they did not get away with. Stories I heard a million times before.

Dennis didn't like it if I called him dad. It made him feel old. He wasn't old; he was only 35. Mom got pregnant with me at the age of 16, Dennis was a few weeks shy of 18. They tried to do the right thing and be a couple, raise me together. They had the biggest plans together. None of them came true. Mom was 17 by the time I was born. Mom lived with grandma at the time, and when we were released from the hospital, we went home to grandmas. Dennis wanted to move in with us, but grandma would have none of that. He could come over to see the baby until 10 pm. After 10 pm he was to go wherever he pleases, but not remain at grandma's house. She was very strict about that; she didn't want to have another grandchild living in her house. Dennis came over all the hours he was allowed to be inside the house. Not for me, mind you, but for Mom. I don't even think he ever changed my diaper or wiped my behind. I wouldn't even be surprised if he never even held me as a baby.

Dennis constantly called or texted Mom. He had this sick need to know where she was, who she was with, and what she was doing, all the time. Didn't take long for Mom to grow sick and tired of that. She ended the relationship, and it was hard for Dennis to let go. He kept sending her text messages, email messages, calling her, and leaving a voicemail message. All of them stated that he loved her and was willing to work for it. He said he would change that they could make it work. Not a single message referred to family none of them mentioned me. He didn't care that much about there being a baby, he just wanted her back and to fight for her.

Dennis started doing what he did best. Stroking his ego and boasting about what he had. He started bragging about this great new addition he currently had in the process of being built onto his house. The new addition, the house already was massive. He lived there alone most of the time unless he had a new girlfriend move in. Who knows, maybe Linda was the one. Maybe she would last. Most of the rooms in the house weren't even used for anything other than to stall out his stuff. He collected items from all over the world, of all ages. He offered to give everyone a tour of his newest addition, not revealing what it was just yet. We all got up and followed Dennis to the very end of the house. I didn't feel like a tour and hear Dennis tooting his own horn, but everyone went, so I joined in as well. Dennis led us into a dark room and told us to wait close to the doorway. We could hear two sets of footprints shuffle in the dark towards the center of the room. The lights turned on, and we were standing in the skeleton of what was to become an indoor pool and sauna room. Dennis and Linda climbed into the already dug out pool area and were standing in its center. "welcome to the soon to be new pool area" He started to explain that one side of the room there would be sunbeds, on the other a big sauna cabin and we could already see how big the pool would be. I excused myself from the rest of the speech and went to the bathroom.

In the bathroom, I stared in the mirror. I looked miserable. I washed my face a bit and tried to freshen up. The ground trembled a bit as if a big truck drove by. Not possible, Dennis' house was quite a bit from the road and closed with a gate. But who knows what else Dennis has arranged for his birthday. Maybe he ordered a big crane, and we all get the chance to bungee jump. He usually came up with something or revealed something always trying to make his party be one you wouldn't forget easily. When he turned 30, he had this huge bouncy castle set up in his backyard. It was to prove that no matter how old he would get, he would still be young at heart. I made my way back to the new swimming pool room.

As I made my way back to the party, the ground started shaking again, and I ran into the pool room. When I made it into the room, the ground started shaking more obviously. This wasn't a truck; this was an earthquake. Everyone decided to make their way back into the house, everyone except Linda and Dennis. They were trying to get out of the pool and asked for help.

Just as I turned around to see what I could do, the ground started shaking more violent, and the roof of the structure came down. It knocked both Dennis and Linda back to the bottom of the pool. They were stuck under a pile of rubble. They tried to get out from under it when one of the concrete beams came down. It landed on Dennis' head. His head split open like a ripe tomato. Blood and brain matter landed everywhere. Linda, now covered in Dennis' blood and brain tissue, started screaming hysterically and frantically tried to get out, in her efforts to grab onto something she grabbed onto a plank that had a few nails sticking out. As she tried to pull herself out of the rubble, the plank catapulted towards her head. The three nails sticking out, all pierced her right eyeball. The shrieks of fear, pain, and agony were unbearable. By now, the ground had stopped shaking. Emergency services were already alerted and on their way. In shock, I stared at the scene. One of Denis' friends tried to shield me from it, but I saw it unfold, right before my eyes. My dad is dead. I felt horrible, not sad, horrible. I just saw my dad die, right before my eyes and I didn't feel sad, and that felt horrible. Linda became unresponsive. Not knowing if she was dead yet or not. I jumped into the pile of rubble and started to dig her out. Their friends joined in, and soon we had her out of the rubble.

She was still breathing but unconscious. The plank with the nails was still pinned to her head. The plank covered most of her face. Someone wanted to remove it; luckily, someone else yelled for them to not touch it. They could do more harm. You know, how in movies or theater they always scream out if there is a doctor in the room, and someone heroically steps up and saves the day. Here I was in a house filled with doctors in various medicine and even two surgeons. Nobody stepped up and saved the day. Here I was, holding the head of Linda in my hands, who was probably dying, telling her it was all going to be okay. I've seen my father die; I saw it as if it was in slow-motion. I've seen where every single drop of blood landed. How Linda got covered, her face, her head, and a part of her back, covered in blood and brain matter in no time. The sound the plank made when it hit her face, how her seemingly lifeless body looked when we got it from under the rubble.

The emergency services arrived. The paramedics stabilized Linda and decided to take her to the emergency room in the next city. They had trauma surgeons on call, and everyone agreed that the board needed to be surgically removed.

After I refused medical treatment, I asked if I could go home. A very understanding police officer offered to bring me home. I didn't say a word for the drive home. I was just thinking about what I had to say to Mom. Luckily I didn't have to explain anything to Mom. When she saw a police car pull up, she ran outside. When she saw me get out of the car, she gave me a puzzled look. She asked the police officer what happened. She explained everything that happened to Mom. Mom put an arm around me and took me inside the house. She sat me down on the couch and started to make me a cup of coffee. She returned with the coffee and sat next to me. She didn't say a word, neither did I. She put her arm around me again and somehow that broke me. I started crying my eyes out. "Why? How?" I didn't understand. How he could die at his own birthday party. How cruel is this world? Why did he need to go and stand in the center of that pool, what on earth did that add to his story? Since when do we have earthquakes? In the 16 years that I've lived in this town, there never has been an earthquake. "He finally got what he wanted." I sobbed, "He finally had a birthday party no one will ever forget."

Mom hugged me and held me for what seemed like forever. She said all the comforting words. How he didn't suffer, that he would live on in our hearts and memories, that he would want us to remain strong, that it was okay to feel what I am feeling. There are stages of grief, and anger was one of them. I kept crying over his loss in a way I never imagined I would. Dennis might not have been much of a father, but he still was my dad. We did spend time together, and I did love him. No matter what, he was still my dad. That night I cried myself to sleep.

Linda was rushed to the emergency room; they decided to waste no time and prep her for surgery. Even though I didn't know her that well, I was hoping she would pull through. But I have to say that it looked really bad when we got her out from under the debris. That plank was quite literally nailed to her eyeball. She was covered in so much blood; it was hard to tell which was hers and which was my dads'. All these freak accidents that kept happening around town, Dennis was the third person to die in as many weeks. Fourth, if we count Mr. Nelson. Linda was still fighting for her life. She was undergoing quite some extensive surgery. None of us knew if she would make it. After the surgery, she went to the intensive care unit, where they kept her in an induced coma. Allowing her to wake up normally at this point in time, would be cruel. They had to cut open a part of her skull and remove her right eye. After taking off the eye, the plank could be removed as well. Luckily the nails on it weren't long enough for them to reach her brain. She would have been instantly killed if they would have pierced her brain. After surgery they covered her face in bandages, she looked like a mummy. Poor Linda, doomed either way. If she would pull through and survive, she'd be horribly disfigured for the rest of her life. The other option would be that she didn't pull through and died. Oh, hell no, don't let her die as well. I can't handle another funeral!

CHAPTER FIVE

When I woke up, I was hoping it was all a bad dream. I got up and started to get ready for school. "Where do you think you are going?" Mom asked when I sat down at the breakfast table. "To school, where else" was my answer. Mom said she didn't think that was a good idea. I should take some time to mourn. I had no time to mourn. This was my senior year; I didn't want to mourn. I wanted to see my friends; by now, they would have heard what happened. I wanted them to hear the story from me, and not some blown up out of proportion mouth to mouth story where in the end, a nuke probably blew up in the living room. I was going to school, and that was the end of it.

My friends were quite surprised to see me at school. I arrived a bit late for class so I wouldn't have to talk to anyone before going in. During class, there was no chit-chat amongst us, as there normally would have been. I managed to keep up with the lectures pretty well. It wasn't until lunchtime we actually had a conversation. Everyone tried to steer clear of the topic. It was Nigel who dared to bring it up. He asked me how I was doing and that he sure didn't expect me to be in school already. I said that I surely had better days, and that missing school wasn't going to bring him back or make me feel better I really wanted to get into a good college, and for that, I had to have excellent grades. In all honesty, maybe I was just looking for an excuse not to give in to the madness I was feeling, the anger, the rage, the sadness. At least for now, it worked.

As Dennis' only living next of kin, apparently, I was also the one who had to make the funeral arrangements. I sat down with the funeral director to make arrangements for the funeral services and understood next to nothing of what he was talking about. He first asked if Dennis left behind a pre-arranged funeral plan, if it was going to be a burial or a cremation, in case of cremation what I wanted to do with the remains, or perhaps he would have liked to donate his body to science. Where was the service to be held, what kind of service it would be, traditional or memorial? With or without the casket present? Should he be embalmed? What kind of music and readings I would like, who would participate in the ceremony and how many visitations? Should it be an open or closed casket, that one was a no-brainer, no pun intended. I needed to choose a casket or urn. How the obituary should look, and of course the payment details, I had no idea what I was about to pick, or how to pay for it.

Luckily Mom sat down with us and helped to make the arrangements. I had no idea how much work it was to arrange a funeral, and it's all on short notice. I felt so overwhelmed. How do people manage this, have a conversation about how to dispose of your recently perished loved one? The conversation mostly referred to Dennis as the deceased. Completely depersonalized him. As if we were talking about an object and not about my dad. The deceased, the body, I snapped. "Can we stop talking about the body, the deceased, his name was Dennis, IS Dennis, and he is my dad." Silence filled the room until the funeral director apologized and said he would refer to him as Dennis from now on. Mom put her arm around my shoulder and whispered in my ear that we would get through this. Before we were all done, he asked if Dennis left behind a last will and testament. I looked at my Mom. I had no idea if he did. Mom said she would get in touch with Dennis' lawyer, if he had one, surely the lawyer would know.

After the funeral director left, Mom got on the phone with Dennis' lawyer. The lawyer hadn't heard of his passing yet but did confirm that there was a last will and testimony. Mom quickly asked him if there were any notions in regards to his funeral. He didn't include funeral details; he didn't want to jinx his luck in life. Well, that didn't do him any good now, did it? The lawyer invited us over that afternoon for the will to be read. I looked at Mom with watered-down eyes and asked if I really had to go, if I really had to listen to someone else talk about my dad as an object. Unfortunately, she said that I had to go.

The lawyer started to read out the will. None of his girlfriends were ever added to it, not even Julie who he had quite the romance with, she lasted 3 years, but he never added or removed her from his will. In his will, he left everything to me. I now owned his home, his items, and his cars. He also had life insurance, that would pay out $1.000.000 to his next of kin. I was dumbstruck. "I... I..." I stuttered. I am 16! I can't afford a house and things and cars. I don't want any of it! I want Dennis to be alive! The lawyer was quick to state that I could disclaim the inheritance, only required one signature. Mom interrupted him and once more pointed out the fact that I was only 16. Under no law could I engage in any kind of contract. In the final clause of the will, Dennis had arranged for all the money to be put in a trust until I would turn 21. But what about all the things that were not money? The house, the cars, the things? The lawyer shrugged and said, you can do whatever you want with those. All of it was mine now.

I realized something and looked up at Mom. What about Linda? She just moved in with him; I can't make her homeless. I looked at Mom and the lawyer and asked if in some way I could let Linda live there without charging her rent or anything but still get Dennis' things from the house. The lawyer looked at me, confused. He recovered himself and answered that he could draw up a contract that would allow me to take ownership of all of Dennis' belongings and allow her to remain the occupant on the merit that she was his girlfriend and living there prior to the accident. At a fee of course. I told him to do so.

Ms. Belle was the first to come to our door and offer her condolences. She invited herself in and offered to make us a cup of tea. Tea? Is she trying to poison me? I drink coffee, not tea! She smiled her crooked smile and said, you sure look like you could use some nice, hot, calming, chamomile tea. Well, she sure looked like she could use a plastic surgeon, several to be honest, but I am not saying that out loud to her either. Chamomile tea, who does she take me for. Coffee, dark roast, and not frikkin tea. I excused myself and took the dog out for a walk. I was going to take a longer route in hopes of Ms. Belle having disappeared by the time I got back. I went to the fountain in the town square. I loved the sound of the running water. When I turned around and started to walk home again, I saw Mrs. McHenry. She didn't notice us walking by. She was surrounded by the pigeons, but not feeding them. It was like she was having a conversation with them. Weird. I heard her sneer, "Curiosity killed the cat." I didn't even look in her direction! We just kept on walking.

Unfortunately, Ms. Belle hadn't left yet by the time I got home. She asked me how I was doing. Told me to sit down for a chat. I was in no mood for a chat with Ms. Belle, but I did go and sit down. She started talking about how sorry she felt for me, and how horrible it must be. She spoke of Mr. Kelly, Nicolle, and Mr. Nelson. If there was anything she could do, I only had to say it, and she would do it. But then she started to ask questions, weird questions. She wasn't there when Nicolle lost her life, so she asked what happened and followed it up asking what Nikki looked like after they removed the lawnmower. She asked me what I had seen at Dennis' house, what exactly happened, if there was a lot of blood, how Linda looked like with a plank nailed to her head, what was left of Dennis, how his head looked. Her questions got very uncomfortable. I yelled for her to stop and ran up the stairs to my room.

She always was nosy, that wasn't new, but her focus on wanting to know those details, it was quite disturbing. I decided to not return downstairs again and call it an early night. Besides, I had a lot of things to do tomorrow, school, finalizing the funeral arrangements and, if she was stable and allowed, go visit Linda. After quite some tossing and turning, I managed to fall asleep.

The next day after school, I went to the antique shop to ask Adam at what time I was to start on Saturday. When I entered the antique shop, I didn't see Adam. I called out his name, but there was no response. I stood there and waited for a good ten minutes before Adam ascended from what appeared to be a basement storage. He apologized and said he was doing some inventory, and that the bell that usually rings when you open the door to the shop fell off this morning. He hadn't found the time to fix it yet. I didn't even know he had a basement storage.

I asked him at what time I was to start on Saturday. He looked at me with a hint of disbelief. He saw right through me. "Listen, kiddo, you might try to grab onto anything you can right now, so you don't have to deal with everything that happened, but it will wear you down," he said. He told me he fully understood why I was doing it, but also stated he was not going to facilitate a mental breakdown. I was welcome to come over on Saturday, but he would not put me to work or pay me for that matter. This Saturday, I was welcome as a friend and customer, not as an employee. He saw the disappointment on my face and told me that I could start the next week.

He asked if I needed any help with the funeral arrangements. He was happy to help where he could. He even offered to help me pay for it. I thought that was really nice of him, but there was no need. If there was one thing Dennis did manage right, it was his money. He put aside enough for the event of an unexpected death. He put enough money aside that I could get him a solid gold casket if I wanted to. Maybe I am exaggerating a bit now, but I had no worries on that front, the funeral expenses were fully covered.

Adam offered to give me a tour of the shop. He took me to the storage room in the back, which had quite a few novelty items that he sold in his shop, I guess they would fit the oddities section for they sure weren't antique. Some coffee mugs with weird texts, some bottle stoppers that looked... ehm... rather questionable. In each and every one of them, it was a figure where the actual stopper resembled a phallus. Toilet paper with weird prints, even an ice cube tray mold that was shaped like dentures. I couldn't help but smile, looking at all these items. The shop itself needed no introduction. This past holiday, I practically lived in the shop. I was there almost every day. Listening to another one of Adams stories to go with another one of the items.

Next, he opened the door to what he called "his sanctuary." We entered the basement storage. There was this huge basement underneath the shop. It was filled with many items. These clearly were antique. From dresses to dolls, to surgical instruments and books. Adam said these all needed to be cataloged, and some of them required some additional research. That's what I would be doing for the better part of my working hours. I truly looked forward to that. The shop opens at 09:00 am on Saturdays so that would be the time I was expected to start as well. "Next week!" he added. I thanked him, he gave me a warm smile, and we said goodbye.

Most of the shops were closing up as the restaurants at the square were welcoming their first dinner guests for the evening. I noticed the fountain wasn't running at the moment and some workers were cleaning it. People would throw coins in the fountain; sometimes they would clog up the waterworks. Funny thing with coins and fountains, someone thought up that if you throw a coin in a fountain you can make a wish and it will come true, someone else believed it, and for some reason, more and more people started doing it. Now it's more of a custom thing to do, I guess. I can't help but wonder if any of their wishes came true. Every once in a while, all the coins would be removed from the fountain and donated to a charity.

With the fountain not running, the square was a lot quieter than I am used to. But there was something else I was missing. The pigeons! There were absolutely no pigeons. As I looked around the square, I noticed Mrs. McHenry wasn't there either. I always was half expecting Mrs. McHenry to be out there feeding the pigeons. But Mrs. McHenry nor the pigeons were at the square. I was only hoping that it wasn't a bad omen, like in a biblical sense, that all the pigeons decided to go away, not awaiting some kind of plague or impending doom. I figured Mrs. McHenry already fed them today and they just went back to their nests or whatever. I continued on my way home.

Dinner was almost ready, and Mom was feeding Sean his bottle. Roger wasn't home yet. He was on his last round of deliveries. I sat down with Mom and Sean. She told me the funeral director had called her, and she informed him we wanted a burial. We needed to go there tomorrow to pick out a casket. Yeah... that sure is how I'd imagine spending my Wednesday afternoon, picking out a casket for my dad. The date for the funeral was set for Friday.

When Roger got home, we sat down for dinner. Roger was complaining about his work and how demanding those shop owners were. How some of them wanted him to park his truck out of sight and walk with his deliveries to the store. "Do they think their customers believe the stuff arrives in their stores like magic?" he exclaimed. Even though his complaints were pretty trivial, right now, I loved to listen to them. A bit of normalcy in this crazy time was a welcome change. After dinner, I asked if I could take Sean out with me in his pram when I went to walk the dog. It was fine, as long as I had him home in time for his next bottle. Taking Sean with me might have been for selfish reasons, but it did work. Everyone I ran into was only talking about how cute the pram and the baby were. No one asked me how I was holding up, and I made sure I'd steer the conversation clear of that subject.

We crossed the town square; the fountain was working again. There were still no birds to be seen though, but it was almost sundown, so it didn't strike me as particularly odd. We made our way to the forest at the edge of the town. I told Sean about the trees and how most of the outer ring trees were planted by 5-year-olds. Not that he could understand, but I enjoyed telling him as if I was teaching him all the things about our town. When I decided to walk home, I glanced at the population sign. 2997 was crossed out, and 2996 was added. Maybe they should just replace the sign completely and no longer add population count. It wasn't that interesting to know anyway, and for some reason, someone felt the need to be very accurate on its exact number.

I kicked against a rock that landed in the soft bedding of a garden and took my dog and Sean back home. I greeted Mom and Roger, got Sean out of his pram and gave him to Mom. Told her he behaved very well and enjoyed all the attention he got from our neighbors. After that, I went for a quick shower and another early night.

The next morning Mom and I went to the funeral parlor. Choosing a casket. I had no idea how many different kinds of caskets there were. You had wooden caskets, metal caskets, semi-metal caskets, biodegradable caskets. Sizes from infant to oversized. Apparently, no matter what kind of casket you are to choose, it will degrade over time and eventually deteriorate because of the weight of six feet of earth and heavy machinery that is used to dig graves. To make sure the ground at the cemetery doesn't become uneven. We also needed a grave liner or burial vault. I gladly would have remained oblivious to the world of caskets.

The funeral director struggled with the next question. He wanted to know if we wanted to lay Dennis out, for us, ours and his friends to come and say their goodbye. Not that I do not have faith in the mortician and I am sure she can work some magic, but to make Dennis even remotely presentable after his head was crushed by that beam, would require nothing short of a miracle. I looked at the funeral director with a look that said nothing other than "you got to be kidding." He corrected his question and let us know that Dennis could be laid out in the casket of our choosing without people actually able to see what was left of him. I agreed to that option. People could come in and have a quiet moment with Dennis laid to rest in his casket. Finally able to tell him a story without him interrupting, I smiled a bit at that thought. The visiting hours were set from 1 pm. until 5 pm. We got the word out to all friends and neighbors. With the funeral to be held the day after tomorrow, they could visit him this afternoon and tomorrow afternoon, if they felt a need to. It would be the last time anyone could be alone with Dennis. I bet Linda would have loved to be able to spend one more moment with Dennis, but she was still in intensive care.

The poor thing was going to miss the funeral completely. I didn't want her to feel left out completely, so I made sure she was mentioned in the obituary and in the service to be held. As we left the funeral parlor, Mom went back home, and I made my way to school. I still did not want to take the entire day off. I only missed the first two hours; there were six more classes today. With everything going on, I still managed to focus on school remarkably well.

My friends commended me on my strength. I wasn't strong. I was just good at utilizing escapes. The school was an escape. School was the place where I was still treated normally. Teachers didn't look at me with pity in their eyes. Other students didn't treat me special. My friends and I did speak about what happened and what's going on, but as we normally would, not in an "Oh my, I am so sorry for you" kind of way. I dreaded the last bell; it meant I had to go back into the town, face the people, the neighbors, everyone that knew Dennis. In their eyes, I was the poor child that lost a parent, and I needed all the support and sympathy. I didn't want any of that! I wanted them to leave me alone, let me go back to my life where no one except those close to me cared about my feelings. On my way home from school, I ran into Ms. Belle. I felt a bit uneasy, seeing how our last meeting ended. She was aware of my awkwardness and apologized for our last meeting. She said her curiosity got the better of her, that she forgot how traumatic it must've been. She was just curious by nature and just genuinely wanted to know. I accepted her apology and told her about the funeral parlor and the visiting hours. She said she would make sure to pay Dennis a last visit and we both went our separate ways.

When I got home, Roger was sitting on the couch, playing some stupid console video games. Really? A grown man, on a workday, and dressed only in his boxers on the couch playing video games? Mom sure picked out a gem. I asked where Mom was, she went to the store and took Sean with her. Convenient, at least that way, Roger didn't need to get dressed or take care of his son. Why was he even home? It's not a holiday, is it? No, it wasn't a holiday, Roger just didn't feel like working, so he called in sick telling his boss he needed to support his wife and stepchild in these difficult times, his employer was fully understanding and gave him the rest of the week off. Unbelievable! "Let's see if those items will make their ways to the shelves like magic" he scoffed. Again, unbelievable! Using Dennis' death and my grief to get time off. I liked Roger less and less each day. I wished he was the one that died, instead of Dennis. A horrible thought, I know, but I had it none the less. Roger acted as if he owned our house as if he worked hard for it and everything in it as if he was the one to make sure there was food on our table, that the electricity and mortgage were paid. He did none of that though, sure he probably contributed by paying for the groceries now and then, but Mom paid for everything else. It was her house, and she paid the mortgage, the gas, the electricity, the cable. It was all in her name and came all out of her bank account. Roger spent all the money he made on himself. On videogames or other stupid things like a drone.

It didn't seem to bother Mom though, she fell in love with him, and by all means, I couldn't figure out why. I had no desire to hang around with Roger. I took the dog and decided to go to the forest at the edge of town. It was a small forest with a babbling brook. I loved to walk through it with the dog. Listen to the sound of the trees rustling in the wind, the birds twittering the sound of twigs breaking as I stepped on them. Nothing could clear my mind more than a stroll through the forest. On my way back home at the town square, I ran into one of Dennis' friends. He said he just went to Dennis to say his goodbyes and complimented me on the choice of casket. "Dennis would have loved it," he said. I didn't really know how to respond to that so just said thank you. I really did choose a casket that was fit for Dennis. It was a black and golden two-tone gauge steel casket with a white velvet interior. He was going to spend eternity inside of it, and even though I was fully aware that he was dead, I still wanted it to be the most comfortable casket, fit for a king. By now, I was a bit curious as to how they laid out the casket and decided to go and see for myself. I returned the dog home and would go to the funeral parlor.

Mom had returned home from the store by now and was putting away the groceries. I helped her to get the job done faster, with Roger not even moving an inch from where he was seated. Still playing some stupid shooter game. "BOOM HEADSHOT" He yelled out. Mom put down the jar of pickles she was holding and walked into the living room. She looked angry. She scolded him for being an insensitive prick that did not take anyone else's feelings into consideration. How could he scream out something as insensitive like that, seeing how I just lost my father in the way that I did. I never saw Mom so angry at him before. He didn't respond at all. He just sat there like a whipped puppy looking at the floor. I don't even think he realized what he said until Mom came in and yelled at him. She came back to me and apologized for his behavior. I smiled at her and said that it was okay, that I already knew he was raised in a barn and never learned manners. Mom tried to suppress a smile and said that wasn't very nice of me to say either. I told her that I was going to the funeral parlor and wanted to say my goodbyes to Dennis. She asked if I wanted her to take me there in the car. I declined, I just wanted to walk. It was on the other edge of town and quite a walk to get there, but I just wanted to walk for a bit.

As I made my way to the room they laid Dennis out in, from a distance, I saw Ms. Belle trying her best to open the casket. I froze in my step, what was I to do? Was I to storm in there and ask her what on earth she was thinking and scare her away? Was I to turn around and pretend I didn't see it? Was I to casually walk ahead and into the room and let her pretend she wasn't doing anything? The casket was laid out on a little altar, so it was higher up, and Ms. Belle stood on a little stepping stool to be able to try and pry open the casket.

Just as I decided to just casually enter the room I heard the casket unhinge, the top flew open with force. Ms. Belle lost her balance, and as the lid of the casket came down with the same force it flew open with, it was her neck that was caught on its edge as the lid bounced up and opened again to remain in that position... Her head snapped off, the lid of the casket acted like a guillotine. The white velvet quite literally turned blood red. Ms. Belles head found its way into the coffin, her eyes wide open and perfectly aligned with Dennis' eyes, as her body slowly slid off the side of the casket onto the floor. I stood in horror and couldn't believe what had just unfolded in front of my eyes. I started hysterically screaming, at the top of my lungs.

The funeral director and two of his assistants came rushing into the room. They sat me down on a nice comfortable sofa in the office of the funeral director. They called Mom and the emergency services. As silly as it may sound, I was hoping Ms. Belle got to see what she wanted to see before... before she was brutally decapitated. Death by casket, in a funeral parlor. This was the fourth death I witnessed. What on earth was going on? Is it me? Am I the bringer of bad luck? Or is it really just random? Poor Ms. Belle. She was dying to find out what Dennis looked like, so much so, she actually died while finding out. I still see her headless body, slowly sliding before it dropped to the floor. There wasn't as much blood as I thought there would be, not that I have any experience on beheadings, but in the movies, there is always a lot of arterial spray and blood reaching floors, walls, ceilings. There was none of that. No blood sprayed out after the body fell to the floor, a little pool of blood started forming around it, and there was quite some blood inside the casket.

"The casket, it's ruined!" those were the only words I spoke after being seated on the couch, and I started sobbing. The funeral director told me not to worry about that; he would make sure everything would be in order for my dad's funeral. Mom came and took me home, the only thing I said to her in the car was that Dennis' head wasn't flat. I was convinced there was nothing left of it, but the mortician actually made it look like a head again. It was still a big mess, and it looked nothing like Dennis anymore, but it was a head again. When we got home, Mom took me up to my room and gave me one of her sleeping pills. Even though it was still the afternoon, it would be better for me to get some sleep she said. I don't even know what I was thinking at that time, I just took the pills and drank the water, and I laid down and must have fallen asleep.

It was already 11 am when I woke up the next morning. I jumped out of bed, thinking I was late for school, but then the events of the last week hit me. They hit me hard. I sat back down on my bed. I looked around my room. My room was still the same. My desk was still cluttered with books and notes, clothes on the floor instead of in the laundry basket, my wardrobe with the doors barely closing because I just tossed in the clean clothes instead of folding them neatly before putting them away. The pictures on the walls hadn't changed either. Everything was exactly the same as it was the night before, the day before and not very different from a week before. I got up, brushed my teeth, and slowly walked downstairs. Mom was playing with Sean when she saw me come down the stairs. She said she called the school and signed me off for at least the rest of this week. I shrugged and walked into the kitchen to get me a cup of coffee.

I sat down at the kitchen table and grabbed the newspaper. "Curiosity killed the cat" read the headline. It told the story of how Ms. Belles' curiosity ended up costing her life. It didn't state anything about the gruesome scene or her beheading. It just stated that when she tried to have a peek inside the casket disaster struck, how she lost her balance and broke her neck in the fall. Yeah, she broke her neck all right... it snapped right off! Poor Ms. Belle. No more nosy neighbor. How is it possible to have such morbid curiosity? Even though she creeped me out the other night, she usually was very kind and helpful. Maybe that was only to find out as much as she could about a certain subject, but then again, maybe it was just out of the kindness of her heart. I will never know what her motives were or why she had this need to know everything. I do know that I will miss her. The small talk every time I ran into her. The doorbell rang and interrupted my thoughts. When I went to open the door, I saw the silhouette of a woman through the glass.

When I opened the door, I froze into place as if I was nailed to the floor. In the door opening stood, Ms. Belle! This wasn't possible, I've seen her head roll into the coffin, no doctor in the world could fix that. The lady at the door smiled, that's how I could tell it couldn't be Ms. Belle. Ms. Belle had a crooked smile, with yellow teeth; this lady had straight pearly whites. "I am sorry to scare you," she said. "Tamara was my twin sister; I am supposed to go and clean out her house" I was still staring at her not saying a word.

The same long curly hair, the same shade of grey, the same height, the same figure... everything except her teeth was like an exact copy of Ms. Belle. Mom came to the door and said she was expecting her. Apparently, they spoke on the phone before, thanks for the heads up Mom. Mom had the spare key for Ms. Belles' house. She invited the lady into our house. She introduced herself as Nancy, Nancy Davies. She was married and had a son. Her husband and son would come over later to help her clean out the house. For some reason unbeknownst to me, I heard myself say "If you want, Mrs. Davies, I'll be glad to help" She smiled at me and just said, "Please, just call me Nancy, I'll let you know if we need help." She winked at me as she walked into the kitchen with Mom. I remained in the living room and played a bit with Sean on his blanket. How lovely it must be, to be oblivious to what's happening in the world around you. If I could go back to being a tiny baby, I would in a heartbeat and instantly stop growing. I'd remain oblivious forever.

CHAPTER SIX

The phone rang, it was the hospital. Mom answered the phone, and with a heavy heart, I was waiting for her to end the call. Maybe they failed to stabilize Linda, maybe she died last night. With all the events happening, good news was not something I expected. Mom got off the phone and said that Linda was awake and able to receive visitors. She had even asked for me. I let out a sigh of relieve, but I was also doubtful, of course, I wanted to go and see Linda, but what was I to tell her? Was I to tell her that Dennis' lawyer would draw up a contract so she could remain in the house? Was I to tell her that Dennis didn't leave her anything in his will? How would she react? What would she look like? What would she remember? I was slowly freaking myself out.

The more I thought about going to see her, the more I dreaded actually going. "Well? Come on, let's go." Mom was already at the door with little Sean. Ready to drive me to the hospital. I asked her about the things I was thinking about. She told me not to worry. Just go in there and talk to her, just see how she is doing. When we arrived at the hospital, my feet became really heavy, as if my shoes were filled with lead. I walked up to the room Linda was in and stopped at the door. For some reason, my heart was pounding in my chest. Did I really want to go in and see what was behind the door? I did owe it to Linda and my dad to go in there, but could I? Could I face what lied behind that door? "It's okay, you can go in there, she's awake" the friendly voice of a nurse telling me to go in. Now I had no choice, I could hardly turn around and run away now, she probably heard the nurse. I opened the door and stepped inside.

Linda was in her bed, her head almost fully bandaged, only her left eye and mouth weren't covered. She looked at me and tried to form a smile. I walked up to the bed, I couldn't find any words. Asking her how she was doing seemed like a stupid question. I didn't even bring anything, like flowers or a fruit basket, should I have? I sat down next to her bed. "I am glad you weren't hurt." Linda broke the silence. "How are you holding up kiddo?" She was asking how I am doing, while she's the one in shambles in the hospital. I told her I was trying to keep it all together. Told her of all the funeral arrangements I had to make and how I had no idea what Dennis would like for his funeral. Linda smiled and said she had no clue either. Dennis always exclaimed that he was going to live forever. He took very good care of himself, mind, and body. Nothing could kill him.

I was hesitant if I should tell her about the passing of Ms. Belle, but she already knew. She read the newspaper. I decided not to fill her in on the details. I asked if she would be able to attend the funeral. We could wheel her out in a wheelchair and load her into a van. Immediately stating that with my luck, the van would probably crash and kill everyone inside except me. Linda looked at me and said, "Oh my, you are not blaming any of this on you, now are you?" I guess I was blaming it all on me. I was near all of them when these accidents happened. Linda told me to stop being silly. I did not make the roof cave in, it wasn't a solid structure, to begin with. If anyone was to blame it should be Dennis, for going down into the pool area and standing in the center of a room that wasn't made to be stood in yet. I should stop blaming myself. Linda and I talked for a little more until it was time for her to rest some more. I went back to the entrance, where Mom was waiting for me. When she drove us home, I asked her to let me out near the forest. I wanted to clear my head some more.

Mom let me out of the car near the edge of the forest. I followed the trail leading into the forest. I looked up at the sky, which was clear blue, not a single cloud, it was a sunny day. I looked up at the trees, I saw some squirrels fighting over a nut. I imagined them being husband and wife and her telling him he had enough nuts. I loved the forest, the trees, and the animals. I took off my shoes and rolled up the legs of my trousers, I stepped into the water of the brook. It was cold, very cold, but also rather refreshing. After a little while, I got out of the brook and sat on a rock nearby, waiting for my legs and feet to dry. As I was sitting there, everything was calm. There was no stress of things that still needed to be done, no one asking me how I was doing. I loved being alone. After I put my shoes back on, I went on my way into town again. I knew I was about to pass our population sign and was sure the number would be crossed out again. Unless it would have been Ms. Belle, who did that, but I could not imagine. As I neared the population sign, there was a lot of commotion. As I got closer, I could see why.

The number 2996 was indeed crossed out, the number 2995 was added, but was also crossed out. Below it, with bright red paint, the number 66 was added, and the first line of another six started. Next to this number, however, there was a hand pinned to the sign. As the coroner, who was already at the scene, removed the hand, it revealed the number 2994. Behind the sign was a dead body. I couldn't make out who it was just yet, and the eerie thought of it being Nigel or Amy crept up to me. They both lived close to the edge of the town, and it didn't seem like the hand of an adult. As I got closer to the body, I could see that it was ripped open from the neck all the way down. Completely disemboweled as all its intestines made a trail from the sign as to where the body was laying. As I got closer, I dreaded to look. But when I did look, I was able to have a look at its face, and a feeling of relief came over me. It wasn't any of my friends this time. In fact, it wasn't anyone I particularly cared about. The person that was lying dead behind the sign was Ricardo. He was scum. Him and his friends were the nuisances of the town. Always causing trouble. Riding their scooters where they didn't belong, harassing the elderly, scaring the little ones. I am ashamed to admit that this death didn't faze me at all. This death also seemed to be far from an accident. His hand severed from his body, pinned to the sign with a pocket knife, probably his own pocket knife. It looked as if he was changing the sign to something stupid but got interrupted. I sure wasn't eager to find out by whom and made my way home as fast as I could.

When Mom asked if I managed to clear my mind, I told her what I had seen at the sign. "Another death," she exclaimed. "People are dropping like flies around here lately." Immediately after she said that she wished she bit off her tongue. She turned around and looked at me and said she didn't mean it like that. I knew what she meant. I thought about it before. At least this time I wasn't there to witness any of it. It did get me thinking though, 3 people dead within a week. Dennis was only 35, Ricardo was around my age, maybe a year or two older, and Ms. Belle was heading towards 60 I believe. None of them were at an age where you'd think their end would be near.

That evening after dinner, I met up with Nigel, Amy, Emma, Chris, and Marcy. They told me I didn't miss much at school, two of the teachers called in sick, one class was just repeating stuff we already had last year, and the other wanted to give a pop quiz but spent all his time searching for the test paper. At lunch, there was a fight between the scooter scum, as we had nicknamed them, after lunch, they had gym class, and that was about it. I asked if they heard about Ricardo. Me calling him by his name already got everyone's attention. I told them what I had seen when I left the forest. Apparently, without Ms. Belle, the news around town didn't spread as fast, seeing as none of them heard about it yet. They said he got into a fight with 2 of his buddies at lunch, but that wasn't really out of the ordinary. They were always play fighting and ended up really hurting each other. It was as if every day, they had to figure out who was the alpha male again. We talked some more about everything that happened in the last few weeks. We all agreed on the fact it was strange that so many freak accidents occurred lately. Ricardo wasn't an accident, I quickly added. He was gutted, and his hand was cut off. Somebody did that to him. I can't think of a single accident that could occur with that outcome. They agreed. After making up stories on who could have done this the subject changed to tomorrow. Oh, how I dreaded this subject.

Tomorrow was Friday. The day of Dennis' funeral. I told them how hard it was to arrange everything and that I still had no idea what came of the casket, you know, after Ms. Belle. I also told them Dennis left me everything in his will but put it all in a trust fund where I was to receive it at the age of 21 or after graduating from college, whichever came first. "Wahoo so you're rich now huh," Nigel said. I looked at him and only said: "No, Nigel, I might come into money at the age of 21, but I still lost a parent." Nigel looked away from me in shame. Before I let him mutter his apologies I told him I understood his reaction, but that I would give away every last penny and sign away all possessions if that would bring Dennis back. I never knew how much I cared about him until he was gone. Sure, he wasn't much of a dad, but he did succeed in being a friend. My friends all said they would be there tomorrow. And if I needed anything, I should not hesitate to ask. It still felt so unreal. Tomorrow we would bury my father. That would be the end of it, no more visits to Dennis, no more running into him at the town square, no more awkwardness during PTA meetings, no more bragging and boosting. It was all over, and tomorrow would finalize that.

I had no idea how I would hold up. Would I be strong and brave and sit through it like a champ, or would I break down and cry like a toddler whose candy had been stolen. The casket, what became of the casket? I know the funeral director told me not to worry about it, but Dennis could not be buried in another woman's blood! I decided to say goodbye to my friends and return home. On my way home, I called the funeral director. I told him I was sorry to bother him, but I needed to know if the casket was cleaned. He managed to suppress a laugh and answered that they replaced all the lining with brand new white velvet, and it was good as new. I don't know why it was important to me, but it was, and his answer made me feel more at ease.

When I got home, Mom was engaged in a conversation with Mrs. Kelly and little Nora and Sean were on the blanket. Roger was on the couch, again playing some stupid video game. I guess Mom got him to wear his headphones. I greeted Mom and Mrs. Kelly and grabbed something to drink from the fridge. Mom asked if I wanted to join them for a chat, I really didn't. I told her I just wanted to go up to my room and listen to some music before going to sleep.

I woke up bright and early the next morning. I already laid out my nicest darkest clothes the evening before. As I was looking at my clothes, I was wondering who we all were dressing up for. We would all be there in our best black suits and dresses. It's not like Dennis would still care. As if he'd be looking over his funeral in spirit form and decide to go hAunt the person who didn't dress up nice enough. I went downstairs. It was still dark outside, and the only light burning in the living room was the red light of the television. It was so quiet, the birds outside hadn't awoken yet. I made a pot of coffee and turned on the television to watch some reruns of yesterday's news broadcast. Ricardo's brutal murder was mentioned. The police created a task force to solve his murder. They had received tips that it could be gang-related. I scoffed, gang-related. This town might be pretty far from a perfect town, but if there is one thing we do not have, it is gangs. There was also a bit in there about Patrick. Apparently, his trial would start on Monday, all the preliminary hearings were concluded, and a jury of his peers had been selected. Trial by jury, I wouldn't be surprised if he got off. Playing the victim card, the, she seduced me card or the, she has the legal age of consent card. You don't climb on a 16-year-old when you are a 44-year-old man. I was hoping the jury would see through that.

I heard footsteps on the stairs, a light tread, it was Mom. She asked me how I was holding up. Right now, I was holding up just fine, looking at the misery in the world with a cup of coffee. I had no idea how I would hold up during the memorial service, though. Mom and I talked some more until Sean woke up demanding attention. She got him from his crib and attempted to wake up Roger. Roger claimed to be not feeling well and asked for a few more minutes. She came down with Sean and asked if I wanted to feed him his bottle so she could take a quick shower. I had no problem feeding the little worm. After her shower she tried to wake Roger once again, again he asked for a few more minutes. She went downstairs and took over Sean from me. I went to have a quick shower as well. I got into my black clothes, Mom was all dolled up as well. We looked as if we were going to some kind of gala or maybe an opera. But nothing was further from the truth. Roger still hadn't made his way down yet. Mom went up one last time. I could hear her yell at Roger but couldn't make out the words. When she returned she just smiled and said we had to go, we didn't want to be late.

When we got to the memorial center, the room was filled with flowers. Beautiful colorful flowers. I wanted to be one of the pallbearers, but everyone advised against that, so I opted not to. Might be a bit much to carry my dad's casket into the room. 6 of my father's closest friends would be the pallbearers. Funeral bouquets with ribbons telling Dennis to rest in peace. Gone but never forgotten. Forever in our thoughts, you will be dearly missed and more. The one I chose was in the center on a pedestal, it had a long ribbon that read "Time may pass and fade away, but memories of you will always stay." The room filled up with many people. I never realized he touched that many people. His friends went front and center, and all said some nice things about him. Mom went up there and thanked him for the most beautiful gift he could have ever given her, me. She thanked him for the good times, for always being there when needed, for still remaining a friend even after they decided they would not work as a couple.

After Mom, it was my turn to go front and center. I stood there and looked around the room. "I didn't really prepare anything," I said. "I tried to write down beautiful words and memories, and I would love to tell you what a great father he was. Truth is I can't. Dennis was many things to me, but not a father. He was a shoulder to cry on if need be, He was a listening ear if need be. But never once did he correct me, tell me off, or allowed me to call him dad. Does that mean I had a bad father? No, it certainly doesn't! It means I had a really good friend, who also happened to be my father! He left the punishing and telling off to Mom. He only had me over every fourteen days for a weekend and every other holiday. He wanted to fill my life with joy and fun memories, he sure did. I barely have any bad memories of Dennis, and for that, I am happy. Thank you, Dennis, for always being there, and for always being my friend!" As I stepped away from the microphone, there wasn't a dry eye in the room. Some tears found their way down my cheek as well. After the service, we went to the graveyard. As the casket was lowered into the ground, everyone threw a single red rose onto it. I was the last to throw a rose and the first to pick up the shovel and toss a heap of dirt onto it. Apparently, it's a tradition for closure. It felt weird.

The entire day was weird. I was prepared to have a heavy and depressing day. But it wasn't. After the bit at the graveyard, a lot of people went back to our house. We were talking about Dennis, about the things he did and still wanted to do. It was a day filled with love and memories. It was a day Roger missed completely. He was still in bed when we got home, still claiming not to feel well. I secretly wished he would get some kind of flesh-eating disease and die, with the best dermatologist in town dead, he stood no chance what so ever anyways. This day was all about Dennis, and there was no room for anger towards Roger. My friends all came to pay their respects and support me. Emma was the last to return to her house. It was fairly late in the evening when the last people left our house. I helped Mom clean up all the dishes, never had I been so thankful we had a dishwasher. After Sean was sound asleep in his little bed and the last bits and pieces were cleaned up, I sank into the couch. I was dead tired. This day wore me down. Roger never once made his appearance. All I could do was hope that one day, Mom would realize that he was a bum, a freeloader, and leave him. But for some reason unbeknownst to me, she loved him. I never made it up the stairs that evening, I fell asleep on the couch and woke up there the next morning when Mom came down the stairs with Sean.

It was Saturday. I didn't have to work, that wouldn't start until next week unless someone else is going to die on me and Adam thinks it wise to postpone it for another week. I asked Mom if she could drive me to the hospital later on. I wanted to tell Linda about the funeral, about the lovely words that were spoken and the sea of flowers. That we guided Dennis to his final resting place. I wanted to see how she was doing if she had any idea when she could leave the hospital. Mom agreed to take me there in the afternoon.

Roger finally made his way down the stairs. He didn't say a word. "Aren't you ashamed of yourself?" I sneered at him. "You might not have liked the man, but he was my father if anything this proves you are a piece of shit!" "You better watch that foul mouth of yours or else..." he recanted, but was interrupted by Mom who was dying to know or else what?! I turned to Mom and told her that he was a waste of space, he didn't care for anyone other than himself. He didn't ever take care of Sean, if I were to drop dead right now, he'd probably step over my dead body and go play video games. "Mom, please look at him, he's a bum, and he's living off of your money but is pretending he is the breadwinner" I pleaded for her to throw him out. She just told me to go to my room.

I left the kitchen but didn't go to my room. I heard them fight. Mom was yelling at him that I was right. He didn't care for anyone other than himself. That he was only with Mom because she brought home the bacon. Since Sean was born, he never even fed him, let alone change his diaper, wash him, or even hold him. She said that she had put up with a lot in the name of love, but that yesterday was the straw that broke the camel's back. For something that was so important not only to me but to her as well, he couldn't even get out of bed! She had enough! She told him she wanted a divorce and that he should pack his things and leave.

Roger yelled at her that it was all lies, that I was the one that planted those in her head. It was fine, he would pack up his things, and he would go. She would come crawling back to him anyway. No way could she handle two kids on her own. She laughed, it was the evilest laugh I ever heard from her. "Really?" she said. I think I am better capable of taking care of two kids than the three I am taking care of now. I quickly made my way up the stairs to my room and still heard yelling going on downstairs. Were they really getting a divorce? Finally! She never should've married him in the first place. No idea what kind of natural herbs they were on when they decided to get married. Good luck Roger, maybe you can convince her to drink some tea tree oil tea with you and make it all better. Roger and his stupid homeopathic, herbal, nature is everything kind of nonsense. At some point, I heard a door slam shut, really loud. I figured it was safe to go back downstairs again.

I expected to find Mom sad and sobbing at the kitchen table, but when I entered the kitchen, she wasn't there. Instead, I found her in the den, wildly going through some drawers. I asked her what she was doing. Looking for her prenuptial agreement and the number of her lawyer, apparently. Never in a million years would I ever think I would say this, but I heard myself say, "Mom? Did you really think this through?" She looked at me with more determination in her eyes than I could find words to describe and said "I should have done this a long time ago, I hoped having a child of his own would awaken his father feelings. I should have known better." She continued her search. As I saw her searching for these papers, I felt a slight panic. Yes, I didn't like Roger, he was an idiot, and he didn't do anything what so ever that we could possibly describe as useful but... he has been there for the last few years. "Found it!" She yelled out and started to dial the number of her lawyer immediately. "Mom, you are wound up and angry, please calm down before you do things you'll regret." Mom looked at me, and told me if it would make me feel better, she would wait with the call until tomorrow.

This will toss all our lives around. Sure he's a bum, and I should be the biggest supporter of a divorce, but I worry for Sean. I am afraid that if she divorces him, he will show less and less interest in Sean. At least now he has Roger in his life. I know, Mom raised me on her own, and I think I turned out quite alright, but I still had Dennis in my life. I am afraid Roger will just leave and stay gone. I wonder where he even went. He ran out the door, didn't take any of his stuff. Maybe he went to build himself a little cabin out of twigs in the woods and will eat bugs and wash himself in the brook. This situation was weird. On the one hand, I couldn't stand Roger, and hearing Mom say that she wants a divorce, felt like a wish come true. On the other hand, I didn't want to be the one who set that in motion, I want little Sean to have a father in his life and I certainly don't want him to blame me in his teens, when puberty strikes, for not having one.

I am going to try and convince Mom to at least talk to Roger. They made Sean together, so at some point not too long ago there still was love, right? What is wrong with me, why aren't I happy. I am finally getting what I wanted, and now I can only think of reasons why I don't want that to happen. None of them are very good reasons. If I can't even convince myself, how am

I going to convince mom?

Now I was the one sulking at the kitchen table. "What is wrong?" Mom asked when she came into the kitchen. "I don't want to be the bringer of bad luck," I replied. "Everywhere I go, people appear to be dying, and now I am causing you and Roger to get divorced." "Let me stop you right there," she said. She started by stating, not saying, it was a true statement, that I was in no way, shape, or form responsible for her wanting a divorce. She continued to tell me that the love had gone soon after she fell pregnant. It seemed as if Roger lost all interest in her. At first, she thought he was afraid to harm the baby, but he stopped showing interest in her, or the baby pretty soon. At some point, she saw a message he sent to one of his friends. It read "the goose is cooked, we got one in the oven, I am settled for life" at first, she thought that he was happy and announcing the pregnancy to his friend, but then she also saw the reply the friend sent. That one read "Good, now she will never get rid of you, and you can do as you please, well-played mate, well played" Rogers only reply to that message was "I know, thank you." This was the point at which Mom wanted to end the relationship the first time, but had high hopes that the baby would melt him.

After Sean was born, he didn't melt. If anything, he became more annoying. Roger got all the attention he wanted, he was acting up like a spoiled brat and stopped doing anything. He didn't even take out the trash anymore. The only things he did was, get up, go to work, come home, play videogames, eat, and go back to bed. On weekends the go to work bit was skipped, but the rest of his activities remained the same. With him missing Dennis' funeral and memorial service, not even showing his face downstairs, Mom had enough. This was a time of need, where we needed him and he definitely showed his true colors.

He is never going to do anything for Sean, and I don't want Sean to see an adult male that deems video games more important than his kid as normal. He has got to go, and you, my dear, have nothing to do with that. This is all my decision, that I blurted it out after you had a little run-in with Roger is pure coincidence. I would have told him today anyway, your little brawl just accelerated the announcement. She told me I had no reason to feel bad. She also told me to forget about this nonsense about being the bringer of bad luck. She pointed out I wasn't there to see Mr. Nelson die, and I've only seen the aftermath of Mr. Kelly's death. She ended with, "If anything, you are my good luck charm, you always keep me safe!" To this day, I am still wondering how I ever kept Mom safe, but hearing those words sure did make me feel better.

Later that day, Mom took me to the hospital to see Linda. Mrs. Kelly was watching little Sean, so we could both visit this time. Mom told her that Dennis had a worthy memorial, that many people showed up, and there were lots of kind words. I asked when she could leave the hospital. Linda said they wanted to keep her there for at least another month. She had some rehabilitation to do. She lost any and all feeling to a big portion of the right side of her face. She could no longer feel her eye socket. She had trouble moving her left arm. And she also suffered a broken ankle that was still healing. I told her I would come by and visit her as much as I could. She smiled and said she'd like that.

After the visiting hour was over Mom and I headed back home. It was good to see Linda again. Her head was still covered in bandages, so we still had no idea what she looked like underneath, neither did she. She told us she didn't want to see it yet. I could imagine that you are not anxious to look at the disfigurement you have to live with for the rest of your life. I couldn't imagine having to stay in the hospital for at least a month. I should have asked her if I could bring her anything to pass the time. I didn't know what though, a book might not be what she wants right now, and she still has to adjust to having only one eye. Mom and I were talking about our hospital visit when all of a sudden, a man ran out of the woods and onto the road.

Mom hit her breaks as hard as she could, I hit my head on the dashboard before the seatbelt did its job. Mom was too late in stopping the car though, she hit the man, and he launched off of the hood of the car, flew a few feet through the air, and landed on the antlers of the majestic buck that was seemingly chasing him. He landed with such force that the antlers pierced him through and through. He landed face down, they went in through his stomach and out through his back. They slit through him like a hot knife through butter. Blood was pouring out. He was still alive, he was squirming, trying to get off. Around his neck he was wearing a pair of binoculars, the cord of his binoculars was woven in a hangman's noose around his head and the antlers. The more he squirmed to get loose, the tighter the knot around his neck became. He was wearing a camouflage jacket. We couldn't make out who he was. Then he started to scream, it was filled with so much panic and pain.

"Roger!" Mom yelled out and stormed out of the car. The buck was trying to make his way back into the forest, but with so much weight on his neck, his legs just collapsed from under him. We called the emergency services to send an ambulance right away. Mom was telling Roger not to move and to hold still. Roger was squirming, still trying to get off. The buck was also squirming trying to get him off. It tried to stand up while scraping his head over the floor. Roger must have been in a lot of pain. At some point, they succeeded, and Roger was off of the antlers, bleeding profusely on the ground. The cord of his binoculars, however, was not. The buck got back onto his feet and took off in a sprint. The cord of the binoculars applied so much force at once that it crushed Rogers's trachea. Roger started suffocating straight away. His death struggle was tough to see. He was gasping for air, trying to cough, but there was no way he could still breathe. The buck dragged him along into the woods for a little distance until the binoculars' cord broke and Rogers' lifeless body was left next to a nettle bush with a bloody trail leading up to him. When the paramedics came, there was nothing they could do, Roger died at the scene. Mom kept yelling out that she killed him. "It... it... it happened so fast, he ran out of the woods... I... I tried to stop... he launched... the buck... holy hell... I killed him... I killed my husband... I... I killed Roger!" After the paramedics gave Mom something to calm down and a small overall checkup, the police took us to the police station to record our statements. The captain was convinced it was an accident and said he'd think the district attorney would feel the same. We were offered guidance counseling, both Mom and I refused. We just wanted to go home.

When we got home, the first thing Mom did was call Mrs. Kelly. She told her something had happened, and she would fill her in on the details tomorrow, but she wanted to ask if Sean could spend the night. That wasn't a problem at all. It was just Mom and me at the house for the rest of that day. "Mom?" I said, "You do realize that you didn't actually kill him, right? I mean, he ran straight in front of the car, there was nothing you could do" Mom looked at me and gave me her warm "everything is going to be okay" smile. She said, "Oh sweetie, yes, I know I didn't actually kill him, but it happened so fast, and I do feel responsible." We talked about it some more. The way Mom was handling this did show me she wasn't lying before. The love was gone. Yes, she was sad that he died and felt guilty because her car hit him, but she wasn't devastated or acting like she just lost the love of her life. Her reaction to Rogers' death was 100% different from Mrs. Kelly to Mr. Kelly's death.

We ordered a pizza, and after the pizza, we did something we had never ever done before. Mom brought out a bottle of vodka, and we drank, and drank, and drank until we were drunk to boot. I couldn't tell you what we talked about or did. All I know is that the next day I woke up with a terrible headache. When I finally made my way to the bathroom that morning, it struck me. Oh no, Roger is really dead, Sean will definitely not have his father in his life. Oh bloody hell, this means we have to arrange another funeral, pick out another casket, and decide all the shit we had also done with Dennis. Oh hell, I don't want to go through that again. When I managed to crawl down the stairs and make my way into the kitchen, Mom was already there.

On the table was a cup of coffee, a glass of water and 2 paracetamol. "Take the pills and drink the water first, and then enjoy your coffee," Mom said. She was looking fine. No hangover there. I wanted to ask her how come she was looking fine, but I was already struggling to try and keep my eyes open. It felt as if there was a marching band in my head, trying to get out by playing really loud and marching into the sides of my skull. I was afraid my head would just explode. Why on earth do people drink so much if this is the aftermath? I decided that the aftermath was totally not worth it. Especially considering I had no memories of the night before. I decided to just sit at the table for a while and stare at a little black spot on our white wall. I am just going to sit here at the table until the pain goes away. Yes, that's my plan, and I am sticking to it.

CHAPTER SEVEN

At some point, my headache toned down to a bearable pain. I got out of the kitchen an attempted to walk back up the stairs. I stood at the bottom of the stairs and looked up. They might have been Mount Kilimanjaro at that point. There was no way I was going to climb them. I turned around and made my way to the couch and sat down. I felt so horrible. Mom came and sat with me. I asked her how she was doing. She was still in shock. She couldn't believe what happened yesterday. How Roger all of a sudden ran in front of her car, how he launched off the hood, how he tumbled through the air and landed right on top of that what he was running from. The poor buck that must have gotten the scare of his life as well. I wonder what happened to him if he was injured by the impact of Roger. When he finally succeeded in getting Roger off of his antlers, he took off into the woods. Roger, killed by the thing he was always pretending to protect, nature.

I looked at Mom and said something that I probably shouldn't have said out loud, but I said it anyway. "Well, at least now you won't have to divorce him" after I heard me say that I realized how stupid and harsh those words were. Mom just looked at me. Before I could tell her I was sorry, there was a faint smile on her face, and she said that I was right about that. She added that a divorce was less work and easier to arrange than another funeral, though. Wow, we were heartless about Rogers' demise. I never cared for him since day one. To me, he was this selfish hypocrite hippy. Pretending everything was about nature. Not eating meat, not eating or drinking dairy products. But he did wear a leather jacket and shoes made of leather. When pointing that out, he just replied that the poor cow or sheep or whatever kind of leather it was, it was already dead and it was of no use to let it go to waste. I stated that the meat in the stores wasn't exactly still living either, he would reply that it's not the same thing. The meat in the store were animals that were bred for the purpose of being meat and that his leather products were just a byproduct of that. It was all a load of rubbish. The only thing that made me sad about his passing was little Sean.

Sean would never get to know his father, he would never be able to form an opinion about him. But on the other hand, he would also never be disappointed by him. He would never find out what kind of lazy bum he was. He wouldn't know about the disinterest he had for him. I would make Roger out to be a hero for Sean. Sean would grow up thinking his father was the greatest. Hell, I'd even make up a story about how he saved that buck from a bear trap and that in its fear and panic the buck accidentally killed him. I would protect Sean better than Roger ever could anyways, and now I could even make Roger out to be the great role model which he never was. Mom interrupted my train of thought. She made me something to eat and said she was going over to Mrs. Kelly to talk about what happened and to pick up Sean. She asked if I would be all right by myself. I told her I'd be fine, if I would eventually make it up the stairs, I might try to get a little more sleep, take a shower, and go out. If I wouldn't make it up the stairs, I'd probably be still sitting here if she got back home again. She laughed, called me silly and left. I turned on the television, not to really watch but to have some noise in the background as I started to eat the food.

At some point, the television drew my attention. They spoke

about Roger, and the news anchor also made a remark about there being a lot of freak accidents happening around town lately. She said something about hearing an old wives tale that the town was cursed. The town cursed? That's an interesting angle, here I thought I was cursed, but it could be the town. The town wasn't huge, so if something were to happen around town, there is a big chance a lot of people will witness it. I tried to comfort myself with that thought. It wasn't me, it's the town! Having eaten something, already made me feel a lot better, I managed to get up the stairs and laid down for a little nap. That little nap lasted 2 hours. I took a shower and got dressed. When I came downstairs, Mom wasn't home yet. I decided to write her a note saying I went out to hang with my friends.

I went to Nigel's house. We couldn't believe the stuff that was going on around here lately. I told him that I heard the news anchor say the town was cursed. That she heard it as an old wives tale. Perhaps we should investigate it. We should go to the library and look into the town's history. Too bad today was Sunday, and the library was closed. We decided to go to the forest instead and went over to our favorite spot in the forest. It was a fallen tree next to the brook. There was a clearing in the forest here where a lot of animals came to drink. A squirrel was washing his nuts in the brook, acorns to be precise. When we sat there and were talking, I heard the sound of a larger animal approaching. It was a deer. Nigel asked if perhaps this was the deer that killed Roger. I didn't think so, this was a doe, and Roger was killed by a buck.

Not long after the doe started drinking, a huge buck showed up. I froze in position as the animal stared directly at me. "This is him," I whispered to Nigel. The antlers of this buck were stained with a brownish color, Rogers dried blood I am sure. It still had the cord of the binoculars around them. The buck ignored the doe and the brook, and slowly stepped towards me. It came so close it pressed its nose against my shoulder. I looked at its antlers. Yes, this definitely was the buck that killed Roger. Why was it behaving so docile? When I found my guts again and dared to move, I removed the binocular cord from his antlers. It was almost as if that was exactly what the buck wanted me to do because it went straight for the brook to have a drink after I removed it. Nigel and I just stared at each other, not saying a single word. After a while, both deer headed back into the forest. It still took us a good 5 minutes, after they disappeared from sight before we spoke again. "That was intense and weird," Nigel said. Indeed it was. This was the buck that was seemingly chasing Roger out of the woods and caused him to die. I was sure it would try and chase us away as well. I didn't expect it to be so docile. We decided to leave the forest.

We walked by the population sign. The number 2994, which was written in a bloodstain where Ricardo's hand was pinned, was now crossed out and the number 2993 was added. I couldn't believe the sign was still up. Flies were squirming around the blood pattern on the board. "Gross" was all Nigel had to say when passing the sign. I asked him if he didn't think it was weird that somebody keeps crossing out the number. He just shrugged and didn't think anything of it. Sometimes people have weird desires. Apparently, we have one inhabitant that has an uncontrollable urge to keep the population count accurate. "What if that person killed Ricardo for messing with the sign?" Saying that seemed to peak Nigel's interest. Next time someone dies, we should stake out the sign, and we will find out who changes the sign. Funny how this little town in the middle of nowhere, where nothing ever happened now appeared to have its own mystery. Quite some strange freak accidents and what seemed to be a murder. Nigel was sure we could be better detectives than our police force. We should include the others so we could take shifts at the sign if somebody were to die again. I would tell the plan to Chris and Emma, Nigel would inform Marcy and Amy. We would set up a stakeout schedule. At least we would get to the bottom of who was changing the sign and perhaps catch a killer in doing so. The next few days were quite uneventful. We went to school, did our homework, and worked out our stakeout schedule. Now we only had to wait for someone else to die.

Mom took care of all the funeral arrangements by herself. This time it was a cremation. She kept it all quite sober. Roger was baptized, so she went for a traditional service in the church. His funeral was on Wednesday. I would have loved to not show up and return the favor. I didn't want to pay my respect to a man I didn't respect. I went to the service anyway. For Mom, not for Roger. There were a few funeral bouquets, and the church wasn't filled completely. People were scattered through the church, so it did give the feeling of a full church, but if you would put them all next to each other, I don't think you would fill up half the church. As with any funeral, some people stepped to the front and said some nice words. His love for nature was praised and that he always delivered his goods on time. I didn't hear a single word about his personality, that he was a nice and warm man, that he helped anyone out, no funny anecdotes, just his love of nature and that he was good at his work. Well then Roger, there you have it, that's your legacy.

After the service, only Rogers' parents came back to our house. Mom spoke with them and asked if there were any of Rogers' things they'd like to have. His mother only asked for his pictures, his father had no desire to take anything. Mom asked about the remains. If they were okay with them being scattered out in the forest. His mother's eyes welled up with tears. "Yes, he would have loved that, he loved nature so much," she said, his father agreed. They drank a few more cups of coffee while talking with Mom and playing with Sean. Unlike Roger, they did show an interest in the little fella. They even asked me how I was holding up. They might not be my grandparents, but besides grandma on mom's side, I never had any grandparents, and they filled the gap up quite nicely. At some point, his mother asked if it was okay if they still came by on occasion to see little Sean. Mom was stunned by this question. "Of course that is all right Myrtle, you are his grandparents, you have a permanent spot in his life!" she replied. After a while, they went home, and Mom decided to take a nice hot bath. I remained downstairs with little Sean, who had just discovered how to roll over. Oh my, if he's rolling over already how fast will he be with sitting up, crawling and walking? I picked him up and put him in the playpen. I sat on the couch and turned on the television. Perhaps there was a nice movie on or something.

Zapping through the channels on the television I found absolutely nothing worth watching. Amazing, we have almost 600 channels on television, granted a lot of them are foreign and I can't understand a single word they are saying, but still, there was only rubbish on. Movies that were so ancient that everyone had seen them a million times. Some television shows that might be fun to watch if they weren't interrupted by a 10-minute commercial break every 15 minutes. As I was about to turn off the television, I heard an announcement about a trial special. It was Patrick's trial. At least that was about somebody I knew, so I might watch that. I had already forgotten that his trial started last Monday. Apparently, it was already over, wow that was fast, and today was its recap. The jury was in deliberation. As soon as they came out with a verdict of either guilty or not guilty, it would all be over and done with. It started as any documentary starts. With a so-called expert stating that the jurors might have a hard time to come up with a verdict on this case. He repeated the indictment. Patrick S. was indicted for sexual harassment, abuse of power, lewd acts with a minor, sexual misconduct, and they added statutory rape to the charges as well. Patrick S. had, on several occasions, seduced his intern Brody B. to perform sexual acts on him. Brody had testified that, more than once, Patrick had sodomized him against his will and threatened to give him a bad review for his internship if he didn't comply. I couldn't believe what I was hearing. All this time we thought Patrick had done the naughty with some underage girl, but he actually went for his male intern? I knew Brody from around town. He wasn't someone to stand out in a crowd, he usually just kept to himself. He didn't have many friends, if I saw him outside, he was usually playing with his dogs. Can't remember ever stopping and have a chat with him. Poor Brody. His parents testified that they saw a difference in his behavior since he started his internship at the newspaper. He was turning more and more into himself. One time when doing the laundry, his mother found a blood-soaked pair of underpants. Not knowing how to confront their son about this, she let it slide. One evening during dinner, when his father tried to comfort him for something, he curled up into a fetal position and started pleading not to touch him. That was when the entire story came out.

Brody told them about Patrick and what he did and made him do. My stomach must have turned over quite a few times listening to this recap. Patrick also took the stand. He pleaded not guilty to all charges. He claimed all sexual contact was with consent, that Brody freaked out when his parents found out and made up this elaborate story about being forced. Why would he, as a well-respected journalist within the community, risk his position for some sexual gratification? A few more witnesses were heard. All testified about the change in Brody's demeanor. There wasn't a single character witness for the defense though. In the end, the expert stated that with all the testimonies, the jurors might have a hard time to come to a clear verdict. Without there being any physical proof it was a, he said, he said and would come down to who the jurors would believe more. I was sick to my stomach when the program was over. I looked over to little Sean. I would personally kill anyone that would do that to my little brother. Forget the police, forget the court, they don't get to do time, they will die a horrible death!

Mom finished her bath and joined me on the couch. She asked what was wrong and I told her about the special I just watched. "Oh honey, why do you watch that?" she looked at me with a bit of sadness in her eyes. The only reason I ended up watching that was because there wasn't anything better on. Now I just felt horrible. Horrible that this was going on under all our noses, but none of us noticed. None of us took enough of an interest in Brody to notice any change. A part of me wanted to go over to his house and invite him to hang out. But the sensible part of me prevented that from happening. I don't think Brody was looking for a pity party or for friends who only become friends because something bad had happened. If I were Brody, I would probably want all of this to be over and forgotten and go back to normal. I decided to take the dog out for a walk, perhaps I would run into Brody and chat him up casually.

I decided to walk towards the forest, that way I would pass by Brody's house. He wasn't outside. Perhaps he was hiding, with the trial going on and everything. As I approached the garden, I noticed a for sale sign. Yeah, I guess I would want to move my child away from the town this happened in as well. I decided to just walk around the town a bit. I ended up at the town square. It was dark, the fountain was lit up by the lights at its base. It gave the water a yellow glow, like fire. It was a Wednesday evening, so the bars weren't filled, and the restaurants were still serving their last dinner guests. It was quiet in the town square. I haven't seen Mrs. McHenry in a while. I don't know why it struck me as strange. She wasn't always there, but lately, I've seemed to always run into her and now... I guess it must have been over a week ago since I last saw her. I had no idea where she lived, or I might have gone and check up on her. Maybe she died and is now rotting away on her Livingroom floor. Waiting to become another newspaper headline. Something about neighbors calling the police because of the horrible stench that came from her house.

When I returned home, I asked Mom if she knew where Mrs. McHenry lived. Mom thought long and hard, but she had no idea. I told her I was a bit worried because I hadn't seen her in a while. "Oh, don't you worry about Mrs. McHenry dear, she can hold her own," Mom said. I guess... but it still felt a bit uneasy. I could tell you where most people in the town lived, even if I didn't know them very well. If I couldn't tell you an exact address, I could give you a good idea in which part of town they would live. But not with Mrs. McHenry, she could live near the edge of town or in the dead center of it. I had no clue. Maybe there would be a trail of breadcrumbs leading from the town square to her house, just like Hansel and Gretel. Impossible, the pigeons would have eaten all the breadcrumbs. Perhaps follow a trail of pigeons instead, I smiled. What a silly thought, a trail of pigeons. Now that would be something! I would just ask around town, someone would know where she lives. And Mom was right, no need to worry, she's probably just fine.

I had to figure out what to do with Dennis' belongings, but first, I needed to know what Linda wanted to do. If she was planning on returning to the house, I wouldn't touch a thing. We were to see her again this evening, and I really should bring it up this time, but I had no idea how to do that. Hell, I am a sixteen-year-old having to ask a grown-up woman if she plans on staying in my house. My house... that will never be my house! I might own it on paper, but I have never lived there, nor will I ever. I took the bus to the hospital this time. I didn't want to bother Mom, besides she was busy with Mrs. Kelly anyway. I went into Linda's room, but her bed was empty. A little strike of panic ensued, but I was put at ease pretty swiftly when they wheeled her in again. She was out for some more examinations. I asked her if she was improving after she got settled in her bed again. She answered that she was, baby steps, but still, there was some improvement.

"Linda... I..." I stopped and sighed. Linda was looking in anticipation of what I was struggling to say. I took a deep breath and said, "Linda... I need to know if you plan on returning to the house when you get released here," Linda laughed. "Is that what you were struggling to ask?" she asked. "No, I have no plans of returning to Dennis' house, it never was my house anyway even though I did move in," she answered. It's the house where Dennis died, where she got severely injured, she'll carry the marks of that for the rest of her life. I asked her if she could make me a list of her belongings and of the things that belonged to Dennis that she wanted to keep. She said there was no need to make a list. All her belongings were in the empty guest bedroom, Dennis didn't want to mingle their stuff yet, so her things were kept separate in the guest bedroom. As for Dennis' belongings, there was nothing she wanted to have. All of it would remember her of that fatal evening. I told her I would clean out the house and put it up for sale. She asked if she could ask her mother to contact me about picking up her belongings. She would stay over at her mother's house after she was released from the hospital. She would need some time to adjust to her new situation, her Mom would take care of her. At least now I knew what to do with the house and the stuff in it. When the visiting hour was over, we said our goodbyes and I promised to come by and visit again soon.

Tomorrow I would start my job at the antique shop, thankfully Adam didn't make me wait another week due to Rogers' passing. I would have hated Roger even more if I wasn't allowed to start tomorrow. I was home alone once again. It was kind of nice having the couch free. No Roger sitting on it, playing video games. I watched a movie I had seen a million times before, but it was better than watching some documentary about a rare plant that only blooms once every 30 years and smells horrible, or the reality T.V. shows. After the movie, there was an announcement for the news broadcast. They had an update about Patrick's trial. The jury had reached a verdict. Great, now I had to sit through all the commercials because now I wanted to know what the verdict was. I almost fell asleep during the commercials, the recognizable tune of the news pulled me away from the dreamlands and landed me back into reality. I first had to sit through the global news. Mostly reporting about ongoing wars and conflicts about to happen. I can't help but wonder if any of these soldiers can still remember what they are fighting for, or if they really do support the cause for which they are putting themselves in danger. I guess they are all just fighting for their next paycheck.

At the end of the broadcast, there was time for local news. Patrick was the local news main story. The anchor told a bit about the trial and that the jurors only needed to deliberate for a little more than a day to reach their verdict. My Aunty Gale, who was a reporter, came on screen, reporting live from outside the courthouse. She said that it was an intensive trial. A lot of emotions riled up in the courtroom during the testimonies. As the chairman of the jury read out the verdict, at first, it was quiet in the courtroom. Then it showed a clip of inside the courtroom.

It showed the chairman of the jury going by every complaint. "As to count 1 of the indictment, sexual harassment, we the jury find the defendant, guilty as charged." A gasp could be heard through the courtroom. The camera panned in on the parents of Brody. They both had tears in their eyes and eager to hear the rest of the verdict. The chairman continued. "As to count 2 of the indictment, abuse of power, we the jury find the defendant, guilty as charged. As to count 3 of the indictment, lewd acts with a minor, we the jury find the defendant, guilty as charged. As to count 4 of the indictment, sexual misconduct, we the jury find the defendant, guilty as charged. On count 5 of the indictment, statutory rape, we the jury find the defendant, guilty as charged" The judge then asked "So say you all?" all the jurors replied with a "Yes, your honor." He scheduled the sentencing hearing for next Monday. The camera cut back to Aunty Gale outside. She spoke a bit more about the verdict and how it wasn't surprising that the jurors came to a guilty verdict on all charges after seeing the testimony of Brody who was brave enough to stand up and testify in court against his abuser. After that, the broadcast returned to the anchor in the studio, and I decided to turn off the television, I had to go to work tomorrow so I couldn't stay up late. I felt somewhat satisfied that Patrick got convicted. On that note, I went to bed.

When I woke up, bright and early, the next morning, I made myself a little breakfast and a cup of coffee. Mrs. Kelly was looking in through the kitchen window and started knocking on the back door. I let her in. She was completely out of breath. "Where is your mother?" she asked. "You need to get her and turn on the television. It's horrible." I asked her what happened. She told me to just get Mom out of bed. I did as I was told and got Mom out of bed. "Oh god, I am so sorry," Mrs. Kelly said. Mom was confused and asked what she was sorry about. Mrs. Kelly looked in my direction again and told me to turn on the television. I asked to what channel. Any channel would do. Again I did as I was told.

Apparently last night a lunatic broke free from the courthouse after his conviction. He was convicted of first-degree murder. He snatched up Aunty Gale, her cameraman, and a few other innocent bystanders and held them hostage, all this time the camera was still rolling and broadcasting live. The terror on all the hostages' faces was plain for all to see. Mom was worried about Aunty Gale. It was her older sister, the one that helped her get a job when she needed one. Mom worked for the same news station as Aunty gale did, as a newsroom editor. Both of them were the cause for me wanting to become a journalist. Mom could tell the best stories of the clips she edited and of all the footage that didn't make it into the broadcasts. Aunty gale started out as an international reporter, but when she started having kids, she wanted to stay closer to home. The network complied with her wishes, and she became a local reporter. It did not have the flair of an international reporter, but she enjoyed her work a lot. My attention got drawn by the television again. Everyone was so afraid, even the idiot holding them hostage looked as if he was in a panic.

Aunty Gale tried to stealthily crawl towards the door. The hostage-taker noticed her and went berserk. "You think you can just crawl out of here little lady? No woman will ever leave me again unless I tell her it's okay!" he yelled out. There was a rage in his eyes, pure hatred seeped through in his looks. He hit Aunty Gale in her face with his gun, he hit her again. At this point, Mom was screaming at the television for him to stop. I could see the pain on moms face. "Why aren't they cutting to commercials?!" she exclaimed. "No one should see this happening!" The hostage-taker hit Aunty Gale again, and she finally fell down on to the floor. He walked away from her, only to come back, holding a metal rod. "No woman will ever leave me again!!" he shouted as he hit her with the metal rod. We could hear Aunty Gale yell out that she was sorry and we could hear her beg and plead for her life. He kept hitting her with the pipe. A pattern of blood spatter was forming against the wall and on the ceiling. Every hit Gale screamed louder, and her cries were tough to swallow for anyone, but for Mom in particular. She was watching a madman hurting her sister, and there was nothing she could do. As Gales' screams got louder, the man seemed to get more and more agitated. We heard the sound of bones breaking. At some point, Aunty Gale stopped screaming and crying, she passed out due to the pain and stress I reckon. We could still hear her gurgling in her own blood. As the man stood over her, holding the metal pipe over the location of her heart, we all heard him say, "now, you may leave me." He lifted the rod and stuck it straight through her heart. "NOOOOOOOOOOOOO!" Mom screamed at the television. She was hysterically crying. I didn't know what to do. The picture went to black. Tell me that wasn't real, please, someone, tell me that wasn't real!

Mrs. Kelly and I tried our best to calm Mom down. Mom wanted to go to the courthouse, help her sister, and get that bastard. Mrs. Kelly and I had a hard time convincing her to stay home.

There was nothing she could do over there. I went into the kitchen and put on a pot of coffee. I called over to the antique shop for I didn't have Adams' personal number, but there was no answer. I couldn't go to work and leave Mom alone in this state. Not that I could do anything for her, I was distraught as well. I just saw my Aunty being murdered in front of my eyes through television. Everyone saw it. Only just now I realized that our phone was ringing, and had been ringing for quite some time. "Leave it!" Mrs. Kelly said with so much authority that I immediately left it. "Everyone saw that happen on television, every reporter that is awake will start calling Gales family now," she said. I guess she was right. This was horrible and aired live on television, this made for a sensational news story. I didn't want to be part of that circus. Mrs. Kelly suggested that we'd all go over to her house, we agreed. Mom picked up Sean, his formula, and some of his toys, and off we went to Mrs. Kelly's house. On our way there, Mom called grandma on her cell phone. Reporters were already calling grandma's landline, she had heard the news and was heartbroken. Mom told her where we went and invited her to come over as well. Grandma arrived half an hour later. The pesky reporters already made it up to her house. She had to sneak out to be sure they wouldn't follow her. This was madness, had they all completely lost their minds? Let us mourn in private, why do you want us to share it with the world. It was only 8:15 am, and the reporters were gathering around our house like vultures. They had no idea we were somewhere else. At least that way we had a little bit of peace and quiet.

By now, my friends started sending me texts as well, asking how I was doing, how Mom was, and how shocked they were about what happened. Believe me, none of them were as shocked as I was. I don't think I will ever get rid of that image. The pure rage in that man's face, the force he applied to the rod, the screams of Aunty Gale, the gurgling sound she made when her mouth was filled with her own blood, and she was struggling to breathe. Aunt Gale never saw that final blow coming, she was already out cold by then. How could they let this madman escape! If he was on trial for murder, why wasn't he in shackles? How on earth could this have happened? I really wanted to get rid of those images and to be honest, I didn't want to sit with Mom and Mrs. Kelly all day either. I decided that there was still time to make it to the antique shop before 9 am. Maybe Adam didn't watch the news, or perhaps he would assume I hadn't seen it yet. Either way, I was going to the antique shop.

I arrived shortly before 9 am. I walked in, trying to act like everything was fine, I yelled for Adam. Adam came to the front of the store and asked me what I was doing here? "Well, I work here, remember? I am starting today?" I tried to play it off. Adam questionably examined me. "Hmm no, I don't see any evidence of a fall," he said. What kind of fall? I hadn't fallen. "The fall in which you must have hit your head so hard that you can no longer think straight. " He said when I asked what fall. Silly me, thinking I could fool Adam. Clearly, he had seen it, and he wasn't dumb enough to think I hadn't. He wanted to know why I came to work. I decided to be open and honest. I told him my motives were purely selfish. I didn't want to deal with any of it right now, and I would take on anything that would get my mind off things. I didn't want to be at my house because of the reporters. I didn't want to hide at Mrs. Kelly with Mom and grandma because, well, none of the subjects they speak about interest me, and I know little to absolutely nothing about most of them. I couldn't just roam around town, people would just keep telling me that they saw it and how shocked they were. "Please Adam, let me stay and work, I just don't want to think about the real world for a little while" Adam looked at me, there was a little sparkle in his eye. Adam finally agreed to let me stay today, on one condition. I would have to clean out the basement, dust the shelves, sweep and mop the floors. Do I look like a cleaning lady to you? I hardly look like a cleaning lady!

Somehow I think he tricked me into this one, but he said that the basement would be the best place to hide from those pesky reporters. I figured he was right about that, they would never look for me in the basement, so I started dusting the shelves and sweeping the floor. Not until I was about to mop the floor the thought occurred to me that no pesky reporter would come and look for me in the antique shop either. I had to hand it to Adam, I fell for that one, hook line and sinker. Well played sir, well played. I finished cleaning the basement and made my way back up into the shop. Adam was admiring his priceless, not really priceless it had a tag just like anything else in the store, dining set. It looked so comfortable and made for a king. I still wouldn't dare to ask him if I could sit on it. I think he would have a stroke if I would even suggest that. Adam noticed I was finished and told me I could head out for lunch somewhere if I wanted. It was 1 pm, lunchtime. I went to buy a simple sandwich and ate it at the restaurant before returning to the antique store. I enjoyed the sound of the fountain as I walked across the square. I looked around and still didn't see Mrs. McHenry. I should stop making myself nuts over nothing. She was probably doing just fine.

Lay Dee

CHAPTER EIGHT

When I returned to the antique shop, Adam was engaged in conversation with a man that was unfamiliar to me. He was about 6 feet tall and quite a chubby fella. He was bald, unsure if it was by choice or by nature, he had a well-trimmed beard which gave away his ginger hair color. Adam introduced him as George. George was a pre-sales consultant for an IT company. I nodded as if I knew what that was. George recently moved into old Mr. Nelson's house. Well, previously Mr. Nelson's house. George had bought it and moved in with his wife and 3 children. I asked if he heard what happened to the previous owner. He confirmed that he heard about the horrible accident and that he was sad a young lady lost her life. I told him I lived across the street from him, in the house next to the one where the accident took place. George said he noticed there were a lot of reporters and news crews around my house. Before I could answer, Adam intervened, he told George that something had happened to a family member of mine and those rats were now swarming around my house in hopes of getting another scoop or reaction to the event.

Adam told me to head into the basement and start to do research, price, and catalog the items down there. Now that was something I was looking forward to doing. Cleaning the basement was not a job I enjoyed very much. But researching the items, that I did love to do. Every single one of the antique items in Adam's shop had its own story. There was this silver handheld mirror with matching comb, at one point in time it belonged to Marie Antoinette. She was the queen of France until she was convicted for incest and treason in a questionable trial. She was sentenced to death by guillotine. The comb and mirror were accompanied by a small portrait of Marie Antoinette holding them. Like most items, these also came with a certificate of authenticity. I couldn't help but wonder who came in and authenticated them and based on what exactly.

When I got back into the basement, there was this huge pile of items that weren't cataloged. It looked like a great big pile of junk. I decided to sort the pile out. When I was finished I had 3 smaller, but still big, piles of junk. One pile of big items, one with smaller items and one with small items. I looked at the piles, somewhat disappointed. At this point, Adam came into the basement, saw the expression on my face and the 3 piles, and he started to laugh. "Yes, I made that mistake once as well" He explained that it was of no use to sort the big pile out into little piles. It was better to just grab an item and start researching it. In the back of the basement, there was a little desk with a computer that on its own could be marked as an antique. It had specific software installed that made it easy to look up the items. It also had a connection to the internet in case one felt that the software didn't include enough detail or couldn't find the item, you could give it a shot with your favorite search engine.

I started with an antique table, it had a marking edged in its base. I scanned the marking and told the software to search for it. This software is amazing, it found a lot of marks that were similar to this one, and one that matched perfectly. I looked it up and got the name of the maker. Now I could search for his known work to see if this table was amongst it. It was! I found the exact same table. What I did not expect to see was the price on it. In pristine condition, this table was worth $5.300. I wouldn't label it pristine though. It clearly had some scratches and markings that didn't belong, but it surely was of good quality. In good condition, it still went for $3.700. For some reason, I heard Roger's voice in my head saying, "Ha, for that money, I could buy myself a brand new table and 6 chairs!" The thought of that made me chuckle. I looked up some information on the maker. Apparently, he was Danish and considered a modernist for his time. I put all the info on the card and priced the table. I looked up a few more items. I was really enjoying to read about their maker and where they came from. Many of the items had well-documented backstories.

I came across a pile of old books. I love books. They were all first editions of something or another. Most of them seemed to be maps or travel guides. Found a traveling guide from the 1900s of northern Germany. I wondered who would come in and buy that. None of them were really worth a lot of money, though. 20 bucks here 15 bucks there. These books would not make Adam rich, no sir. At the bottom of the pile, there was a very old looking book. I looked at its cover, it showed a rather desolate land. In big red letters was the number 3000 written on it. I read the back cover. This sure was a weird book. The synopsis, at least I think that's what it was meant to be, read as follows:

A book to protect the world, and keep all well
A book to protect the world, from the gates of hell
The words inside, you'll have to heed
The words inside, you need to read
Become a guardian, be brave
Become a guardian, keep everyone safe

It gave me an eerie feeling. As I was about to look it up on the computer, Adam called for me. I went back up the stairs. It was time to close shop and go home. I had a lot of fun looking up everything and asked if I could come back on Monday after school. Adam was a bit surprised that I actually liked looking up things. I told him about me wanting to become a journalist, and that research was a big part of being one. He said that it was the part he most dreaded. Sometimes he would have an item with a unique story, but most of the time they were well documented boring items. As to answer my question, he told me to focus on school during the week. I was welcome to come by anytime, but save the work for Saturdays. I reluctantly agreed. Adam asked if I was okay with going home. I wasn't really, but I had no other choice, perhaps now after an entire day, the attention might have died down. I thanked Adam for allowing me to work today. We parted ways, and I was about to head to Mrs. Kelly's house.

I decided I didn't want to head back to Mrs. Kelly's straight away. I called Mom to let her know I would be going for a walk before heading back there and asked her how she was doing. She said that the big circus of reporters was slowly dying down. She didn't have the heart to turn on the radio or television anymore. She was still at Mrs. Kelly's, and grandma was there as well. They were about to start cooking dinner, and she asked me to not make it too late before heading over there. I promised her I wouldn't.

When I hung up the phone, I noticed that I had received a message from Nigel. It read, "We were too late with the stakeout, the sign has been changed, but it's been changed to a higher number." A higher number would actually make sense. Since George moved in with his wife and kids that meant the population count has grown by 5, well, 4 since we have to deduce Aunty Gale. I decided to go and see for myself, I would pass the sign on my way to the forest anyway. I saw that the number 2993 was crossed out and that the number 2998, which was added underneath it, was also crossed out. The new number that was added was a bit odd, though. It should be 2997 with the loss of Aunty Gale, but the new number read 2995. I sent Nigel a message. I asked him about the numbers. Since he lived close to the edge of town he told me to stay put, he'd be right over.

Stay put, sure... I'll stay put... near the sign where Ricardo was killed, on my own, in the twilight dusk. Not unsettling at all. I heard some twitches behind me break, the sound came from the forest. I turned around, afraid to come eye to eye with the person who killed Ricardo, but all I saw was a little bunny hopping away. I nervously chuckled at myself. After the bunny disappeared from sight, it became silent, dead silent. I can't remember it ever being so silent. Then, out of nowhere, I heard footsteps approach and a voice "Hey." I almost jumped 3 feet up into the air. "Oh man, you scared the living daylights out of me," I said to Nigel as I turned around. He told me he didn't see the 2995 number before, he only saw the 2998 number. I told him that Mr. Nelson's house was sold. A family of 5 moved in which would explain the 2998 number. We couldn't figure out the 2995 number though. As far as we knew, no one else had died yet.

I looked at Nigel and said, "Oh no, Mrs. McHenry" Nigel looked at me puzzled. I told him to think about it. She was pretty old, and she was always on the square feeding the pigeons, and I haven't seen her in quite a while. Might even be two weeks ago that I had last seen her. Nigel started thinking, long and hard. He also didn't remember seeing her lately. Maybe she passed away as well. I felt a bit sad at that thought. That would be another person I somewhat cared about and was an icon to the town, that would be no longer amongst us. Nigel pointed out the obvious. "The number is still off by 1 if it would be Mrs. McHenry." He was correct. I asked him if he knew how the hostage situation ended. He said he had no idea. There was no more news about it on television, the news channel was airing their test pattern and a statement on the screen that they would not be airing today due to technical difficulties. We decided we would get to the bottom of this mystery another day. I had to head back to Mrs. Kelly's, dinner would probably be close to ready by now.

When I arrived at Mrs. Kelly's, Mom and grandma were still setting the table. They asked if I had a good day at work. In light of things, I didn't want to say that I had a great day and that I didn't think about what happened at all. That I was too busy researching the past to be bothered with the present. I just told them I had a good first day, and that everything was still new to me, so I was still learning the ropes. I asked how their day had been, and if any of the reporters found them at Mrs. Kelly. Mom said they didn't, but that one of them did call her on her cell phone. I asked if she scolded him, but already knew she didn't, it's Mom we are talking about. She told the reporter that she appreciated their interest, that she had seen the horrible footage, that we all were shocked and would greatly appreciate it if they would respect our privacy and allow us to grieve in peace. The reporter thanked her for her statement and slowly but surely, the circus of reporters at our house started to disappear. Grandma was so sad and so in shock. She tried to not let it show, but it was pretty obvious. I felt so sad for her. Yes, I was sad too, I lost my Aunty, but grandma lost her eldest.

During dinner, she said that parents are not supposed to bury their children. Gale was no longer an international reporter, she became a local reporter to take care of her kids and be with her husband. She took herself out of the fire lines and into the safety and comfort of our little town. It wasn't fair. I hadn't even dared to think about uncle Artie or the kids. They are probably devastated. I hope none of them seen it happen. I asked Mom about it, she said she hadn't been able to contact uncle Artie just yet. He's probably busy at the police station. Since I had spent most my day in a basement I heard no news about the hostage situation, did it end? Mom answered that it did after Aunty Gale was killed the police stormed the place and shot the man. He died on the way to the hospital. Our attention was drawn to the street when all of a sudden, all the remaining reporters jumped in their cars and drove away at high speed. We looked at each other a little bit confused but also quite relieved. We were free to return to our house without having to deal with those reporters. After dinner and cleaning up, we thanked Mrs. Kelly and headed back home. Not a single reporter in sight. Mom asked grandma to spend the night, just to be sure she wouldn't run into any reporters on her way. We set up the guest room for grandma to sleep in.

Mom's phone rang, it was uncle Artie. He took the boys on a fishing trip on Friday evening. He only just found out what had happened. I couldn't help but feel glad none of them saw the spectacle on television. Mom told him to bring the boys and come over. He hadn't told them yet, he didn't know how to tell them that their mother was dead. She was fine Friday evening when they left. I could not imagine what he was going through, and he was right, how do you tell your kids that their mother is dead, killed by a madman. They were still very young, but old enough to understand. Ryan was 6, and Lucas was 8; they were always happy and cheerful, oblivious to the evil in the world. Now there was this news, this reality no 6 and 8-year-old should ever have to deal with. That is not the age at which the world shows you its ugly side. They should be playing with their toys and worrying if they were nice enough to get presents from Santa. That should be their only care in the world. Uncle Artie was fighting his tears with all his might and tried his best to keep a normal posture for the boys when they arrived at our house. Mom gave the boys some chocolate milk and set up the second guest bedroom for them to sleep in. After they finished their chocolate milk, I offered to take them to bed. They still had no idea, for them, this was a surprise sleepover, and they were having the best time.

After they brushed their teeth and got into their pajamas, they asked me to read them a story. I was browsing through our collection of children's books. I noticed that all the fairy tales had one thing in common, there was always an evil stepmother or a witch, but there never seemed to be a mother. I decided to stay away from the fairytales and read them a story about a little fox. There were only other animals in this book and no mention of parents or evil witches. Just a happy story about a little fox. After the story, I tucked them in and told them to be quiet and go to sleep. Before I made it to the stairs, they were already calling me back into the room.

Ryan said he couldn't sleep, he was afraid of the dark. I didn't have a night light for him, so I told him there was nothing to be afraid of, that the dark helped to find the way to dreamland. He should close his eyes and look around in the dark. There should be a rainbow that is only visible in the dark. Sliding over this rainbow would land you into dreamland. By now Lucas way paying attention as well, he asked what dreamland was. I smiled and answered his question. Dreamland is the land made of dreams. In dreamland, you can find anything you like and do anything you please. The clouds are made of marshmallows and cotton candy, there are fields where lollipops grow. In the center, you would find a chocolate fountain you could swim in. Houses were made of gingerbread and cookies, there was a train made of cake and a chocolate tunnel. Your stuffed animals come to life in dreamland, and you can actually talk with them if you want to fly you fly. Anything you want to be there, is there. By the time I finished telling them about dreamland, Ryan was already there, and Lucas was well on his way. I quietly left the room and went down the stairs again.

Mom, grandma, and uncle Artie were all sitting at the kitchen table. Uncle Artie was broken. He sat there crying in disbelief. I don't think I have ever seen him like this. He was always the funny man. The comedian at the parties, the one who pulled the lamest pranks and laughed the hardest. He wasn't now, now he was just a big broken mess. He just lost the love of his life and the mother of his children. He still had to tell the boys in the morning. He had to be the one to crush their perfect world, grandma interrupted him telling him that he isn't the one responsible for crushing their world, that madman was! "It's all the same." Uncle Artie replied. "It doesn't matter, for the rest of their lives they will remember the moment that I told them their mother has died. That is what will be edged in their memories, and I don't know how to do it. I don't know how to tell them that the perfect world they are living in, isn't perfect at all. How, please, tell me how am I to tell them that their mother is dead, I don't even think Ryan knows what death is!" He started crying again. I had no idea how to react to this. There was my uncle, a man I looked up to most of my life, completely broken and crying at our kitchen table. Mom and grandma both laid an arm around him. They told him they would be there when he tells them, and help in any which way they possibly could. I offered my room to uncle Artie, and I spend the night with Mom in her room. I went to bed before they did. As I was staring at the ceiling, I couldn't help but wonder about the population sign. Who else had died this weekend? Aunty Gale and the madman that shot her made up for 2 deaths, but there was an addition of 5 and a subtraction of 3. Who was the third one? Maybe the one responsible for the numbers had just made a mistake, and with that thought, I fell asleep.

When I went outside the next morning to grab the newspaper, it became obvious that the sign changer did not make a mistake. The front page had 2 headlines. The one at the bottom read "Reporter killed during hostage situation" thankfully it was a plain text article, no stills of the live broadcast. I wasn't surprised at this article, just happy they didn't turn it into something tasteless. The headline at the top, however, was accompanied by a picture. It's true, a picture says more than a thousand words. It showed a corpse hanging from a flagpole with all the intestines dangling out. The end of the intestines was pinned to the flagpole with a pocket knife, and the head of the deceased was pinned to the top of the flagpole. Somehow it reminded me of Ricardo's murder scene. His hand was pinned to the sign with a pocket knife as well. There was a trace of blood down the white flagpole. I recognized the house and the garden. This was the house next door to Nicolle and Paul's house. I had to read the story to find out that it was indeed their neighbor that was dangling at the top of the pole.

Mr. Thompson was a horrible man, if a ball landed in his backyard, he stabbed the ball with a knife. We never got any of our balls back. If we were playing on the street, he'd always come out to yell at us for making too much noise and that we'd better not touch his car, or else. He was always angry, and Nicolle was terrified of him. Their parents always encouraged us to play on the other side of the house, and not in front of Mr. Thompson's house. He was the kind of neighbor you would love to hate. As we grew older and bigger, we just laughed at him as he came outside to try and scare us off. When we were about 12 or 13, we stopped respecting him completely. We would call him gramps to his face. He once threatened to call the police because we were riding our bicycles to close to his car. Paul stepped off of his bicycle and went right in his face. "Listen, gramps, I ride my bicycle wherever I damn well please if you don't like it, move. I am pretty sure no one will miss you, or better yet, just die already," he said. Mr. Thompson turned red with anger and rage and went straight over to Paul and Nikki's house. We all feared that there would be some severe punishment. None of us were taught to disrespect the elderly, we were thought quite the opposite. "Bitch!" is the word Mr. Thompson screamed out as he walked away from Paul and Nikki's front door onward to his own house. I guess he didn't get the reaction he wanted out of their Mom.

A few moments later, he came out with a garden hose and started to water the plants in his garden. The next one to ride past his car was Nicolle. He turned around and put the hose on her, this made her lose her balance and the control of her bicycle, she drove it straight into his car and broke her arm in the process. The police were called, and Mr. Thompson got arrested for reckless endangerment or something like that. He had to pay a nifty fine and a rather large sum to Nikki for pain and suffering. Nicolle remained scared of the man till the day she died. None of us liked him, but to see him in the newspaper, dangling like a flag on a flagpole with his guts out like party streamers, that wasn't what I wanted for him either. This must have been why the reporters all left our house in such a hurry the night before. I handed Mom the newspaper when she came down and told her to put it away before the boys got up. She looked in horror at the picture and quickly stuffed it in one of the drawers. I wished Mom luck with the tough day ahead of them.

At lunchtime, both deaths were the topic of the day. Every kid in school was talking about it. Because the hostage situation took place fairly early on a Saturday morning, not many of them had actually seen the madman kill my Aunty. The few that did see it talked about it to their friends in detail. I just pretended not to hear any of it, of course, they were talking about it, and I couldn't blame them. They also talked about Mr. Thompson. Most of them saw the newspaper article and the very graphic picture. Some said they couldn't believe the newspaper actually printed that photo and others rebutted that in this day and age it would appear on the internet anyway, for the newspaper to remain in the playing field they had to become more graphic. True as this might be, on the internet, I still had a choice to not click the link showing me the picture. Finding it on the front page of the newspaper was a different story, it was there, and you had no choice not to look at it. You could try not to look at it, but your peripheral vision would still piece together the horrible picture. This was a newspaper that in many homes would disappear into a drawer until the children left for school before it was read. This image was not friendly for children at all. The newspaper received a lot of critiques and released a statement later that day in which they apologized and promised to never put images like that on the front page but instead, put them inside somewhere with a notice of graphic content on the front page.

We spoke about Mr. Thompson. We all agreed that he was a nasty man, and we all rather seen him go. But this was shocking, to say the least. After school, we all hung out at the town square for a bit. It was a sunny day and busy at the square. "Have any of you seen Mrs. McHenry lately?" I asked them. They were all thinking, but none of them could say for sure that they had seen her last week. I asked if any of them knew where she lived. They all shrugged. "She can stay gone, for all I care," Amy stated. She answered our puzzled looks by saying that with the disappearing of Mrs. McHenry, there was a lot less flying rats. "Pigeons are not Rats" Nigel came to their defense, he topped it off with letting everyone know he would take over the bird feeding if Mrs. McHenry remained missing. He made us all chuckle. Not Amy though, she didn't like the birds. Ever since she was playing in the park as a little girl in her Sunday dress and one flew over and dropped a number two on her. It landed dead in the center of her lovely pink dress. She cried her eyes out for hours. Ever since then she steered clear of birds and if some flew over she made sure she wasn't underneath them. If it were up to her, they'd all be shot. We all started speculating about Mrs. McHenry and where she could have disappeared off to. We all decided to ask around town to see if we could find out where she lived. On that note, we all returned to our homes.

Uncle Artie and the boys had left back to their own house. The boys took the news pretty hard. There is no way to sugarcoat that a madman killed their mother. Mom told uncle Artie that he and the boys were welcome to stay for as long as they liked, but uncle Artie said they had to get used to their new situation, staying would only be delaying the inevitable. I still couldn't believe all the stuff that's been happening lately. This used to be such a boring town where nothing ever happened. Now people were getting killed, either by the hands of other people or freak accidents. I asked Mom if she didn't think it was strange, how all this seemed to be happening in this short time span. Mom just shrugged, she didn't think anything of it. She told me to watch the news more often. The world was filled with freak accidents, murder, diseases, and many other things. That this was a boring little town didn't mean it would be free of the ugliness in the world. We haven't had a murder happen here since the 1800s. A serial killer went on a killing spring in the early

1820s. It was well documented, but the killer was never caught. After that, it became a boring little town. Nothing of much excitement ever happened. The only thing of excitement was the annual fair, and that was about it. I never knew there was a serial killer active here. I decided I would do some research on it one day if I had the time. For now, I had to focus on helping Mom, grandma, and uncle Artie.

I walked into the kitchen to pour me a cup of coffee when the doorbell rang. Mom got up to open the door. It was George with his entire family. His wife, 2 daughters and a son. He introduced himself and his family to Mom and said they moved into the house across the street. Mom welcomed them inside and called me over to meet the new neighbors. When I entered the living room, George mentioned that we already met at the antique shop. He introduced the rest of his family to me. His wife, Natascha who seemed like a nice lady. His son, Logan who clearly was the youngest of the bunch. The little girl, Elena who seemed like a cheeky little girl. Last but not least, their oldest, Jessie. She was around my age and clearly was here against her will. She clearly had no interest in meeting the neighbors while she could be out with her friends. She wasn't paying attention to anyone in the room what so ever. She was on her mobile phone messaging back and forth with her friends. I could only imagine what they would be talking about. After about half an hour she asked if she could leave, after hearing her Mom say she could, she was out the door. The rest of them stayed for quite some time talking with Mom.

I played a bit with the little ones who had quite the interest in my little brother. Asking if he could walk or talk or do anything besides laying there. "No, babies can't do much, they can only be loud, eat, sleep and fill their diapers," I said. "eeeeeeew" they both screamed out at the same time while pinching their noses. I chuckled at this scene. Mom asked if they'd like to stay over for dinner, but they had already made plans. They stayed for a little while longer and then headed back to their own house. Mom started to make dinner, and I sat down to do my homework.

The news came on. They apologized for being off the air the entire day yesterday. They were facing technical difficulties that they couldn't bother to deal with. They were all distraught over the loss of their dear colleague and the inability to kill the live broadcast of the event. They made a great item about Aunty Gale and the reports she did. A lot of the work she did abroad and the small town madness she reported on in town. She had quite the career as a journalist. They ended it with a beautiful picture of her, underneath it the year she was born, and the year she was killed and the words: You will be missed, greatly. Then the news broadcast returned to normal. The anchorman was clearly moved by the item about Aunty Gale. There were tears welling up in his eyes, and his voice was just a tad higher in pitch. He quickly found himself again and continued onto the item of Mr. Thompson's death. It was clear he was murdered, but the police were in the dark about the killer. Urging everyone who had seen or heard anything suspicious to come forward. A special tip line was opened that everyone with information could call. Even if it was something minor and you didn't think it meant anything they, urged us to please call the tip line. The golden tip that would actually lead to the killer would be rewarded with $10.000.

The last item was about Patrick's sentence, which was pronounced today. He was found guilty on all counts he was charged with and still only had to spend 6 years in jail. He got off quite easy if you asked me. What he did to poor Brody. Brody had to live with this for the rest of his life, he wouldn't have forgotten it in 6 years' time. Patrick would be out walking the streets living a happy life by then. There was nothing fair and just about that sentence. I wondered how different the outcome would have been if Brody was a girl. I wondered if he even would have been convicted of anything in the first place. Either way, this was a very unsatisfying outcome, to say the least. After the weather forecast, Mom yelled out that dinner was ready. We sat down, just Mom, me, and little Sean in his playpen nearby. It's been a long time since it was this quiet at dinner. We were just eating our meals, both thinking our own thoughts. "Maybe you are a bit right," she broke the silence, it was a bit odd that there was a lot of deaths lately. Sure there were people dying all the time everywhere. But the way in which most people in town died lately was rather unusual. 3 were murdered, 1 was shot by the police 1 died of natural causes and 5 freak accidents. All that in a very short time span. I agreed with her reasoning and added that I was sick and tired of people that I love and care about are dying. Can't it just limit itself to the Mr. Thompsons in town? There are quite a few people nobody really likes, why can't they be the ones having freak accidents or the ones getting murdered. Mom shrugged, it's always the good guys that go first.

After dinner, I continued with my homework before going to bed. I laid there, twisting and turning, having a hard time to find sleep. I thought about the words I told my nephews how to reach dreamland. If only that weren't total nonsense and would work, I would find that rainbow and never come back to the real world. After some more twisting and turning, I finally managed to fall asleep. In the morning, I found myself the wrong way round in bed. I guess I had quite the restless night. My head was at the foot end of the bed, and my feet were near the headboard.

I was wondering how I managed to do this in my sleep. I got up, took a shower, and got myself ready to head to school before heading down the stairs. Mom was already downstairs, I could hear the coffee maker in the kitchen. When I got downstairs, she was talking to someone in the kitchen. When I entered the kitchen, there was a man in an expensive suit holding a briefcase. I recognized this man as Dennis' lawyer.

He came by to check on us and to see if we had decided what to do with Dennis' belongings. I told him it was none of his business what I planned to do with Dennis' belongings. He agreed that it wasn't, but also added that he knew the estate and if I decided to sell any of it, he would be the man best equipped to help me. He also asked if I was still interested in the contract for Linda. I wasn't, Linda made it clear she had no intention of living in the house again. I looked at Mom, she only shrugged. This was my decision to make. I told the lawyer I had no time for this on a Tuesday morning before school. He could call me later and make an appointment, while I would give it some more thought. With all the commotion going on since Dennis' accident I hadn't really thought about the house, the items in it or the cars. Linda! I completely forgot about her. Haven't called her or been to visit her since the day I asked her if she planned to come back and live there. I asked Mom if she could bring me to see Linda later that day. She promised she would, and I headed out on my way to school.

CHAPTER NINE

After school Nigel, Chris, Emma and I decided to go to the library and do some research on our little town. Apparently, it wasn't always this boring little town in the middle of nowhere. We found a lot of information about the killings in the 1800s. Mom wasn't lying when she said that it was well documented. The first victim was found around Christmas time in 1820 and the last one somewhere in 1823. 35 victims were ascribed to this man, assuming it was a man, but it could have been many more. He disemboweled his victims, and his weapon of choice was a pocket knife, which he always left at the scene. Police had no idea who he was or how he chose his victims. At best, they were chosen at random. There was no common denominator among his victims. He killed both males and females, both the adults and children. The only thing that was ever left behind was the pocket knife used to kill the victims. There never were any witnesses.

During this killing spree, the town was left by a lot of its inhabitants. Many people moved away from the town. A serial killer in our little town, who would have thought. Why wasn't this taught in school? In school, we learned about H.H. Holmes, he was the first known serial killer in the world. I guess that is still true since this one was never caught, nor did he get a fancy name like Jack the Ripper. He killed 35 people, and as abrupt as he started, he stopped 3 years later. It took years for the town to recover. After dark, people were still afraid to leave their houses alone. If it weren't so well documented in newspaper clippings and sheriff's reports, he would have disappeared into oblivion and be completely forgotten.

Emma was the first one to say out loud what we were all thinking. "Ricardo and Mr. Thompson both were disemboweled, a pocket knife was found at both scenes" We discussed the similarities and came to the conclusion that whoever did this must have done research on this killer. We asked the librarian if anyone else recently was interested in the town's serial killer.

Apart from the bored detective that would look into it now and again, there hadn't been anyone asking her for information. She added that, as long as nothing is checked out, and the research is done within the library, she wouldn't have any records of it either. She asked why we were interested in him. "It's for a school project," Chris answered her question. He made up a story that we were set out to search for the first real serial killer. If that title belonged to H.H. Holmes or perhaps we could find proof of a serial killer being active before that. A smile emerged on the face of the librarian. She said that there was a rumor of a serial killer being active in town as early as the 1600s. There wasn't much documentation on it though, she could only hand us over a few autopsy reports. They were hardly legible, all of the dates on the death certificates were issued between the year 1664 and 1666. The only thing about the autopsy report we could make out was the drawing of the corpses and the incision in their abdomen. I had an eerie feeling. Serial killer active in the 1600s then later on in the 1800s now it's the 2000s again 200 years later.

Could it be like a curse? I remembered how the news anchor lady spoke about there being a curse on the town. I asked the librarian about this so-called old wives tale. She said she hadn't heard of a curse on the town before and added "but that doesn't mean there isn't one, I am only the librarian. You should find old Mrs. McHenry, she can tell you many things about the town, and she's been here forever." I told her I would love to ask Mrs. McHenry, but we couldn't find her. We hadn't seen her at the town square for quite some time. Perhaps she knew where Mrs. McHenry lived? Unfortunately, she had no clue either. "Don't you think it is rather peculiar that no one seems to know where Mrs. McHenry lives?" I asked. There is always someone who can point you in the general direction of someone's house. But with Mrs. McHenry, whom is known by everyone, it is still a big mystery as to where she lives. We all agreed that this indeed was odd, but that did not solve the mystery. It was close to dinner time, so we all decided to head back home.

We asked Nigel if we should walk him home, he declined. "I am a big boy, I can find my way home, unharmed," He said laughing. Chris, Emma, and I made our way back home as well. On our way, we were discussing the possibility of someone impersonating this serial killer, which would mean that there would probably be more murders. We discussed if we should go to the police station with this information. None of us felt like spending hours at the police station, though. Couldn't accuse our police force of being the fastest in the country. "Didn't they open up a tip line?" Emma asked. They did! We decided Chris would call it in. "Gut ripper!" Chris yelled out. "Serial killers have fancy names in this day and age, don't they? Let's call this one the gut ripper." Emma and I looked at each other and shrugged, it was fine by us. From now on, we would refer to this serial killer as the gut ripper.

Chris dialed the number for the tip line and told the story of the serial killer from the past, he said that he thought there were a lot of similarities with the recent murders. The person on the other side of the phone laughed, "A serial killer?" they said,

"Young man, you have been watching too much television."
Great, we weren't being taken seriously at all. We agreed that we
did all we could and headed back to our homes. Our research
would have to continue another day.

Mom asked where I had been all day, she had been waiting for
me. I looked a bit surprised at her question, I couldn't remember
we had an appointment to go anywhere. "I've been at the library
doing some research, why?" I asked. "Oh, no reason, I just
thought you wanted me to drive you to the hospital to go and
see Linda today," she answered. My face instantly became red
with shame. Linda! Again I completely forgot about Linda. I
apologized to Mom and asked her if she could take me
tomorrow instead. Mom smiled and said that I was too busy for
a teenager. "You are starting to forgetting things because you are
stuffing too many things into that head of yours," she said.
Perhaps she was right, but then again, it might just be because
this was exciting. Scary on the one hand, but exiting on the
other. There might be a serial killer on the loose, and the police
weren't ready to investigate that angle just yet. Mrs. McHenry
seemed to be missing. The town sign that keeps on being
changed by an unknown someone. There was a lot of mystery
going on. The 16 years I've been alive I have lived in this town,
never did anything exciting go on, and now we have a triple
mystery on our hands. After dinner, I had to continue on my
homework, hadn't done anything with it yet due to our research
at the library. Why do they give us so much homework, anyway?
It took until around 10 pm before I was finished. I quickly took
the dog out for a short walk, headed back home, and went to
bed. I heard Mom on the phone with Uncle Artie. The poor man
has no idea how to cope with the new situation. When the call
ended, Mom asked if I could take the baby monitor into my
room. She would go over to uncle Artie. I agreed. Sean slept

through the nights most of the nights anyway. Told her to wish uncle Artie my best. She left, and after thinking about today a bit more, I fell asleep.

The next morning I woke up by my alarm clock, Sean slept through the night, as he usually did. When I looked to my left to take the baby monitor off my nightstand, it was no longer there. I searched for it on the floor, thinking it might have fallen off, but it wasn't there either. Mom walked by my room, asking me what I was doing, told her I couldn't find the baby monitor. Mom laughed and said she came and took it from my room when she got back home last night. Well then, that explains why it wasn't there. She asked me who the gut ripper was. I looked at her rather puzzled. Apparently, I was mumbling this name in my sleep last night. It was nothing to worry about, I said, it was the name we gave the 1800s serial killer. I told her we went to the library yesterday and did some research on him. The librarian told us there might even have been a serial killer as early as the late 1600s. Mom raised an eyebrow. "Don't get yourself lost in an ancient mystery," she said. "Live in the here and now." Sure, she was right, not like we could solve the 1600s and 1800s murders. I told her about the similarities between the killings then and the 2 unsolved murders today, and that we did call the police tip line, but weren't taken seriously. "2 unsolved murders with some similarities hardly make for a serial killer," she answered. But if we did feel this strongly about it, we could always see if the newspaper was interested in our theories. They were always up for some sensation and a serial killer, oh my, that would definitely be a sensational story. But she also warned us. "Bringing out the news that we have a serial killer roaming around town might also cause panic and mass hysteria, be careful." That sure was some food for thought. I decided to keep the option of going to the newspaper open. Who knows, maybe the police did have some leads by now. It's not the 1800s anymore, forensics are way more advanced than they were back then. The chances of the killer leaving nothing of himself behind were slim to none. I decided to let the police just handle it without stirring things up. Besides, those reporters should be smart enough to make the same connection we did. I had my breakfast, packed my lunch, and went off to school.

After school, Nigel, Emma, and Chris asked me to join them for some more research. I wanted to say yes and dive into the library again, looking over every single detail of the 35 known murder cases, but I had to decline. I couldn't forget about Linda again. I told them to ask Marcy and Amy instead. Perhaps they would notice things we didn't, fresh eyes and all that. I headed home where Mom was waiting. "Good, you didn't forget today," she sneered. It was well deserved, but I still felt very small the way she said it. In the car we talked about Aunty Gale some more, her funeral would be tomorrow. I told Mom I wasn't sure if I could go. Facing a broken uncle Artie again and little Ryan and Lucas, crying their little eyes out. Only thinking of it broke my heart. Mom stopped the car for a bit and gave me a hug. "It's not fair," she said. "But it's also the ugly reality, your nephews need all the support they can get, and they adore you. It would mean a great deal to them if you are there." She hugged me again and told me it was my decision and that she would understand if I decided not to go. There was a knot in my stomach. Thinking about Ryan and Lucas, I only wanted to pick them up and hug them, tell them everything was going to be alright and this was only a bad dream. But Mom was right, this was the ugly reality. I couldn't stay away, they looked up to me. I had to go, if only for them. The poor little innocent ones that got a wakeup call telling them that the world isn't this magical place we all made it out to be. Maybe we are wrong in raising our children with stories about magic and fairy tales, happily ever after. It's not the reality of the world, but it is what we make our little ones believe. To be honest, the original fairy tales never had the happily ever after. The little mermaid didn't get to marry her prince. In the original version by H. C. Anderson, the prince married a different woman, and the little mermaid threw herself into the ocean to be dissolved into sea foam. No happy ending there. It's just one of many examples I could give. Somehow along the lines, it was decided that fairy tales should be happy, all's well that ends well. Ryan and Lucas don't get their happily ever after, neither does uncle Artie. Perhaps I could salvage some of their ever after. Mom started the car again and drove me to the hospital. She said she'd be back to pick me up in about an hour and a half, she had some errands to run.

I walked up to Linda's room. When I entered the room, she was facing away from me, shielding her right side. "They removed the bandages," she said, "I look hideous." I didn't know how to respond to that. I tried to reassure her that it would get better over time. It was fine if she didn't want to show me, I understood. I didn't come to make her feel insecure. She asked me to not be spooked if she turned around and I promised I wouldn't. When she turned around, and I saw the entirety of her face, she wasn't lying. It did look hideous. There was an empty eye socket where her right eye used to be. You could see the pink flesh in the back of it. It looked as if it was very painful. Her mouth was in a crooked shape you'd usually see witches depicted with. Her face was still bloated, and a bit of the bridge of her nose was missing. She still had many stitches and scarring that made her look as if someone tried to stitch up Frankenstein a new bride. I kept my posture and tried to act as if she looked normal. I asked her how she'd been. "Bored, I've been terribly bored," she answered. She was regaining her strength, movement in her arm returned, and she was ready to leave the hospital. Doctors wanted her to schedule an appointment with the plastic surgeon to see if there could be some reconstruction done on her face, she declined. I might not be easy to look at, but at least I will never forget what happened. These are the markings of a terrible accident I overcame. I will wear them with pride. Her words made sense on some level, but on the other hand, if you could choose to not bear those markings visibly, why wouldn't you? I didn't really understand her choice. "The only thing that will change is the eye, I did agree to a prosthetic eye," she continued. "I don't want to completely alienate the world and scare small children every time I leave the house." I felt so sorry for her.

Maybe Dennis did get the better end of the deal. He died, he didn't have to live with a heavily mutilated version of himself. Linda was stronger than Dennis would have been. I am sure Dennis wouldn't be able to cope, he was so vain and proud of his looks. Linda told me that her face needed to heal completely before they could measure a prosthetic eye. I told her I was very sorry for her and apologized for not visiting sooner. "Nonsense" she answered, "I have a television and newspaper here as well you know" She winked at me, at least I think she winked it's hard to tell since she only had one eye. She asked how Mom and I were holding up with the loss of Roger and Aunty Gale. We spoke some more about the town and the recent deaths. She said she couldn't wait to be released from the hospital and go to the town hall to unregister as a citizen. This reminded me that I hadn't heard from her mother, yet concerning her items at Dennis' house. "If it's all right with you, I'll ask her to contact you this week, with all you had going on I asked her to wait a while." I smiled and thanked her for her consideration. By now an hour and a half had almost past. I told Linda I would come by to visit again when I could and in turn she told me she would give me a call if she was released from the hospital before that. We said our goodbyes, and I headed outside where Mom was already waiting for me.

When we got back home, Mom asked me to help unload the groceries. I asked her if she was expecting world war 3 to break out anytime soon. Mom had bought enough groceries for the entire neighborhood. Mom laughed and said no, apparently Mrs. Mitchell had asked her to get these groceries for her, she was having a cookout with friends. She invited everyone on our block for dinner. She had sold her house, and this was her way to celebrate. I helped Mom unload the groceries, and together we went and dropped them off at Mrs. Mitchell. There wasn't much time for pleasantries, there was a group of 8 ladies waiting for these items so they could start cooking. The guests were to determine who cooked the best meal, so Mom and I were "ordered" to leave immediately. We weren't allowed to see who would cook what, to prevent a bias judgment. I couldn't help but laugh at the scene. 8 elderly ladies, wearing an apron standing behind a chopping block. It was almost like stepping into an episode of one of those cooking shows. We delivered the groceries and went on our way back home. I looked at Mom and asked if we had to go and have dinner over there. Mom smiled and said that it couldn't hurt, besides, she sold her house. It might be one of the last times that we saw her. In the light of having another hard day ahead of us tomorrow, a bit of harmful entertainment couldn't hurt. We ran into Chris and Emma on our way, they asked if we were going to Mrs. Mitchell for dinner. Yes, we were going, Mom told them. "Please tell me you are going too" I practically begged them. "Yes," they said, "our moms are making us go too." Mom chuckled and said, "See? We are all alike, pesky moms making our teenagers do things they don't like to do." I told Chris and Emma that I'd see them later. At home, I decided to take a shower first. After my shower, I laid out my clothes for tomorrow. Never did my pitch-black clothes get so much airtime as they did lately. After getting dressed for dinner, I headed downstairs.

Mom wasn't downstairs, and I hadn't seen her upstairs either. I couldn't imagine her going over to Mrs. Mitchell without me or without telling me, so that's probably not where she went. I decided to just watch some television while waiting for her. Again there was absolutely nothing that piqued my interest on the television. Only a lot of reruns, or shows that I didn't like to watch anyway. It was a minute to 6 pm, the news broadcast would start soon. Perhaps they had some news on who killed Mr. Thompson. I decided to change the channel, so I could watch the news. The news anchor opened with a story about riots in prison. There wasn't much information on it yet, but it seems prisoners started to riot, holding a guard and a visitor hostage. The press secretary of the police force didn't release any names for the visitor or officer that were caught in the riots. My first thought was a shameful one. I was happy that I didn't know anyone in prison or anyone who would visit anyone in prison, nor did I know any security guards. No matter the outcome, this wouldn't affect me. A second later, I did think about the poor families involved and how this would affect them. I felt horrible at myself for my first thought. The news continued. The next item was about the city council, they had invested and bought the old monastery at the town square some months ago. Their plans to renovate the building and open it as a retirement home were almost completed. The elderly citizens of our town would no longer have to leave their beloved town. I wondered if Mrs. Mitchell would consider staying if she knew that the new retirement home in town would open soon. I heard the back door open and close. "Are you ready to go?" I heard Mom yell from the kitchen. She was holding Sean motioning for me to hurry. I asked her where she went. "Had to pick up Sean from Diane's." Of course, Mrs. Kelly had been watching Sean today so she could take me to the hospital and run some errands. I gave myself a last look in the mirror, and off we went to Mrs. Mitchell's cookout.

It was a fun but uneventful evening. All 8 ladies made some lovely dishes, but everyone knew in advance that the desert would win. Not everyone likes a pot roast or steak or chili and whatnot, but everybody loves dessert. Mrs. Mitchell was responsible for the lovely apple pie. She got most votes for the favorite dish and won her own cookout. After dinner, the ladies mingled with the crowd. George also showed up with his wife and the two little ones their oldest was spending the night over at her boyfriends. On a school night? Mom would never let me sleep over anywhere else on a school night. Mrs. Mitchell came over and asked us if we were having a good time.

Mom and Mrs. Mitchell engaged in conversation while I set out to find Chris and Emma. Perhaps we could find a way to leave the cookout without anyone noticing. How about we just told them that we had to go and do some research for a school assignment? That wouldn't fly, Mom would ask me what the project was about. I decided to just go and ask Mom if it was okay for me to leave. Without asking any questions, she said it was okay. Easier than I thought it would be. I told Chris and Emma to just do the same. They were also allowed to go. We decided to go to the forest and sit in the clearing near the brook.

It was already dark outside, but we all had flashlights on our phones. We sat at the brook for about an hour. Just talking about nothing in particular. Not once did the subject stray to what was going on in town at the moment. When we headed back, we passed by the population sign. The number was crossed out again and replaced with the number 2994. "Maybe it already subtracted Mrs. Mitchell now that she is leaving." It was a plausible explanation Emma came up with, but somehow I didn't think that was it. The town seemed nice and quiet, not like a disaster or catastrophe took place. Maybe there had been another murder? Mrs. McHenry was still missing in action as well. Mom was already home when I returned. She asked if I had fun with my friends, I did have fun. It was nice to have an evening together without talking about any weird stuff for once. Mom agreed. Talk of the evening at the cookout was the new nursing home. Most of the ladies agreed it was a waste of money. They wouldn't even consider moving in there. It used to be the Sacred Heart Monastery, nuns lived there. Most of them went to school when nuns were still the teachers. They hated their guts. "Not a chance in hell I will spend the remainder of my days in a monastery, I don't care if they remodeled it or not" Mom mimicked the voice of Mrs. Mitchell. Clearly, she didn't care about staying in town as much as the city council thought she would. She'd rather await her turn at Ever Shades. I chuckled. Mom asked what was funny. "It doesn't matter how old you are, no one likes last-minute changes," I told her. She smiled, and at that note, I went to bed. We had quite the day ahead of us tomorrow.

Next morning I went to grab the newspaper after I made me a cup of coffee. "Child molester dies in prison riot" was the headline. It was accompanied by a warning that read: Explicit content inside. I was in no mood to read this right now. I decided to just have my coffee in silence. The newspaper was only filled with bad news anyway. Someone should come up with a good news newspaper. One that was only filled with happy stories. That dealt with the beauty in the world and not only it's ugly side. If you watch the news and read the papers, you might think the world is a cesspool of death and decay. Heroic acts are mentioned, in little footnotes, or one paragraph stories tucked away to the side. The main stories are always about something bad. About soldiers getting killed during the war, murders taking place, robberies, scams, heists, riots, hardly anything good. I was getting annoyed with the news, I was probably just looking for something to blame my feelings on. Today we had Aunty Gale's funeral to go to. I've attended quite the number of funerals in the past couple of weeks, but none had me feeling as heavy-hearted as this one. I buried my father and my stepfather, but this one got to me the most. Mom came downstairs, holding little Sean. I asked her to hand him to me instead of putting him in his playpen. I sat there hugging my little brother telling him I'd do everything I could to keep him from experiencing these feelings. He just gave me his baby smile. That's a smile that can melt ice. A little toothless baby smile. Funny how that looks cute on a baby yet quite the opposite on an elder. After breakfast, we got ready and headed over to the church. Front row seats for us again, it's never a good thing to have a front-row seat at a funeral.

When we entered the church, I saw Uncle Artie, Ryan and Lucas already seated. The little ones looked so smart and handsome in their little black tuxedo and tie. They looked so sad, it broke my heart to look at them like that. The last time I've seen them, they were still happy and living in their little safety bubble. The next day that bubble burst into a thousand little pieces. I can't imagine how they felt when being told that their Mom had died. Mom walked over and hugged Uncle Artie. Ryan was sitting to his right and Lucas to his left. I sat down next to Lucas, and Mom sat down next to Ryan. "Mom is dead, she's in a casket, and they will carry her in later," Lucas said. "She will turn into a star in the sky so she can still see us" that was a beautiful thought. I told Lucas that my father was a star as well. Lucas asked if he would play with his Mom and help her make friends with the other stars. "Of course he will, he will make sure your Mom is a happy star with a lot of star friends" I tried my best to control the tears I felt well up in my eyes. I hugged the little one. The organ started playing, and the pallbearers came in carrying the casket. Lucas looked at it with big eyes. "My mommy is sleeping inside there forever," he whispered. Bless his little 8-year-old heart. I was fighting my tears, I had to stay strong for the little ones. Little Ryan was crying his eyes out, he wanted his mommy. Lucas was being brave and seemed to have found comfort in thinking his Mom would become a star. Ryan just wanted his Mom to come back. Both Mom and uncle Artie tried to comfort him.

After the service, we all went over to Uncle Artie's house. Sean was put in a makeshift playpen, and the adults were talking about Aunty Gale and all the things she had done and still wanted to do. I took the boys outside to play some games. Can I see Mom in dreamland? Ryan asked me. He caught me off-guard with this question. Of course, you can still see your Mom in dreamland honey, anything and anyone you want to be there will be there. Dreamland is your magical go-to place, where you are the king and make everything happen. "I want to go live in dreamland," Ryan said. "Yeah, I want to live in dreamland too, but we can't just yet. We are not ready to move over and stay in dreamland" I tried to explain that we still had to do a lot of things in the waking world. I had no idea what I was making up and how to make it sound logical, but Ryan accepted my explanation. I told him that if it was dark outside and the sky was clear, he should look for the brightest star in the sky. That would be his mother shining her light, especially for him and his brother. This was the most serious talk I ever had with a six and an eight-year-old. We played a bit with their toys and then it was time for us to head home. I said goodbye to the little ones and told them to come over soon, we'd play some basketball or other games if they'd like. Uncle Artie thanked me for trying to keep their mind off things. That wasn't a problem at all, it was not right that their mind had to be taken off these things in the first place. It wasn't fair. Aunty Gale didn't deserve to die and definitely didn't deserve to die like that.

After we got home, Mom asked if I had any plans for the rest of the day and evening. I told her nothing in particular. She wanted to head over to Mrs. Kelly to unwind or something like that and asked if I wanted to watch Sean. I didn't mind. Sean was such an easy baby to look after. Besides it was close to 8 pm, he would only get one more bottle and then it was time for bed anyway. I could do that. Mom left me some money so I could order some food since we hadn't had dinner yet. I still had a knot in my stomach and wasn't hungry at all. Mom left, and I played a bit with Sean. He was at the point where he tried to grab things if you held them in front of him. I wondered what he would grow up to become. Would he be a big badass boy that you wouldn't want to mess with? Would he become a nerd, a go-to guy if you need help with your homework? Whatever he would turn out to be, I would always be there watching over him, making sure nothing bad would ever happen. I didn't care if he would think of me as being obnoxious. He was my little brother, and it was my duty to protect him! I fed him his bottle when it was time, and after that, I changed his diaper and put him in his crib for the night. I was getting a bit peckish and ordered a pizza, I turned on the television and caught a commercial stating there would be an exclusive interview with an eyewitness to the prison riots. "The hostage speaks, what went on in prison during the riots" story at 11. The prison riot, I totally forgot about that. I was intrigued, I might stay up and watch it. Nigel texted me the homework assignments we got today, so I decided to work a bit on those. I finished shortly before 11. Mom just came in as well and asked me why I was still up. Told her I wanted to see the story off the prison riots. Mom rolled her eyes, she wasn't up for more misery today. She kissed me goodnight, and she went off to bed.

The Story started at 11 sharp. There was a show tune, and the host appeared on the screen. "Tonight, exclusive on The Story, a man tells us about his experience in the visitors' space of a prison after a riot broke out." The camera zoomed out and gave us a blurry picture of the guest. I always hated it if they started shows like that. As if they wanted to add mystery before zooming in on the guest with perfect pixels. After the camera zoomed in again but now on the guest only I recognized him. It was Mr. Ramón, he worked as a manager at the local newspaper. He started as a reporter as well and made his way up in the company. The host opened with, "Can you give us a detailed description of what went on at the prison, sir?" Mr. Ramón said yes, but also had his own question. "How much detail do you want me to include?" He was to include all of it. He started to tell his story. "I went there for an interview with one of our former reporters who had recently been convicted of various charges" At this point, the host cleared his throat as if to make clear that he should not forget to mention what they were concerning.

Mr. Ramón continued, "Of various charges concerning the abuse of his 16-year-old intern. He maintained his innocence all throughout the trial. I went over to interview him and get his reaction on the outcome of the case and his sentence. He claimed the intern came on to him and that he even rejected him a couple of times, but that the intern was persistent. He agreed to grant me an exclusive interview because, at one point, I was his manager. This was a medium secured facility. It meant you had one armed guard on the floor, and visitors and inmates were not divided by a wall or glass or anything. It allowed physical contact. I was sitting at a table, waiting for Patrick to arrive when I noticed there were far more prisoners in the visiting room than there were visitors. Especially when I realized I was the only visitor. Patrick was escorted to my table by another guard who then left the room. After that, it all happened so fast. Two of the inmates tackled the one guard bearing arms that was inside the room. They took his gun and his taser. One of the inmates kept pointing the taser at the guard and said if he would only move an inch, he would have a lot of fun tasing him. The guard couldn't do anything about what happened next."

Mr. Ramón cleared his throat and went on with his story. "One of the inmates went up to Patrick and spoke only one word. He said the name of Patrick's victim. It was followed by quite a long silence. After that, he inhaled deeply and said with a growl in his tone that he was his nephew. Two of the other inmates came over and yanked Patrick off his chair. Let me tell you, I've been sent out to the frontlines of war twice, but never have I been as scared as I was in that room. There must have been around 20 muscled angry inmates in that room, and the only guard on the inside couldn't even raise the alarm. By the time the guard on the outside noticed something was wrong, it was too late. The inmates controlled the room. To the side, there was three of them discussing something. After they were done, two of them walked up to me. I almost literally wet myself. They told me not to worry, as long as I behaved I would get out unscathed. They told me to watch and make sure to report on what I was about to witness. Seeing how Patrick was a reporter, he surely would want there to be an article about it that was accurate. Patrick's face was stricken with fear, the fear of death. Death would probably be the only thing he wished for because that would have been a lot more merciful.

At first, all the men took turns on punching him in the mouth. Blood spatters flew everywhere. They knocked all of his teeth out. Patrick begged for them to stop, but they wouldn't listen. One of the inmates, a shorter one who wasn't exactly ready to apply to Mensa if you catch my drift, came up to me very excited and said 'it can't bite if it got no teeth.' I didn't have to wonder for long what that meant, because when I looked up, I saw that one of the inmates had undressed the lower half of his body and was now forcefully inserting his penis into Patrick's mouth. Patrick was choking on it and coughing up blood. The inmate yelled out for him to suck it, or nibble at it, he didn't mind. Patrick was crying, out of fear, pain, and humiliation. I couldn't do anything to save him, and the prisoners kept yelling for me to take a good look, I didn't dare to look away. The guard cried out for them to stop, in return, he got a kick to the stomach and was told to butt out. All the men took off their clothes, and all had a turn into putting their penises into Patrick's mouth. After the last guy had his turn, I hoped it would be over. It wasn't, oh holy hell it wasn't. Patrick, who by now had lost all will to live and therefore all will to fight, was pushed over a table. They pulled down his pants. Patrick still was begging for them to stop and not do this. The kids' uncle went first.

He told Patrick to feel really special as he had never done a bloke before and hoped it would feel very nice. Without any warning, he stuck his penis up Patrick's ass. Patrick screamed out so loud, this must have been the worst pain he ever felt. The kid's uncle didn't stop, oh no, he kept on thrusting till he was finished. There was a lot of blood and excrement coming out from his ass with each thrust. Patrick's asshole tore up quite a bit. I thought, after this, they would leave him alone. Again, I was wrong, dead wrong. All of them had their turn. All of them kept calling him their little bitch and asking Patrick if he liked how it felt, and that this was exactly how the kid had felt.

On some occasions, Patrick passed out. They stopped if he did and started to pour water on his face. When he regained consciousness, they continued. They made sure Patrick endured every moment of this torture fully conscious. After the last inmate had his turn, the first one took over again. They kept at it for hours, until finally, Patrick died. He must have been praying for the sweet release of death. After they made sure he was no longer breathing, the one with the gun, put the gun down, the one with the taser, put the taser down, and they all went to lay face forward on the ground with their hands behind their heads. The riot was over. It was the most bizarre thing I had ever witnessed, and I am still in shock over what I've seen. I will never unsee the fear and pain in Patrick's eyes, forget the sounds of regurgitation of blood, none of it, nor the foul smell that emitted from the scene. He was terrified and in so much pain. One hell of a way to go."

The camera panned in on the host again, who was just drinking a bit of water. There were a few more questions on how he felt and what he could and couldn't do if he thought about ways to save Patrick and whatnot. I have to be honest, I only heard half of the questions being asked and none of the answers. The way he described the scene, it was as if I was there. In my mind's eye,

I could see it. Patrick was begging and screaming for his life. The blood, the smell, gross. And indeed, what a way to go. I have to say I wasn't feeling sorry one bit. Don't touch young boys and you won't be in that situation. The sign! Now it made sense, Patrick was the citizen that was subtracted. Even though he was currently in prison serving a six-year sentence, he was still a citizen in our town. He still owned the apartment he lived in. To take my mind off what I've just seen, I decided to watch some cartoons on television, just some light-hearted nonsense before going to sleep. Tomorrow was a new day, who knows what it might bring.

CHAPTER TEN

The next few days, nothing noteworthy happened. We did some more research on our towns' history but could not find anything that would point us in any particular direction. No more murders took place, the news around the prison riot died down pretty quickly. People didn't really seem to care that much. A convicted child molester died, and most of them thought it to be poetic justice in the way he died. Humans are a scary breed. If we deem it justified, it's okay for someone else to suffer. If it is someone that wronged us personally or someone close to us, we wish the most gruesome horrible death upon them. But even monsters have others that love them. These others will be hurting too, but apparently, that serves them right for loving a monster. The world is turning more and more into a grim place. People are dying of starvation, in other countries people are dying of obesity-related health issues.

We often dream of times long gone, but never as they actually were. We have this inept ability to romanticize everything. It was always better, more beautiful, and easier. That must be how fairytales came about. Unfortunately, real life is not a fairy tale, and the good guy doesn't always win. Sometimes it's the monster that wins, and other times it isn't even clear which one the monster is. In a competition, fight, discussion, or whatnot, we tend to root for the underdog. I guess that's because we truly still want to believe in fairytales. The underdog actually winning is the closest thing to a fairy tale we get. I don't ever want to bring kids into this world. If I ever get a partner, I'll make it abundantly clear that having children is not on the agenda. What's the point, they just start dying as soon as they are born. Some will do that sooner than others. It's Friday evening, and this was a horrible week once again. I would love for next week to be without someone dying, no funerals, it's been enough. It's time for faith to go bother some other town. I want to do fun things with my friends again. I am 16, at least let me live a little! At least tomorrow it is Saturday, and I get to work in the antique shop again. I liked it last time, it really helped me take my mind off things. I decided to take a shower and go to bed. I was tired, dead tired of all the misery and death that had surrounded us this past couple of weeks.

Next morning I did not turn on the television, I did not want to see the news, read the newspaper or hear it on the radio. It was going to be a news-free day. If I don't hear about all the bad things, there are none, as I am about to start believing that there is no more good left in the world. I had some breakfast, a cup of coffee and all of that in blissful silence. When I finished it, I put on a playlist, put on my headphones, and made my way to the antique shop. Adam was already there, so was George. Adam was going online with his business. He wanted to know the possibilities, and apparently, George was the person that could tell him all about it. He could have a website with an online store and an auction section where he could auction off some Items, set a base number that had to be reached before the sale was authorized. That way no one could buy an item he priced in the store at $100 for $1.

I did not care for this conversation much, I wanted to get back into the basement and research the items down there. Adam had different plans though, he asked me to clean out the shop window. I was to go and redecorate it. Now you could say what you want about the antique shop, but Adam always puts a lot of work into the decoration of his shop window. It always displayed a story of its own. On Halloween, it displayed the most horrifying items. The shrunken heads made their way to the shop window with some books on witchcraft and cannibalism, voodoo dolls and how to make them. I loved the October shop windows. But we were still pretty far from Halloween. This month the theme was going to be autumn related, as that was right around the corner.

I put in some books that showed forests on their cover and put down some fake autumn leaves. Some wooden carvings of a squirrel and some mushrooms that were made around 500 years ago, according to their attached labels. They didn't look like much to me, but then again, 500 years ago they didn't have the tools we have today. I put in some sculptures and china of boots. Some ancient and modern fishing rods. When I was done, the shop window appeared to tell the story of the trees losing their leaves, the squirrels collecting food for the winter, and about people apparently going fishing and swamp dredging. I was proud of my work when Adam came to check on it.

He started laughing when he saw my result and the disappointment to his reaction in my eyes. It was a good attempt but a bit messy. The trick is to pick a theme and stick by it. If I wanted to go for trees and woodland creatures he had plenty of sculptures, books and other items I could use. Same goes for people going fishing, although he wasn't quite sure what that had to do with autumn. We redecorated the window together. He had an old poster depicting a lot of trees in autumn colors which we used in the background, my leaves were allowed to stay as filler on the bottom. We put down some sculptures of hedgehogs and squirrels some acorns and walnuts. Framed pictures of trees and deer in antique frames. He actually had some books on autumn, and what it does with nature, they made their way to the shop window as well. I have to admit that when we were finished, it looked a lot better than the one I had set up. A children's book with a sun on its cover flourished in the center and acted as the autumn sun in the shop window.

By now, it was time for lunch. I decided to head into town and get me something to eat and asked if I should bring Adam something as well. He declined. I just had a club sandwich at a little restaurant on the other side of the town square. I was looking around the town square for Mrs. McHenry, but she wasn't there. After lunch, I went back to the antique shop, and Adam asked me to continue researching the items in the basement.

The pile of items seemed bigger than the last time I saw it. Where does Adam get all these items from? I stared at the pile, wondering where to begin, let's just start at the top again. There were so many items, ranging from cutlery to tableware, to pots, furniture, paintings, statues, books, and many more things. I was able to find most things with the computer or at least similar things. I printed out many information cards and stuck a price on them. I was enjoying myself quite a bit when I stumbled upon this book again. Last time I was just about to put it through the software when Adam came down to tell me the day had ended. I scanned the book for an ISBN number, it didn't have any, which wasn't that odd seeing as they only became the standard in 1970. I scoured the book for details on the year it was made or the author. It had none. There was no index page telling me anything about who might have written it or when it was published. The title search yielded many results that had the number 3000 in it, but nothing that resembled this book. I opened the book on a random page and decided to type over a bit of its text and do a random search on that.

3000 souls are what it needed, right above his head.
3000 souls are what it needed, 3000 and the world was dead
3000 souls are what was offered, 3000 souls were on display
3000 souls are what was offered, but no longer than a day
3000 souls found havoc around them, and the demons cheered
3000 souls found havoc around them, until 500 of them disappeared

This random search yielded no results what so ever, and this text was weird. The entire book was in rhyme, but it made no sense what so ever. It was truly bothering me that I was unable to make out where this book came from, who wrote it and when. I forgot about the other items and was focused on this book. I had to find out more about it. I tried an internet search, perhaps the internet would yield results. I only found results to religious texts. Nothing that came even close to the wording in this book. I started to get pretty annoyed. It was as if this book didn't exist, or at least, never was published to the public. I couldn't find the slightest trace of it. I decided to read some more, perhaps I could make out a time of when it was written or a clue as to what the story was about. The fact that it was written in rhyme didn't help either.

2500 souls remaining, looking rather sad
2500 souls remaining, never felt so bad
2500 souls were safe, calm became the town
2500 souls were safe, the devil got no crown

Great, this bit of text made even less sense than the other bit. Apparently, the devil needs 3000 souls above his head? For what? This must have been the strangest book I've ever laid my hands on. If this was a unique book, the only in its existence, I most certainly could imagine why. None of it made any sense to me, let alone to anyone else. I lost track of time trying to research this book, I probably could have done about 10 to 15 other items during this time. Adam came down to the basement to tell me it was closing time again.

He could tell I was annoyed and asked me what was wrong. I told him about the book and my ineptitude in finding its whereabouts. Adam told me not to worry about it, he couldn't always find where an item came from or what it was worth, he would just make up a story and price it as he seemed fit. I shouldn't hit myself over the head with it. "I tell you what kid, why don't you take the book home with you, read some of it and then next week you can print out a story card and price it with what you think it's worth" and he handed me the book. I gladly took on this assignment. I was going to find out what this book was about and everything I could about where it came from. Next week I'd have a fitting story to go with it!

I put the book down on the counter when I arrived home. I looked around the house for Mom and Sean, but neither were there. When I walked into the living room, I noticed there was a note taped to the television, smart one Mom. It read that they were spending the night over at uncle Arties, she left me some food in the fridge that I only needed to reheat if I was hungry. Great, got the house all to myself. I wanted to tell Mom about my day and the book, instead, I am greeted by an empty house and only the dog to talk at. I phoned Amy, but she didn't answer, so I ended up calling Chris and asking him if he wanted to come over. I told him that I borrowed a strange book from the antique shop that I needed to investigate and asked if he wanted to come over after dinner so we could investigate it. Chris was always in for a mystery-solving hunt, so he said he would come over straight after dinner. I did the same with Nigel, Marcy, and Emma, all of them said they would come over. I sent Amy a text message since she still wasn't answering her phone. I went into the kitchen and heated up the meal Mom had left for me in the fridge. After that was done, I took the dog out for a walk. We went all the way to the town square. Still no sign of Mrs.

McHenry. It already turned dark by now, and the fountain in the center was lit by the surrounding lights. It made the water look like a fountain of lava as if flames were bursting out of the ground. I looked at it for a little while, the sound of the water had a calming effect, yet the color it got because of the lights gave it an eerie touch. After a while, I turned around and headed home again.

I checked my phone to see if I had gotten a reply from Amy. There was no reply, nor was there any indication that she had read the message. Maybe she was taking a bath and left her phone downstairs, who knows. I washed the dishes and tidied up a bit before my friends came over. I got my laptop, so we could look up things and went into the kitchen to grab the book from the counter. On my way back to the living room the doorbell rang, it was Nigel. Typically, Nigel, he lived the furthest away but was always the first to arrive. Soon after him, Marcy and Emma arrived and last, but not least, Chris showed up. They all took a seat, and as I was about to unveil the book, Emma asked if we weren't waiting for Amy. Nigel said he walked by her house, but it was all dark as if they weren't home. Could be they went away for the weekend. I couldn't remember Amy said anything about it, but then again she might have, and I probably didn't listen. I would see her tomorrow morning anyway, we set a date to go swimming tomorrow. We decided to not wait for Amy and just go ahead. I started to explain the mystery.

"I got this book from Adam to research where it came from, how old it is and who has written it" I started. "I've tried the better part of the afternoon to find out anything I could about it, and have found absolutely nothing. There is no mention of it online or in Adam's special antiquities software." I laid the book down on the table. They all stared at it and said that its cover looked creepy, heavily dated, but still creepy. Nigel recognized a bit of the desolate land, he said it looked similar to a plot of land behind his house. Nothing had ever been built there, and nothing seemed to grow there. We looked at each other, and all had the same idea, we all took our phones as flashlights and set out to the plot behind Nigel's house. He was right. There were similarities between this stretch of desolate land and the plot we were standing on. But then again, I think every stretch of desolate land would resemble this picture. It didn't really give us any identifiable markings. We decided to sit down as it was still warm outside, and the full moon provided enough light for us to not even need our flashlights. They asked me to read something to them. I opened the book on the page I had already started reading and read the next bit to them.

3000 souls are never good, not longer than a day
3000 souls were never good, for they'd come out and play
3000 souls are dangerous, you will lose your head.
3000 souls are dangerous, with all the humans dead.

Wow, this was getting more and more sinister with every part I read. We all gave our thoughts on what it could mean. "Perhaps if 3000 people died, a demon would come and destroy the world?" Emma stated, "No, no," Chris interrupted. "Over the course of humanity a lot more people died than 3000, maybe 3000 really bad people need to die and then the earth explodes." Marcy just shook her head "good people, bad people, a whole lot of both sides have died over the centuries, and the earth hasn't exploded nor is there a demon walking the lands, it has to mean something else" She was right, but what could it mean? Was there even a meaning, or was it just a lunatic that had written down some words to make a scary rhyme? It could be any of it. And what's with this one day stuff? The more I read, the less I understood. They asked me to skip to the last passage in the book and read that one. I flipped the pages and found the last passage. It read:

> 3000 souls open the gates, to a realm of fear
> 3000 souls open the gates, the demons will come here
> 3000 souls need drastic decline, truer words were never spoken
> 3000 souls need drastic decline, before its chains are broken
> 3000 souls are one too many, 24 hours is the maximum time
> 3000 souls are at least one too many, if need be commit a crime

Well, lovely, that didn't tell us anything, well, it told us the author of this book of rhyme must have been completely out of his or her mind. It was getting a bit chilly outside, and the wind was starting to blow. We decided to go back home and try to search for more answers tomorrow as it was already getting rather late. We were close to Nigel's house, so we dropped him off first. As we walked by Amy's house, it was indeed completely covered in darkness, not a single light was turned on. After we walked Marcy home, we went back to our street. Emma's Mom was standing in the doorway already. "Ah, there you are, I was just about to come and get you, we need to wake up bright and early remember?" Emma nodded and whispered something about having to get the best fruit from the market tomorrow. Every last Sunday of the month there was a fruit market in the town square. Poor Emma, having to go there bright and early with her Mom. Chris also went home, since we were all going swimming tomorrow he decided to make it an early night as well. "Sure, just all leave me alone again," I said jokingly as I headed towards my own house.

When I opened the back door, I noticed that all the lights were turned off. I flipped the light switch in the kitchen, but it didn't work. Great, now the light also broke. As I made my way to the supply closet to grab a new light bulb, I noticed my dog staring at something in a corner of the living room. This corner seemed darker than the rest of the house. I called her name to get her attention, but she wouldn't stop staring. I brushed it off as the dog being silly once again and made my way to the supply closet. The breaker box was also in there, and I noticed that the main switch was set to the off position. I turned it back on, and the lights in my house came on again. When I turned around, I got the scare of my life and jumped about 3 feet into the air while letting out a scream many horror directors would long for from their actors.

"Oh my, I didn't mean to scare you my dear" a familiar voice came from the dark corner of the room. "Didn't mean to scare me? Didn't mean to scare me! Are you kidding me? The entire house was dark, and the main switch was flipped to off, and yet you didn't mean to scare me, huh? Could have fooled me" She stepped into the light and apologized once more, it was Mrs. McHenry. She said she wasn't sure who lived here and that's why she turned off the lights. If it would be someone bad, landing her in a potentially dangerous situation, she could make it out before the lights were switched on again. All that was fine and dandy, but why on earth was she even in my house!? "You have been chosen my dear, it was a long deliberation, but the vote fell on you" As if it was the most normal thing in the world she was explaining I had been chosen, all right, I'll play along. "I have been chosen? By whom? To do what?" She pointed to a white dove on her shoulder "By her and by them," she pointed towards the window. There were more pigeons on my windowsill than I could count, luckily they were on the outside. Imagine the cleaning I would have to do if they were all indoors. The sight of that many birds, sitting motionless, some on top of each other, staring inside through the window, staring at me, it gave me the feeling I wanted to freak out. But I was also intrigued. Why was Mrs. McHenry standing in my living room telling me I had been chosen by a dove and some pigeons? We all noticed she started to blurt out crazy things the last couple of weeks but breaking and entering to tell a coherent crazy story, that was a new one.

"You still haven't told me what exactly I was chosen for," I said. Mrs. McHenry looked at me in wonder. "All will become clear with time my dear" I guess that was the only answer I was getting, because she turned around, walked out the front door and was gone. I walked after her, but when I opened the door, she wasn't there anymore, neither was the dove or the pigeons. Did this really happen? Maybe I was just hallucinating. Maybe chasing these mysteries was finally getting to me. I have been worried about Mrs. McHenry, perhaps it was my mind playing tricks on me. Just as I was about to fully convince myself that none of this was real, I got a text message from Chris. He wanted to know if I took over from Mrs. McHenry and dropped some birdfeed on my windowsill. Apparently, he saw a large number of pigeons too. The thought of it being a hallucination was so much easier to accept. I send Chris a text back that I would tell him everything tomorrow, I was still trying to make sense of it all for myself. I went back inside and locked the front and backdoor. I checked both of them 3 times before going to bed. I had quite the trouble falling asleep. Mrs. McHenry came into my house, that's how easy it was to break in, and here I was, home alone. That night, my dog got to sleep in my room. No couch for her this evening. Eventually, I managed to fall asleep and wake up the next morning to my alarm clock.

7 am on a Sunday morning. That's no time to get up on a Sunday. I stumbled down the stairs and into the kitchen and made myself a cup of coffee to wake up with. After that, I got dressed and took the dog out for a walk. Packed my swimwear and some towels in my bag. Sent a text to Chris and Emma asking them if they were ready to go. Chris replied that he was born ready, Emma was still typing. She replied she just got back from the market and would be ready in a bit. I looked at the text I sent to Amy yesterday, it still hadn't been read. Strange, maybe she just completely missed it. I sent her another text, it read, "You better be ready to swim when we come for you :)" I met Chris and Emma outside, and we made our way over to Nigel's. Marcy was already there. We were all complaining that it was way too early, but, we also agreed we had to get to the swimming pool early to get a good spot on the field for our towels.

Amy was late. I checked my phone, still no message from Amy and no confirmation that my messages had been read. Nigel tried to call her, but the phone kept ringing until it went to voicemail. Amy always had the biggest crush on Nigel, as did Nicolle. They were both competing for his attention, even though I didn't think Nigel had any interest in either of them. Amy had her ways to get all the attention she wanted. She had the looks and the means to win that competition every time. If Nikki was getting too much attention, she just sent in her younger brother to distract Nicolle. He was 2 years younger and had a massive crush on Nikki if his big sister sent him out to capture her attention he was happy to oblige. Amy would never miss a call from Nigel, she'd bend over backward to answer that phone, yet, it went to voicemail. We waited a bit longer, perhaps she had just lost her phone, wouldn't be the first time that happened. After 10 minutes of waiting, we decided to just head out towards her house and pick her up from there. She'd probably overslept, which also wouldn't be the first time. We rang the bell as we got to her house, but there was no answer. Strange, her dad's car was in the driveway, nothing was hinting at them not being home. We rang the bell a few more times, but still no answer. We decided to walk into the backyard, to try the back door. I walked in front, and as soon as I entered the garden, I fell to my knees.

I was greeted by the most horrific sight I had ever seen. There, in their own garden, on the washing line, there were three corpses. Swinging in the wind, hung out to dry. It was Amy, her little brother, and their father. They were cut open from their necks to their groins. A big pool of blood accumulated below them. A lot of their organs were hanging out, dangling in the wind, still attached to the muscles. Their intestines were used to tie a noose around their necks and tie them to the washing line. There was this trail of blood and drag marks leading from the house to the washing line. Amy's face was completely carved up, someone really did a number on it. Amy, beautiful Amy, there was nothing left of her beauty. Her face now looked as if it had been used as a cutting board by a butcher. The face of her little brother showed an expression of pain and fear, their father didn't seem to have any expression on his face. Whoever did this, must have gotten their father first and by surprise. All of them were gutted, their intestines pulled out and attached to the washing line. It felt as if Amy was the main target, and her dad and brother were collateral damage. Amy was completely carved up. It was as if the killer tried to filet her body and take off her skin but was unsuccessful in doing so and decided to just cut everything up. I could see more bones than flesh on her arms and legs. I felt sick to my stomach. I tried to shield the rest from seeing this and yelled for them to go away. Unfortunately, people rarely listen when you scream out in sheer panic for them to go away. Instead of going away, they all came running towards me, asking what was wrong. They were too focused on me to look into Amy's backyard. Emma was the first to look up, she started to scream hysterically and also fell to her knees. This made Chris, Marcy, and Nigel look up as well. The amount of screaming that ensued alerted some neighbors. Their first concerns were to remove us from this horrific scene.

Emergency services were called. The police went into their house and found their dog gutted as well. It was tucked into its dog basket underneath a doggy blanket. The killer showed more compassion for the dog than he did for Amy and her family. A pocket knife was pinned to the washing pole. Clearly, we had a serial killer active in town. I didn't care about Ricardo, nor about Mr. Thompson, but Amy? Amy was one of my closest friends, how could he do this to her. Why did he have to mutilate her so badly? What did Amy do to anger him this much? If anything, now I was dead set on the police calling this a serial killer! And I would take on this mystery with both hands. I had to find out who this killer was. Amy's mother was currently abroad, reporting on the war in some hot, far away country. Try to imagine receiving that phone call, being safe and unharmed in a war zone, being told that your husband and children have been brutally murdered in the safety of their own home. That thought sent shivers down my spine. The police had called all our parents, and they quickly came to take us home. I didn't say or do anything for the rest of the day. I just sat on the couch, staring into nothingness. All the time, there was one thought going through my head, "why?" Nothing more, nothing less, just why?

Mom made me a cup of coffee and put a blanket around me. "I don't know what to say or do, there is nothing that will make this any better." She hugged me. I didn't want a hug, I wanted to find the sick bastard that killed my friend. I told Mom that I wouldn't rest until I found him. I didn't care how, but I would find him. Mom looked worried and said, "don't get into any trouble, please be careful." Yeah, I would be careful, it's not like I was ready to go hunt down a killer and overtake him. I am 16, what am I going to do. But I could be a detective, I am good at doing research! I would hand all my findings, if any, over to the police and if they didn't act on it, I would take them to the newspaper. No matter what, this time they would have to listen!

I decided to search online for the serial killer of the 1800s, see if there was anything else that the library didn't show. My search yielded around 1500 pages of results. Small town serial killer might not be the correct search term. I entered my town's name + serial killer + 1820. I got 15 pages as a result this time. Some of them had nothing to do with any of my search terms, but I found one website that went deeper into this serial killer.

It spoke about the 35 victims, the knife left on the scene but it also stated that sometimes he went creative with the intestines. Treated them like balloon animals. On some victims they were tied into a bow tie, on others, he formed them into wiener dogs. This must have been a sociopathic psychopath. Back in the year 1820, the town must have been a lot smaller, fewer houses, so I take it fewer families and fewer people. Someone surely must have suspected who this serial killer was. I looked into the archives of our town, to find information on its layout during that time. The town square wasn't there yet, the fountain wasn't there yet, most shops and houses in that area were built later. In the 1820s there was a saloon and a brothel. My eye caught the population count. At the end of 1819, the population count of the town was 2995. Funny how a smaller town housed the same amount of people as it did today. At the end of 1822 there was a population count of 2367, a huge decline happened after the murders. A lot of families moved away, never to come back. I have learned a lot about my town and this killer from my search. I learned that this killer had a thing for the intestines and that his weapon of choice was a pocket knife. He must have had quite the collection of pocket knives for he always left behind the knife at the scene. The killings started around the time the town was to hit a population count of 3000, the killings in the present also started around the time the town was about to hit that same number. The book from the antique store came to mind, it was called 3000, and it had a theme about 3000 being bad. Could this all be linked together? I decided to write down all my findings, print them out, and take them to the police tomorrow. Even if they wouldn't take me seriously, at least I had made an effort. It was getting pretty late, so I decided to go to sleep, I would continue my research tomorrow.

CHAPTER ELEVEN

The next morning the newspaper's headline read: Serial killer loose in town? They summed up the similarities between all 5 victims. All were gutted, all had their intestines removed, and all had at least a part of their body pinned or tied to something. At all scenes, a pocket knife was left behind. But that is where the similarities ended. Ricardo was a piece of scum from the west end of town. Mr. Thompson was a nasty old man that always was having a fit for some reason or another. Always scaring the kids in town and telling them off. Amy was a sweet girl, sure she could have a mean streak, but I couldn't imagine anyone hating her enough to kill her and her family. Amy lived close to the border to the north. Mr. Thompson lived closer to the center. These three had nothing in common. They didn't share the same friends, they didn't hang out in the same places, and they didn't visit the same clubs or stores. There was absolutely nothing to tie them together. It seemed to be random, but I still had this nasty feeling it wasn't.

Every time I closed my eyes, I could still see them hanging on the washing line. Amy was badly mutilated, whereas her father and brother were left intact for the most part. I wasn't going to school today, neither were the others. We were to meet up at the town square later today.

When I walked into the kitchen, Mom had already poured me a cup of coffee. She wanted to know how I was doing. In all honesty, I was upset and angry. How can someone just take another's life in such a horrible manner? Why kill such an innocent young girl with big hopes and dreams for the future. Her younger brother, who sure as hell, never even hurt a fly. He always was on his best behavior if we were over, sure, sometimes he would try to get our attention in annoying ways, but overall, he was a sweet little boy. Their father, a clerk at the post office, was a hardworking man. He lived for his family. All three of them, gone, by the hands of some maniac. I told Mom I was doing okay given the circumstances and that I would be going out with my friends in the afternoon. She warned me not to do anything stupid. Not like it mattered anymore what I did. People were dying all around, freak accidents, murders, there didn't seem to be an end to this streak of death that landed on our town. I just drank my coffee in silence. Mom packed her lunch, got baby Sean, and kissed me goodbye. Her maternity leave had ended, and little Sean was going to daycare. I don't know if I could do that. Leave my child with people that are practically strangers, especially with all that's going on. Who knows, maybe one of them is the killer. At this point, anyone could be the killer. I couldn't shake off this nasty feeling. I decided to get up and take the dog out for a walk in the forest.

The brook always had a calming effect on me, so heading there seemed like the right thing to do. When I reached the clearing, I unleashed the dog so she could run around the forest freely. The first thing she did was jump into the brook. It was a warm day, and the sun was out, under different circumstances, I would probably call it a nice day. But today there was nothing nice about it. Again I was grieving the loss of a loved one. I already knew life wasn't fair, but this was beyond unfair. I lost so many people over the last few weeks, the world has lost many beautiful souls. If people needed to die, why not have it be the scum of the earth! Have the horrible people that no one cares about die. Why take the life of young people that hadn't even begun to live. What motivates this killer, is he going after people he dislikes, that wronged him in some way? Is it completely random? I couldn't shake these thoughts. The brook wasn't calming me down one bit, and on top of that, I seemed to have lost my dog. I called her name, but she didn't come. I kept calling for her and after about 5 minutes and me becoming rather frantic, she came walking towards me. Very calm and wagging her tail as if she was here all the time. I put the leash back on her and started walking. I walked towards the town again and in the distance saw the outline of the population sign. As I came closer, I noticed that the number had been crossed out again. 2991 was the new number added. When I saw the number, this anger came over me. I started to hit the sign, kick it, and scream at it. The sound of my feet and my fists against the sign echoed through the empty street. A dark car pulled up behind me, two men in cheap suits got out and asked what I was doing. "What I am doing? Do you want to know what I am doing? Can't you tell what I am doing? I am beating down this sign! It has angered and frustrated me enough, it has to go, and you can't stop me!" I guess I was wrong there. One of the men reached into one of his pockets and pulled out a badge. He introduced himself as special agent Carlin and the other man as his partner, special agent Hobbes.

He asked why I was vandalizing the sign. Vandalizing? I wasn't vandalizing it, I wanted to destroy it, I wanted it to feel my wrath and let it have the better end of my frustration. I answered that the sign deserved it. Someone felt the need to keep the sign accurate. It declined with a number of three representing the loss of my friend and her family. I was sick and tired of someone changing this sign with every death that occurred or with every family that moved in. I didn't need it to remind me! The agents looked at each other, one started to make a phone call while the other asked me some questions about the sign. I told him that every time one of this town's citizens dies or leaves, someone would change the number on the sign. They would also add to the number when people were born or moved in. He asked some more questions, like when the sign-changing started and if I had any idea who was changing it. I did not. When agent Hobbes got off the phone, he only nodded and said: "we're good to go." Agent Carlin looked at me and said, "well, you're frustrations with this sign are over, for now, we are taking it with us as evidence. Evidence? Of what? Of someone with an obsessive-compulsive disorder to have the population count accurate? I shrugged. They pulled the sign out of the ground, loaded it into their car and left. I continued on my way home.

With Mom at work and Sean at daycare, I was all by myself again. I decided to just go for a long hot bath. Try to wash off everything that happened. I was only in the bath for about 5 minutes when my phone rang. I grabbed my phone from the bathroom sink and answered it. It was Linda. She called to tell me how sorry she was. She read the story in the newspaper and wanted to express her sympathy. I told her I was getting sick and tired of people around me dying. I sure could use some good news right about now. Linda started to say something but then hesitated. "I... I... I might have some good news." Oh, please do tell me some good news. "I am going to be released from the hospital later today! That's the other reason I called. My Mom will pick me up, is it okay if we come by your house, so we can go and collect some of my stuff at Dennis' place?" Of course, that was fine with me, and I was happy she was being released. Finally, some good news. Since she opted out of plastic surgery, doctors saw no reason to keep her there. She could do the rest of the rehabilitation and recovery from the comfort of her own home, well, her mom's home in this case. I asked her at what time she'd be released, but she had no idea. Sometime today is what the doctors said. I told her I was about to meet up with my friends in the afternoon. She would call me as she left the hospital so I could make my way back home and meet her in time. That was fine, I could do that. I could imagine how happy Linda must have been when the doctors told her she was almost free to go. I can't imagine being confined to a hospital room for as long as she had been, going through the pain she went through. Linda was definitely a strong woman. She lost a lot that day.

She lost the love of her life, her right eye, and probably a bit of her sanity as well. But she didn't lose her will to live, and she didn't change, as far as I could tell she was still the same Linda. She had come to terms with the way she looked. She never was stunning to look at, but the accident left her with a horribly mutilated face. Doctors made the best of it, but she could still star in a horror movie as the monster, and even though she was well aware of this, it didn't seem to bring her down one bit. She was just happy that she had survived the ordeal and now slowly could start to take her life back again. We ended the phone call, and I got back into the tub. I tried my best to relax and think of nothing. If my thoughts wandered off, I very actively thought of nothing, just of black, nothing but black. It helped a bit, for a little while I didn't think of all the horrors that had occurred. I must have stayed in the tub for a good two hours, the water was stone cold when I decided to get out. After I got dressed and looked at the clock, I noticed it was almost time to meet up with my friends.

When I entered the town square, I was greeted by a familiar sight. Mrs. McHenry, feeding the pigeons. I had no time to go talk to her, so I had to walk by. As I greeted her, she looked at me as if she was looking through me and said: "Always look both ways, ALWAYS!" Yes, Mrs. McHenry definitely was back, crazy as a bat and all. Talking with her seemed rather pointless at this time anyway. I just muttered out a hello and continued on my way to the diner where I was to meet my friends. Chris and Emma were already there, Marcy and Nigel hadn't arrived just yet. For some reason, I didn't feel comfortable with 2 of them still missing. When I was about to ask if we should call them, they both entered, and we could breathe again.

We talked about what happened and that we needed a system in place. Best would be if we could get like an alarm bell that would alert us all if pressed, but this was not within our possibilities, so we decided to go for the next best thing. Another group chat was started. Every morning, after we woke up, we would check-in, and every evening before going to bed, we would check out. That way, if one of us didn't check-in or out, we would all go and check up on that person. "If I want you all to come round to my house ASAP, I just won't check-in or out," Nigel said jokingly. Our seriously unamused looks made him realize it wasn't a joking matter, and he immediately apologized. Our system was far from ideal and had plenty of holes, but it was better than no system and horrific surprises.

I asked if anyone had been in contact with Amy's mother yet, none of us had. None of us had her phone number either, and she didn't go back to their house after she came back to the country. To prevent situations like this, we all were to list our Mom and or dad's phone numbers as well. We all wanted to know when Amy's funeral would be and wish her Mom all the best, but none of us could. We felt pretty confident about our set-up. Time would tell if it would work or not, but for now, it was the only thing we had. We spoke a bit more about the idea of there being a serial killer amongst our midst and that everyone was a potential next victim. Worse than that, everyone potentially could be this killer. I mentioned my run-in with the federal agents and concluded from that, that the police were now treating it as a serial killer. We talked about the headlines in the newspaper but also noted the similarities between these killings and those that took place about 200 years ago. We had to find out who else had been researching those killings and decided to copy them. We decided to start at the library, ask the other librarians, but since it was close to closing time for the library, there was no point in going there today. We decided to call it a day for now and went home.

On my way home, Linda called, she said she could be released any moment now. She sounded almost like a teenager again, so excited. Her Mom was already there with her; they were just waiting for the release forms, and then they were good to go. I would be home in about 5 minutes, so she was welcome to come over. Mom wasn't home from work yet when I got home, but she must be on her way by now. I decided to clean up a bit here and there. Put all Sean's toys into the toy box, washed the dishes we used that day and cleaned some bits and bobs here and there. Mom came in about 20 minutes later, jokingly asking me if the queen had announced a visit. I looked at her and rolled my eyes "You wonder why you are the one that always has to do the cleaning, but every time I decide to clean something you have to make some kind of remark on it. That doesn't motivate me to do more, you know." Mom apologized, she didn't mean it to be condescending. If I promised I would help more around the house, she promised to no longer make remarks. Somehow that didn't sound like a good deal, it certainly wasn't to my advantage. Guess I got suckered into that one again.

Mom started to make dinner, I was playing with Sean in the living room. Not until Mom called out that dinner was ready had

I realized that Linda was taking an awful lot of time to get here. I put Sean in his playpen as I went to sit at the table. Mom saw my troubled look and asked what was wrong. "Linda, she said she was waiting for the release forms and then she would come over" This was well over an hour ago. "Mom shrugged, maybe she hit traffic?" Maybe she did, it was rush hour after all. Every member of the 9 to 5 community was currently commuting back home. I decided not to worry too much about it, after all, I didn't even know how long it took to get the release forms in order. After dinner, dessert, and doing the dishes, more then another half hour had passed. Right about now, I was getting worried. I tried to call her, the call went straight to voicemail. Mom called the hospital, at first they didn't want to tell her because she wasn't related, but after Mom kept pushing, they told her Linda left the hospital almost 2 hours ago. Maybe she needed to stop on other locations first. I decided to wait a bit longer, not like I had any other option.

The alert for our new group chat sounded, I got up to get my phone from the table immediately. It was an app from Nigel. He linked a video clip which appeared to be from a traffic cam and a CCTV. He captioned it with the words "Oh hell no!"

Intrigued, I clicked the link. It was indeed CCTV and traffic cam footage. It was pretty grainy, but you could make out the highway and cars driving along it. The cameras were situated at an exit. There were a few cars on the exit, next to the exit lane were 3 trucks driving in a row. To the left of them, a car was overtaking them. At some point, the car turned into the lane with the trucks, in between the front two trucks and immediately turned onto the exit. A car already on the exit couldn't stop in time, they had a full-speed collision. The car that was already on the exit lane drove through the guardrail and down a steep slope, it came to a rest on its side. The car causing the collision came to a full stop against a tree behind the guardrail. We could make out someone moving away from the car against the tree before we saw it catch on fire and not long after explode. This video went viral in the last 30 minutes. It was captured from a live feed at the highway.

I know that exit, which is the exit that leads into our town. I walked into the living room and turned on the news channel. There was a reporter on the scene. She reported that both drivers had died during the crash and that a single passenger miraculously was physically unharmed. At this point, she was being checked up by the paramedics, she was hoping to get her in front of the cameras at a later time. The reporter talked some more about the accident, the truck drivers that seen it happen said the car from the left just took over to the right lane without looking if there was any traffic on it already. The oncoming car on the exit could never have anticipated the other cars move. It went from the most left lane to the most right lane in 2 seconds. Traffic on the highway had come to a full stop, and people were advised to take other routes home. Police had not yet released the names of the victims, they wanted to speak with their families first.

I looked up because I saw the red and blue lights of a police car lighting up in the street. A police car stopped on the other side of the street, and two police officers stepped out. They went to old Mr. Nelson's place, well, I should say George's place now. His wife answered the door and let the policemen in. About 20 minutes later, our doorbell rang. It was one of the police officers asking if Mom would please stay over with George's wife for a bit since she said she didn't know anyone really except my Mom, but only from talking a few times. Mom was happy to oblige. I was smart enough to put 2 and 2 together and figured George was in one of the cars. Linda still being absent made me suspect she was in the other car. I tried to ring her again.

To my surprise and my relief, I could hear the phone being answered. This relief was short-lived, though. On the phone came Linda's mother. I could tell by the sound of her voice that she had been crying and was trying her best not to continue. I didn't even say hello, the only words I spoke were "Please, tell me it wasn't her" Linda's Mom started to cry again "I wish I could say it wasn't her, believe me, I wish I could" A silence ensued. Linda's Mom was trying to find her posture again, and I was trying to figure out what to make of it, in my head, the traffic cam and CCTV footage ran again. "What happened?" Linda's Mom took a deep breath and started telling me what happened.

"I went to pick up Linda from the hospital. After all the release forms were signed, we decided to head on our way to you. When we got to the garage, Linda asked if she could drive. When I asked her if she thought that was a good idea, she became really insulted and somewhat hostile, so I handed her the keys. We got in, and everything went fine at first. On the highway was the first time she noticed she had quite some issues with depth perception. I don't know if she was being stubborn or really thought she could make it, but she started to overtake the 3 trucks riding in front of us. I told her the exit was coming up and that perhaps we should stay behind the trucks. 'Nonsense' she said, we could easily make that. We couldn't, in order for her to make the exit she had to hit the brakes, if she hit the brakes she couldn't stay between the two truck and without looking she drove onto the exit. Another car crashed right into us. We went through the guardrail, and the car came to a full stop against a tree behind the rail. Linda's airbag didn't blow up. She took the full force of the impact. Paramedics told me she died as soon as her head hit the steering wheel. My poor Linda." She cried, "My poor Linda, she already had been through so much only to have this as the outcome, she fought hard, but still, she died. I managed to get out of the car and walk up to some people that stopped to help" She took a moment of rest to drink some water and catch her breath...

"That poor man in the car on the exit. He never saw us coming, he was on top of us as soon as we hit the exit lane. His car tumbled down the steep slope. When I saw how the car landed, I was sure nobody would have survived that crash. To my surprise, the driver side door opened. A man managed to crawl out. I don't know how, but as soon as he left the vehicle, the car tumbled over and landed on his legs. The distinguishing sound of breaking bones and a man's scream filled the air. I could hear that over the noise of a beat-up car. I saw how he desperately tried to pull his legs from under the car but was very unsuccessful. He then tried to dig his legs out from under the car, and this seemed to take effect. As soon as he got himself free, he tried to make his way up the slope. It was clear he no longer had any use of his legs, he was pulling himself forward with his arms. He needed help, and he needed it badly. We... we couldn't get to him. When he finally made it to the top of the slope, he crawled through a pool of motor oil and gasoline. He tried to crawl away from Linda's car as fast as he could, but it was too late. Linda's car was already on fire by this time, in seconds the fire had caught up with him. In mere moments he was engulfed in flames, the flames were devouring him. You could feel the pain in his screams. Ever slightly burned yourself? Now imagine that pain times a gazillion, and not only that but over the entirety of your body. There was no doubt he was in pain and agony. There was no way we could get to him without risking our own lives. I couldn't imagine what that poor man was going through. About 30 seconds, maybe a minute later, our car exploded. The man was so close to the car that bits and pieces of him tore off during the explosion. His torso, left arm, and head, still connected with each other, landed in some shrubbery on the slope. The lower part of his body remained in position, and his right arm was currently missing. This one made its way all the way to the highway, and that is what happened here today. Two innocent people lost their lives because one of them had a point to make, or just didn't want to admit to herself what she could and could not do." I felt so horrible for Linda's Mom. They had been through a lot lately, and they were so happy she could finally leave the hospital. Nobody could have foretold this outcome. She asked me to send over Linda's belongings, she couldn't get herself to come and collect them. She did not want to travel that road again anytime soon. I agreed to send over Linda's belongings.

I was unsure if I should call Mom or not. Mom was across the street, consoling George's wife. I could hardly ring her and tell her that Linda was driving the other car and that she caused the accident because she was in a hurry to get to me. I decided not to ring her. She was better off not knowing for now. She should focus her attention on George's wife and kids now. A scooter stopped in front of the house across the street, it was their eldest. I wondered if she already knew or if she was mere moments away from the world crashing down on her. She seemed perfectly happy getting off the scooter, saying goodbye to her boyfriend. I guess she didn't know yet. I didn't want to imagine what was going on inside their house, so I decided to take my dog out for a walk. I could hear the screams coming from George's house. Poor kid, not only did she just hear that her father died in a horrible car crash, by now she already must have seen the footage of it as well. It went viral in no time. I wanted to go over and ring their bell, try to offer my support, but I couldn't. I was a stranger to them, me being there would mean absolutely nothing; besides, I wouldn't be able to keep to myself that it was Linda who was driving the other car. Linda, who was on her way to see me, I didn't want to put myself in a situation where I could possibly be blamed for it all. I just kept walking with my dog.

As I entered the town square, Mrs. McHenry was feeding them pigeons again. "Oh hello dear, are you alright?" she said. I answered that I was fine. She must be having one of her good days, she seemed lucid and wasn't blurting out weird things at the moment. I wondered if I should ask her if she knew that she was at my house the other night, or perhaps ask her where she had been or even where she lives. I opted against all that. I didn't want to talk to her at the moment, I didn't want to talk to anyone at the moment. I walked past Amy's house. There was still police tape around it. It was a crime scene, no one could enter. I walked on till I reached the edge of the forest. I didn't go into the forest, not this evening. This evening I learned that it's true when you think you can't sink any deeper, someone throws you a shovel and tells you to start digging. I turned around to make my way back home. I passed the location where the population sign used to be. The feds took it. I can't say I missed it. Every time I passed by it, there was a feeling of fear, would the number have dropped? Did anyone die? Get killed? Have an accident? I bet if it was still there someone would have adjusted its number again and I would probably get angry again. I returned home about 10 minutes later, Mom was still over at George's place. The alert for the group app sounded. Chris was calling for a check-in. We all answered. Everyone was still alive and in one piece. I tried to wash these last few days, no, weeks off by taking a very hot bath.

My skin turned bright red, that's how hot the water was. It didn't help. I still felt dirty and washed out. I took one of mom's sleeping pills and went to lay down on my bed, I don't know how long it took for me to fall asleep, but I think I was gone pretty quickly.

Only a few hours later, Mom came in and woke me. Apparently, my friends were looking for me. Oh shoot, I missed the check-in. At least we now know it works. I should have told them I would go to bed. I went to the living room where they had all assembled. All of them were here. I chuckled a bit, "You could have just asked Chris or Emma to come and check, they live next door." "And have only one of us stumble upon a gruesome scene on their own?" Nigel asked. Fair enough, finding a horrible scene is awful enough, finding it all on your own might possibly be even worse. It was still early in the evening, and since we were all together, we decided to go for a walk. I brought my dog, and Chris went to get his. That way, the dogs got some exercise as well. I asked them if they heard who the victims of the accident were. They hadn't. "Linda was driving the car that caused it, and our new across the street neighbor, George, was driving the car that crashed into her. Neither of them survived the crash" None of them uttered another word and for a little while we walked in silence. What could anyone say, nothing would bring either of them back or rewind the crash. "Let's head to the forest, clear our heads and there we can let the dogs roam free" Chris suggested. Not only did this break the silence, but it brought the topic to a lighter subject as well. We all agreed to go there.

When we were at the clearing Marcy asked if any of us had been able to get into contact with Amy's Mom. None of us had been successful in contacting her. The house was still taped off as a crime scene, and she clearly hadn't been there since. None of us knew when Amy's funeral would be if there would be a service and if so, when and where. Can't say I'd blame her. She just lost her entire family, getting in touch with your daughter's friends wouldn't be high on my priority list either. We all decided we would try to figure out anything about Amy's funeral tomorrow. Someone should know something, right? Although Amy's Mom never was part of the town. Most of the time, she was abroad for work. If she was home one weekend a month, it would be a lot. I had no idea who to ask if they heard from Amy's Mom. "Look! The sign is back!" Chris pointed at the silhouette of the population sign. I couldn't believe they would put that sign back. As we walked closer, I noticed they didn't. This was a brand new sign. It read "Population about 3000," and someone had already made an adjustment to it. The word about was crossed out, underneath it with a bright yellow marker, the word "below" was added to it. Someone was really adamant about changing that sign, and not having it state we have 3000 citizens.

I didn't have much time to wonder why, because as we were making our way to Nigel's home, we all were spooked by a horrific sound. It sounded like the grunting of a gravely wounded grizzly bear. We weren't far off. It was Mr. Daniels who was stumbling towards us in the distance making strange growling noises. He was the former janitor at our school. He lost his Job after Emma, Nicolle, and Amy were sent to detention. He was to keep an eye on them, and that day Nicolle and Amy were having a fight. During detention, they were still bickering at each other until Mr. Daniels had enough. He got up from his chair and grabbed both Amy and Nicolle's head and slammed them right into each other. Nicolle had to go to the E.R. he broke her nose in that process. Amy got the better end of that deal, she "only" ended up with a black eye. Both Nicolle's parents and Amy's dad went to school and demanded Mr. Daniels be fired, and for the school to pay their medical expenses. Our school was in no mood for a scandal, so they obliged. We all stopped and looked at each other, wondering why Mr. Daniels was stumbling and growling. As he came closer, it became abundantly clear. He was gutted. He was sliced open from his neck to his groin, but not far enough to kill him right away. The opening was just far enough for someone to have fished out his intestines. These were tied around his hands as if it was a tightrope to keep someone captive. The growling was because his tongue was also cut off. He stumbled up until about 2 feet in front of us when he fell to his knees. His eyes rolled to the back of his head, and his body started convulsing. This was a sight unseen and one I wish I could unsee. Blood and guts were dripping from the wound over his abdomen, he was spitting out blood, and there was also foam coming from his mouth. We didn't know what to do, or how to help him, at the same time, the mere sight of him scared us. Who did this? Maybe they were still close. I felt very vulnerable at that time and was happy that I wasn't alone.

I got my cell phone out and dialed the emergency services. The lady I got on the other end wasn't very helpful. I described the situation. That Mr. Daniels tongue was cut out and his intestines were used to tie his hands together and that now he was convulsing on the street. "Listen, kid, I already had a hard day today, and my shift is almost over, I am in no mood for practical jokes and don't you know that you can get a nifty fine for prank calling the emergency services!" That's all she said before she hung up on me! She actually hung up on me. I rang back and got the same lady, by now, I was fully agitated and angry. Mr. Daniels wasn't dead yet, perhaps his life could be saved. I told her not to hang up on me that I wasn't joking and she should send over an ambulance and hurry! "Sure kid, will do," and she hung up on me again. I looked at the rest of the group. I couldn't believe this. I called home and told my Mom what was going on and asked her to call the emergency services, the others did the same. 10 minutes later, about 2 minutes after Mr. Daniels lost his battle for life, the ambulance arrived. After that, the police and fire department also showed up. I walked up to the captain and said I wanted to register a complaint against the emergency services lady. This life could have been saved if she took my call seriously the first time, maybe still if she took my call serious the second time, but instead I had to call my Mom, explain everything to her, and have her call the emergency services for a third time before an Ambulance was set on route. The captain took my complaint very seriously. He had written down some keywords and asked me to come by down the station to make a formal complaint tomorrow. He asked all of us to come down to the police station tomorrow to make a formal statement about what happened here tonight. All our parents had come over to collect us all from yet another gruesome scene. We said goodbye to each other and left for our homes. When I got back home, I went straight to bed. I sent a message to our group chat, stating goodnight and went to sleep. I was ready for this day to be over!

CHAPTER TWELVE

I wanted today to be a normal day. I got up from the bed, took a shower, made me some breakfast, had a coffee, and packed my lunch. I didn't have to go back to school yet, neither of us did, but I longed for something normal. I sent a message to the chat that I was going to school. The others all responded that they were going to school as well. Guess we all longed back to the boring old normal.

Mom came down with Sean, and I realized that I hadn't asked her about George's family yet. I didn't want to seem uninterested, so I asked her how it went. "It went as you would suspect it went," she said. "Natascha was crying her eyes out, the little ones didn't understand, she tried to explain it best she could. At one point their little girl asked that if her father were no longer dead, he would come back, this broke her heart even more. At some point their eldest came home, slightly annoyed that she had to come home, though her mood changed as soon as she saw her Mom in tears. She screamed so loud, she said that it couldn't be true, that George was a good driver and that he would never be in an accident like that. She was screaming and crying, saying that it wasn't true until her Mom grabbed her in a tight hug, and they both cried their eyes out. Natascha decided that they weren't staying here, she told her daughter to pack her clothes and some for the little ones. They hadn't sold their old house yet, and she was moving them back and put this one back on the market instead. I stayed until the taxi came to collect them, she said she would send movers for the rest of their belongings sometime in the upcoming weeks and would arrange for George's body to be transported and buried in their hometown as well. Before she got into the taxi, she thanked me and said that we probably would have become good friends if things had turned out differently. Then they all got into the taxi and left."

Wow, that was quite the emotional rollercoaster Mom had been on. I felt bad. For Mom, for George's family for everyone in town. I gave Mom a hug and asked her if she was going to be okay today. She nodded while taking a sip of her coffee. I grabbed my packed lunch and headed out the door on my way to school. I crossed the town square to take a shortcut. Mrs. McHenry was there feeding the pigeons again. As I rode by on my bicycle, I heard her say, "Cotton, won't stop the bleeding." I couldn't help but wonder what made her this way. I would check and see if she was still there after school and see if she was lucid enough for a chat.

Talk of the day in school was no longer George and Linda's crash gone viral. Most people had no idea who was in those cars, so watching that clip once or twice was enough for it to be forgotten again. No, the talk of the day in school was Mr. Daniels death, and the fact we had a serial killer loose in town. Some kids said they no longer felt safe in town. I could relate. Everyone was afraid to go out after dark, and nobody trusted anyone anymore. Everyone could be the killer. It could be a teacher in school, the bus driver, the librarian, the cashier at the supermarket, everyone could be the killer. None of these killings seemed to have anything in common other than the fact the victims all lived in this town.

I saw Carlin and Hobbes enter the school. What were they doing here? Did they have a lead that it might be one of us? They headed in my direction and stopped next to me. Pointing at Amy's old locker, they asked if that one belonged to her. After I answered yes, they asked me if I could also point them in the direction of Ricardo's locker. I couldn't, I had no idea if he even had a locker. Instead, I pointed them in the direction of his friends. "You see that group of scum over there? They can tell you all about Ricardo and his antics" Hobbes was very observant and noted that I didn't like Ricardo very much. I scoffed, "Of course I didn't like him. He was scum and only out to cause trouble, why would I like someone like that?" Hobbes looked at me as if it actually made sense what I said and they headed off towards Ricardo's friends to have a chat. Good luck with that!

Lunchtime came, and we were sitting at our table in the cafeteria when a lot of commotion came from the nurse's station. You know how on television shows the high school nurse is always this cute attractive young lady? Who was always very loving and caring? I guess our school board didn't see those shows. We had nurse Tessa, but she was called Bertha by most of us. Tessa was a name to be associated with a nice lady and not with a butch like Bertha. She was this fat heap of meat, always looked as if she wanted to tear your head off and eat it. She wasn't loving nor caring. I remember this one time we had to go there because Nicolle fell off a rack in the playground. She had a nasty cut on her leg. It needed stitches, but she just put a band-aid on it and told Nicolle to grow up, it was just a tiny cut. Well, that tiny cut got infected, and Nicolle ended up having to go to the hospital to get it disinfected, even though it needed stitches they couldn't stitch it up due to the infection. Now the wound needed to stay open so the infection could heal. She had to rinse it out twice a day with a disinfectant. It left a nasty scar on her leg, and Bertha never apologized for that. There was also this other time when a boy was brought in after hitting his head really hard after falling from a tree. She gave him an aspirin and scolded him for being stupid enough to climb in a tree. It wasn't in a worried tone, like a mother would, no it was vicious the way she said it. If anything these past few weeks had taught me, it was that commotion wasn't a good sign. I don't think someone dropped off a box of cute little puppies that everyone was excited about and I really wanted to steer clear of the commotion, but our next class was right next door to the nurse's station anyway, so we all decided to head straight towards the commotion.

The boring old normal I was longing for, I would not find today. As we walked closer to the nurse's station, we could see that something was horribly wrong in there. Bertha was laying on the exam table, cut open from her neck to her groin, just like the others. Her intestines had been completely removed, the pile of blood and other fluids were a testimony of that fact, but after they all had been removed, someone filled up the hole with cotton balls, and stuffed them right back in on top of that. The incision itself was covered with band-aids. Marcy and Emma fainted at the sight of Bertha, naked on a table, cut open, with fluids oozing out of the bits of intestines that could be put back into the wound and were just dangling at the side of Bertha's body. It didn't do much to me. I have seen worse these last few weeks. Being around so much death and mutilation apparently makes you numb to the sight of more. I looked over to Nigel and Chris. They seemed rather unfazed as well. "Can't say I am going to be sad about this one," I overheard Chris say. It didn't even shock me to hear those words. I'd bet a lot of kids were happy to see her go. I would have been happy to see her go, as well. Happy to see her pack her bags and move somewhere else. Can't say this made me happy, she must have been in so much fear and pain.

There was a pocket knife stuck to her clipboard. The one she used to write out her advice to students. I walked over to it, and it read, "Stitches not required, band-aid and painkiller suffice" Was this Bertha's writing, or did the killer actually take the time to write out a diagnosis after he was done? Pretty bold move by the killer as well. Killing the school nurse, in broad daylight while agents are snooping around the school as well. That day, school ended early for everyone. As we all were walking towards our bicycles, I remembered what Mrs. McHenry said this morning. She said that cotton wouldn't stop the bleeding, and Bertha was stuffed with cotton balls. Because I wasn't in total shock and horror this time around, I remembered. I started thinking about the other weird stuff she blurted out in the past and started to make a connection between deaths and crazy sayings. I asked the rest of the group to meet up at the diner in a bit, I might have a lead.

On my way home, I avoided the town square this time, no shortcuts. As I got home, I tried to figure out what it is that was bothering me so much. Clearly, Mrs. McHenry couldn't be our killer, she was well over a hundred or at least close to it. Or could she be? And all the things she had said, none of them correlated with any of the murders until now. I started to think hard of all the things she had said and written them down as best I remembered. When I was done jotting down the weird stuff she said, I started to relate it to the deaths that occurred at the time she said it. A disturbing pattern emerged. I had to talk to the others about this. I took my notepad and made my way to the diner. I sent a text to the group saying I was heading there and one by one they replied that they would come soon. Chris first had to convince his Mom that he would be safe leaving the house. Boldly stating that the killer never struck twice in one day, so he'd be safe. Needless to say that this did not go down well with his Mom, but she agreed to let him go, he picked up Emma first, and they came together. Nigel and Marcy followed soon after. They all wanted to know what I found out. "It's not as much what I found out, it's what was already there and I finally connected, I just can't make sense of it all just yet."

I motioned for them to come and sit down. I got out my notebook, but before I started, I made them promise not to think of me as crazy. The promised. "Mrs. McHenry, she is the key to all of this!" They all looked at each other, thinking I had actually lost it. I sighed and stated that their promises were worthless. I got rather defensive at this point, yet I hadn't given them any information as to why I thought she was the key. "Mrs. McHenry the key to all of this? She couldn't even squat a fly, she's old and frail, let alone kill 7 people," Chris said as he looked around the group. The others agreed with him. "I never said she killed them, I said she is the key to it all. She would be the one that can tell us what is happening and why "I turned to Chris, "Remember that evening when you sent me a text asking if I took over the pigeon feeding from her? I never got to tell you what was going on that evening, but she was there. She was in my house, standing in the darkest corner of the living room and had turned off the main power switch, rambling on about me being chosen by a white dove but never told me for what or why" Chris remembered. He decided to shut up and listen to what I had to say, as did the rest.

"I know what I am going to lay out for you, will seem crazy at first, but it will make sense, so please just hear me out. Mrs. McHenry has been here all our lives, we all know her as the nice elderly lady that's always feeding the pigeons at the town square. She has always been kind, saying hello to everyone who looked in her direction, usually getting a hello or a how do you do in return. But a few weeks ago, right before Sean and Nora were born, she started to yell out weird things. She probably said a lot more strange things than I have written down here, but I can only account for the ones I heard or overheard someone else state she said.

The first thing I recall is her telling me that it's coming and that I can't run or hide, that was before all the crazy events happened, and right before Mr. Kelly's death. Right after, she told Ms. Belle that even though the babies were born, but the town didn't reach 3000 citizens yet because it was calm. At this point, nobody outside the hospital knew Mr. Kelly had died, Hell, even Mrs. Kelly didn't know at this point. The next time I saw her, she seemed to warn me that it was very worried because something came to close and that it wouldn't stop until it felt safe again. She never specified what it was, and because she spooked me when she said it, I just went away from her without asking questions. Next time she told me that it trembled in fear and that it was not safe. This was only a few hours before an earthquake took Dennis' life and horribly wounded Linda. The time after that I saw her in a circle with her pigeons, and she blurted out that curiosity killed the cat, I thought that was aimed at me at the time she said it, because of the way she was sitting in a circle with the pigeons looked weird. But mere moments later, Ms. Belle died, and her curiosity was to blame for her demise, and just this morning on my way to school, she said that cotton wouldn't stop the bleeding. Bertha was stuffed with cotton balls and band-aids when she was found"

I looked around my group of friends who were all listening with great attention to what I was saying. Everyone seemed to be thinking about my words, no one said anything for a while until Nigel pointed out that maybe she was just clairvoyant. Most of the things she "predicted" were accidents, she only foretold one of the murders. This was true, and I never claimed she was responsible for all the murders, but I was still convinced she holds the key to solving what was going on here. We decided to go look for her in the town square and have a chat, but she was no longer there. I hoped she hadn't disappeared again. At some point my phone rang, it was my mother, she had heard what happened in school. The tone of her voice was worried and angry but more worried. She wanted to know why I hadn't called her, she would have come home. She was home now and wanted me to get there ASAP. I told her I would soon be on my way. We all had some new stuff to pounder our minds with. We said goodbye to each other. Nigel and Marcy went home together and Chris, Emma and I went on our way home as well. We all left a text saying we got home in one piece in our group chat.

"Why on earth didn't you call me," were the words I was greeted by as soon as I closed the door. "I am sorry, Mom, but you were at work, and I didn't want to bother you" Now I had gotten her angry, "BOTHER ME?! BOTHER ME?!, the nurse at school gets killed, all students get to see her body on display and are being sent home to deal with that gruesome sight alone, and you didn't want to bother me? And believe me, I am not done with your school yet either. Who sends away their students without notifying their parents after something like this happens?" Mom was truly furious. I know I did wrong by not calling her, but it never even crossed my mind to do so. "Mom? I am really sorry I didn't call you, I was with my friends at the diner, we were trying to figure out what's going on, all the strange deaths and murders that are occurring lately, we were looking for a connection and perhaps solve the mystery" "Oh you and your mysteries" she said in a tone of disdain. "That is what is going to get you killed one day, digging too deep into a mystery without overseeing its consequences!" Perhaps she was right, but there was no way I was going to let this one go. I already dug into deep to let it go. I was like a dog with a bone. A few weeks ago, I probably would have laughed at Mom for saying I could get myself killed, but at this time it was a real possibility. I didn't tell her what exactly my friends and I talked about. She would think I am crazy for thinking Mrs. McHenry could be a key part to all of this. Sweet old little Mrs. McHenry. I never told her about Mrs. McHenry's visit to our house before re-appearing at the town square either. Maybe I should have done that too.

Mom was so annoyed with me that she banned me from leaving the house for the rest of the day and told me to go wash up for dinner. I let the others know that I wouldn't be able to meet up with them today, Mom was keeping me grounded for the remainder of the day. Neither of them felt like venturing out on their own or without me, so no more snooping around today. After dinner, Mom and I watched some nonsense rom-com movie and played a bit with Sean until it was time for bed. This was the boring normal I was longing for, but this wasn't the time I wanted it. I had a lead, I wanted to research my lead. I wanted to go out and find Mrs. McHenry and ask her about all of it, but couldn't, Mom was preventing me from doing so. That's the downside of being a teenager, mom's the boss, and you don't mess with the boss. Tomorrow was Friday, but since school was canceled until further notice, it was a crime scene now, after all, I decided that research could wait until tomorrow. I left a message in our chat stating that we should get together again tomorrow to do some digging and signed off by saying I was going to bed. Everyone responded stating they were either going to bed or would soon go to bed. At least everyone was safe, for now.

The next day I woke up to an empty house. Mom had already left for work and dropped Sean off at daycare. I made myself a cup of coffee and grabbed the newspaper from the counter. Bertha made the front page. "School nurse brutally murdered" I scanned the article for clues, but it had none. The police were still none the wiser and federal agents were on the case now. Nothing I didn't already know. I tried to find an uplifting story in the paper, but there was none. The closest thing to good news in the entire paper was the announcement that the retirement home was finished and ready for its first residents. The mayor would open it during festivities on Saturday afternoon, and its first resident would enter shortly after. After I finished the newspaper, I started thinking more and more about the murders.

The people that were killed clearly seemed to be targeted. This wasn't just a maniac on a random killing spree, there had to be more to this. But what on earth could be the connection between them? What did Ricardo, Mr. Thompson, Amy and her family, Mr. Daniels and Bertha have in common? I tried to see if their paths crossed in more than one way. The school! All could be connected to the school, all but Mr. Thompson so there goes that theory. They didn't even go to the same supermarket. The only thing that seemed to connect these people was our town. That was the only thing all of them had in common. I had this feeling that there was a connection and that it was staring me right in the face, but why couldn't I put my finger on it. I printed out a map of the town and started to mark their houses. Who knows, if I were to connect the dots, maybe a pattern would emerge? I started by drawing lines from the places they lived to each other. This gave nothing but some wobbly lines. I then started connecting the places they died. Same result, just some wobbly lines. This was getting me nowhere. I don't know what I was suspecting to draw up, a demonic sign a pentagram, perhaps even an arrow pointing as to where the killer would be? I was grasping at straws here. By now, my friends were all waking up, judging from the alerts coming from our group chat. I decided to check-in as well. We would meet up at the diner for lunch. Till then, I was still breaking my head over what connected these people. There had to be a connection, there had to be.

I took a quick shower before heading off to the diner to meet up with my friends. I was the last to get there. Apparently, we all had been doing the same thing. We were all desperately trying to find a connection, all the links we could come up with were never shared by all. The school fit for some, the gym fit for others, the town only had one library, but two of them didn't even have a membership. There was nothing that we could think of, that linked them all together. Who knows, maybe they all used the same brand of toilet paper. Anything could be a connection at this point. We heard the noise of a scooter, followed by the sound of a crash. It was Raymond, one of Ricardo's scooter scum buddies. Raymond was also the pizza delivery guy for one of the town's pizza places. He drove straight into the shop window of the diner. His scooter lost balance on the curb and catapulted him off. He landed on the window like a cartoon character and slowly slid down. This probably would have been a hilarious scene, if not for the fact that Raymond was dead. He was gutted, and his intestines were tied around the gas handle of the scooter, which still caused it to be accelerating while laying on its side. A pocket knife kept the intestines in place. This was a horrible sight. At this point, Marcy broke down and started screaming, "I am done with this, I am over it. Why is this happening, who is next? When is it my turn?" Emma walked up to her and tried to calm her down. It took quite some effort, but she succeeded.

I noticed that I wasn't as horrified anymore. I looked at

Raymond's body, it was a clean-cut leading from his throat to his groin. There didn't seem to be a sign of struggling. Raymond was a fairly tough guy, worked out at the gym, not the kind of guy I would suspect to go down without a fight. Perhaps he was drugged before he was killed. If that was the case, truly everyone could have done it. It's easy to drug someone and then have your way with them. This didn't help much at all. I looked to the others. Marcy was pretty upset, and Emma was pretty shaken up as well. Nigel was trying to find his footing and Chris was doing the same I was, looking at everyone else to see how they were doing. I called Mom, she probably would kill me herself, if I didn't call her this time. She told me to stay put. Told her I wasn't going anywhere anyway since Mulder and Scully already arrived at the scene. Special agent Carlin came up to us and introduced himself to my friends saying that we had already met before. I took this opportunity to ask if the sign yielded any clues. "Not that I would be at liberty to discuss this with you if it did, I can assure you it didn't" he pulled up one shoulder and made an "I don't know" gesture. He asked us what we saw, we saw nothing. We saw Raymond squashed into the window, slowly sliding down. That's all we saw. After their lines of standard questions, they went outside to inspect the scene. Mom walked in as they went out. "Come on, all of you, get in the van" we all obliged. First, we dropped Nigel off at home, his Aunt was already waiting for him. Second, we dropped off was Marcy, Emma decided to get off as well since Marcy was still pretty shaken up about it. Chris asked if he could come to our house. His parents weren't at home right now, and he didn't want to be alone. Of course, that was fine.

Mom went into the kitchen and started to fix me a cup of coffee, she asked if Chris wanted one as well. "Just a glass of water please, no coffee for me." We sat in the living room. "I can't believe that just happened," Chris looked at me in disbelief. "Raymond was a jerk, and he needed a good beating, but this..." I didn't know Raymond that well, I knew he hung out with the wrong crowd, so I always steered clear of him. Chris continued, "This one summer I got a summer job at the same pizza place as Nicolle did. Raymond's uncle owns the place, so he was strutting around like he owned the place. He kept telling me I had to follow his orders, or he'd tell his uncle, and I'd lose my job. I never took him seriously. His uncle is a great man. Does a lot for the community, including hiring his nephew. At least during working hours, it kept him off the streets. There were a lot of complaints about the pizza delivery guy, but his uncle never stopped believing in him, but this one summer, he went too far.

"He clearly had the hots for Nikki, unfortunately for him, Nikki didn't have the hots for him. Quite the opposite, she found him obnoxious, unlikeable, hostile and ugly. When he tried to get with her once more, Nikki told him exactly that. He didn't like that very much and pulled her back by her hair. He said 'listen, bitch, you're going to do what I say or I will make you lose your job, now get on your knees right now!' At this point, his uncle came in and literally beat the crap out of him. He apologized to us so much, he was genuinely upset with his nephew's behavior. Nikki and I quit on the spot and his uncle gave us our last paycheck and a huge tip with another apology." Wow, he definitely did deserve a good beating all right. How come I didn't know this before? Why did you never tell me? Did the others know? "No one knew, we didn't want to get the poor man out of business because he was trying to save a lost cause. He meant well and he was always really nice to us. We decided to keep it to ourselves and just steer clear of Raymond and the scum he hung out with, so far that has worked pretty well"

Now none of them had to worry about running into any of the others all right. Both Raymond and Nikki were dead now. One died in a freak accident, the other in a freak murder. This killer had no problem going for old or young people. Loved or unloved by the community. He even killed a dog, why the dog. That was one of the sweetest dogs in the world. By no means was it a guard dog. I can't imagine the dog going for the killer, not even when the killer was attacking the family. That dog was known as the greatest coward amongst other dogs. He would even bark at a cat, let alone chase it. My mind was straying again. I couldn't figure it out. Now we had to add Raymond to the equation. He probably had a lot in common with Ricardo but probably very little to nothing with Amy and her family or Mr. Thompson. The school nurse he probably knew and probably not a stranger to Mr. Daniels either. What on earth could it be that linked these people together? Time had flown by, and it was almost dinner time. Chris saw that the light over at his house was on, so he decided to go home, even after Mom told him it was fine if he wanted to stay for dinner. After Chris left, I told Mom that he probably likes his moms cooking better. "Ooh, oh no you didn't, I take it you no longer have to eat tonight, huh?" I apologized, I was only joking. At least it made us both laugh, which was better than the mood we had been in for the last couple of days. Mom continued to cook dinner as it was already getting dark outside. After dinner, I decided to take the dog for a walk.

I went over to Chris' and asked if he'd like to come with his dog as well. Even though I wouldn't be alone if he said no, I'd still be with my dog, I was happy he said yes. For the first time in my life, I actually didn't feel safe walking around town. This serial killer didn't seem to care anymore. He'd grab you during the evening, at night or during the day. We had no clues as to whom it could be. I keep referring to this killer as a male simply because I can't imagine a female killing this way. Maybe that's mind poisoning by movies and television, they hardly have female killers, and if they do have female killers, they kill in clean ways. A single shot to the head, Poison, a single stab through the heart, a push down the stairs, nothing ever as close to this brutality.

Chris asked if we should walk to the forest. Sure, let's head to the forest. We passed by George's house, the trusted for sale sign was back up in the front yard. "Chris? Have you ever wished for something exciting to happen around town? Make it less of a boring old town?" Of course, he had. We all had. None of us meant for it to turn into the working ground of a serial killer though. "I am kind of wishing for it to turn back into the boring old town where nothing ever happens anymore," Chris said. I agreed, and we walked on to the town square.

The square itself was pretty empty. Some lights and music were coming from the bars and restaurants. The fountain in its center was lit up as always. I couldn't wrap my head around it. How could water resemble fire so much? In this light, it looked more like huge flames were spouting out from the ground, like from a volcanic eruption. Chris noted how pretty the fountain looked in this light. He didn't share my thought on it resembling flames at all, to him, it was just colored water. Perhaps I have a bigger imagination than he does.

All the animals sprinted back into the forest when we reached the clearing. We took the leashes off the dogs. They sprinted straight after them. I laughed, there was no way my slightly overweighed pooch was ever going to catch a wild animal. Within mere moments they returned to us at the clearing. Mine had something in its mouth. I called her over and got it out. It was a pocket knife! I looked at Chris, and he stared at me. I looked at the knife again. It wasn't like the ones used in the recent killings though. It looked old and rusted. Maybe some hiker lost it here years ago. I decided to head in the direction the dogs came from, Chris was walking right behind me. In a freshly dug out hole, I guess our dogs did that, we found an entire collection of old rusted pocket knives. I decided to call the police. It took them about 20 minutes to get here. By now, I really had to head home, Mom would have dinner ready by now. I pointed the police officer to the location of the knives and said that I had to go. He wanted to ask some more questions. "I am happy to answer all of your questions officer, but my mother is at home waiting with dinner, and the last thing I want to do right now, is anger, my mother. I can only tell you that we were sitting by the clearing when my dog ran up with one of the knives in her mouth. We walked back here and found this stash, the mud on the paws of both dogs suggested to me that they dug them up, then we called the police, and you all took your time to get here, and now I can stay no longer" I made a waving motion with my hand and headed home, Chris followed behind me. He was slightly impressed by how I talked to the police officer. Well, when you got to go home, you got to go home. 10 minutes later, we both had returned to our houses. Mom was already waiting with dinner. Before she could get angry with me, I yelled out that it wasn't my fault the police took 20 minutes to get there. Intrigued, she sat down, and I told her about the knives. After dinner, we watched some more television, and I went in for an early night. Tomorrow was a workday after all. I said goodnight to my friends in our chat and went to bed.

That night I had the strangest dream. I dreamt that I was flying, high in the sky. I was surrounded by pigeons. I felt happy and peacefully. There was not a cloud in the sky. We were flying high up, and I was having the time of my life. When I looked to my left, I noticed I wasn't the only person flying up in the air over here. I started to fly towards this other person, but the distance between us remained the same. I couldn't make out who it was. The person pointed down and started to descend, I followed. On the horizon, I could see the border of our town, or at least, it resembled our town. There was the town square, but it wasn't the town square just yet. It was open, there was no road. It was a great big hole. It looked like the pits of hell down there. In the center, there was a massive black gate. It looked so heavy, no man on earth would be able to push it open on his own. I wanted to fly closer, but I couldn't. It was like there was an invisible wall I could not pass. To the side of this open pit of death, decay, and fire, there was a group of six people. I couldn't make out any features. I could only see that they were people.

The person that was flying up in the sky with me flew all the way down to the group. I tried to follow but again hit an invisible wall. They started chanting something. The ground seemed to respond to their chants. The more they chanted, the more it appeared to close. By the time they were done chanting the town square was completely closed. The only thing reminding of the fiery pit below it was the glow of light still passing through a single hole in the center of the square. It was the exact location the fountain was standing. I was so confused when I woke up. What kind of dream was that? I know that it hadn't been easy lately, that a lot was going on. But this was one hell of a weird dream. I looked at my alarm clock. I didn't have a lot of time to think about that dream, I had to hit the shower, get some breakfast, and be on my way to the antique shop. I didn't even have time for a coffee when I got down, I kissed Mom and Sean goodbye and went on my way.

CHAPTER THIRTEEN

Adam was counting stock in the storage room when I entered the antique shop. He came to the front and greeted me. "Today, I have a special assignment for you" I looked at him a bit weary, special assignments hardly been anything good. If teachers uttered those words, we would usually end up with a pile of homework or have to write a 50-page essay. Adam laughed, "Come, I'll show you." He walked towards the center of his store, up to his prized possession. "Today, we are going to redress and set the dining set. It has been collecting dust for quite a while now, and the tablecloth certainly could use a good wash too" Great, more cleaning. I already didn't like setting the table at home, now there was also the added stress of definitely not breaking anything. These weren't just plates and cups, this was pricey antique. I wouldn't be able to afford anything I'd break. "I don't know about this Adam, what if I break something?" Adam looked at me, somewhat amused. "Don't worry kid, it's all well insured, besides we'll be doing this one together."

When we took off the tablecloth, it revealed the table in its full glory. It was massive and almost looked as if it was carved out of a single piece of wood. It was in pristine condition. The greater part of the morning we spend dusting it all off, wash it, vacuum the chairs and space it was set up in. When all was done, and the table was set again, it almost seemed to emit a glow of grandeur. "Beautiful, isn't it?" Adam asked, and I just nodded. "Maybe she'll see some use again soon" I looked at him confused and asked, "Have you found a buyer for it?" "Not yet, but who knows." Typically Adam. This entire dining set was priced at 5 million, and even though it was gorgeous, it was way overpriced.

I wouldn't buy a dining set for that amount, not even if I had that much money to spare. It would need to be a magical table for me to invest that kind of money. One that sets itself and cleans itself off, hell, it would even need to help me do the cooking and washing up after. I think Adam overpriced it on purpose. He loved that set, he probably didn't want to sell it at all. We took a break after we were done. My mind wandered off again to the killings. Adam asked what I was thinking about, and I told him about the victims and how they had nothing in common. "Well, they certainly were disliked by the same person" As Adam said that something clicked. We were so busy looking at places and activities they might have in common that I never even thought about persons. As I went over the list of victims in my head, it made sense. I asked Adam if I could have the afternoon off, this wasn't a problem. I thanked Adam and left the store.

As I entered the town square, there was a lot of commotion going on at the other end. Oh no, not again, commotion was never a good thing, but these last few weeks it was a terrible thing. I went to take a look and see what was going on. No corpse this time, it was Mrs. McHenry who was stirring things up. She was preventing the mayor from opening up the new retirement home. She kept yelling, "If they come, you'll set them free!" She was physically preventing him from cutting the ribbon to open the place.

An elderly man was standing there with a suitcase, waiting for the mayor to open up the retirement home so he could take up residence. The mayor kept politely asking her to step aside. At some point, he just tried to cut the ribbon by moving the scissors past her really fast. Mrs. McHenry foresaw this move and stepped in front of the scissors. This lead to the mayor actually stabbing her with the scissors. The mayor, scared by his own actions, dropped the scissors. It wasn't a really deep wound or a brutal stabbing, but the crowd lost it. They all turned on the mayor, how could he stab a poor confused elderly woman? The mayor was too busy apologizing to Mrs. McHenry to pay any attention to the crowd. He called for a paramedic to come and tend to her wound. In this commotion on top of the commotion, the elderly man that stood there waiting must have had enough. He grabbed the scissors from the floor, cut the ribbon himself, and went inside. If nobody had gotten injured, this might even have been funny to watch. Mrs. McHenry luckily only had a superficial wound and didn't need any stitches. In the meantime, the retirement home was opened by its first, and for now, only resident. Mrs. McHenry shook her head. "You have no idea what you have done, what you will unleash upon us" She took one last look at the monastery turned retirement home and started to walk away. I decided to go home and do some more research on what I believed to have found out.

When I arrived home, Mom was rather surprised to see me. "Don't worry Mom, I didn't get fired. I just took the afternoon off" I made myself a cup of coffee. I strongly believed I had figured it out. "Mom? If you knew one of your friends did something really bad, or rather, is doing something really bad, what would you do? Would you tell on your friend, knowing full well it would get them in trouble?" Mom sat down, and after some thinking, she answered my question with questions. "Have you tried talking to your friend? Did you ask why they are doing this? Did you tell them to stop? Is it something you can help them with?" I answered with no, no, no, and a maybe. "If you tell on them, and get them in trouble, will that be for the best? In other words, is getting your friend in trouble worth it? Will your friend come out better?" No, my friend most certainly would not come out better, if my friend came out of those troubles at all, my friend would come out far worse. "I don't think my friend would come out better" Mom looked at me and said "Then don't tell on your friend, try and have a talk first, see if there is anything you can do to help your friend stop doing whatever it is your friend is doing" Yeah, that is easier said than done. Talk to him and make him stop. Sounds so simple. I thanked Mom for her wise words and thought about it some more.

I still could be wrong, but as far as I could tell the victims only had one thing in common. They all had crossed one particular person. I didn't like what this added up to. I had to make a phone call, one that could disprove my theory, but it could also confirm it. Unfortunately, it did neither. I did not get the information I wanted, in fact, I got no information at all. I only got stonewalled by the bureaucracy of yet another hospital.

I decided to write it all down and try to make sense of it. Mrs. McHenry clearly played a part in all of this, but I couldn't quite figure out how. I realized that I wasn't going to figure this one out by just staring at my notes, I grabbed my notes, put them in a bag and set out for the town square. It was time to confront Mrs. McHenry with my questions. I still had no idea why she was at my house and if she even remembered where she was. On my way to the town square, I decided to sit and wait at her spot if she wasn't there, no matter how long that would take. Luckily she was right there, feeding breadcrumbs to the pigeons. "We need to talk!" She looked at me, not even a bit surprised. She nodded, "Yes dear, I think it is time" She got up from the steps she was sitting on and motioned for me to follow her. "Come, let's move to a quieter spot" I did as she asked and followed her. Maybe she would lead me to her house, I wondered what it would look like. Would it be like her, old and dated? Would be fun if she had this modern setup with everything automated. I wasn't about to find out, she lead me to the antique shop. Great, I took the afternoon off, only to return here. Adam didn't even look up when we walked in as if he was expecting us. She walked further into the shop. Behind us, Adam turned the sign to read closed and locked the shop. Mrs. McHenry continued into the little kitchen in the back and asked me to sit down with her. Even though this situation was weird, to say the least, I did comply. I sat down at the table with her.

She remained silent, making me feel rather uncomfortable. I was looking around the little kitchen. It had a little metal countertop, tiles on the walls and floor, a little refrigerator that made a constant whirring noise and my best friend, the coffee maker. The little table we were sitting at was rectangular and with one side against the wall. Mrs. McHenry was sitting on one end, and I sat across from her on the other. There was room for one more person to sit down and I figured we were waiting for Adam to come and join us, but he didn't. Mrs. McHenry got up and started to make some coffee. I was amazed that she knew where everything was. I didn't know Adam and Mrs. McHenry knew each other that well. But considering the events as of late, I didn't think I knew anything anymore. Mrs. McHenry came back to the table and sat down, whilst stirring her coffee, she looked at me. "You must be having quite a few questions by now, and it's time for me to answer them so please go ahead, ask me anything" I was not prepared for this direct approach, or for a lucid Mrs. McHenry. She had been acting so strange lately. I needed a moment to find my composure again. "How about you just tell me what is going on instead of me asking questions. Once you are done talking, if I still have questions, I'll ask them!" Mrs. McHenry chuckled, "Alright, I'll start telling you my story, but first, tell me, dear, how old do you think I am?" I had no idea what to answer, I thought she was well in her hundreds, but I couldn't say that, what if she was only 89 and just aged really bad? She must have seen my hesitation to answer because she started to laugh "It's not a fair question for I already know you will never guess the correct answer. That's okay, all will become clear once I have told you my story."

"Many moons ago I was like you are now. Ignorant, unknowing but always searching for answers, even without knowing what the questions were. I thrived on solving mysteries as they crossed my path. One day I was approached by an old man, he took me under his wing. He helped me to solve the mysteries with his wisdom. A great friendship arose. All of a sudden, the strangest accidents started to happen around town. People started dying in great numbers and due to the weirdest accidents. I couldn't believe that this town all of a sudden, was struck by a streak of bad luck, and I wanted to investigate the accidents. The old man supported me in my quest to find out why this was happening. I explored every angle, considered every possibility, but I couldn't figure it out, for months I've tried. I investigated every accident site, spoke to every witness, but never did I find anything out of the ordinary. Eventually, I told the old man that I was giving up, I was sure there was more to these accidents, but I had no way to prove this statement. He laughed at me and asked me how badly I would like to solve this mystery. I wanted to solve it more than anything, I dreamt about it at night, and it was occupying my mind during the day. 'That's what I thought, she already told me,' is what he said to me. I had no idea who 'she' was and why she would tell him. I wanted to brush it off as the old man turning senile, but then he handed me a book which, back then, already looked old. I believe you have received the exact same book. It was written in rhyme, and I could make head nor tails of it. I asked the old man to explain what I had read, and he continued to tell me his story as I am now telling you mine.

He solved the mystery for me, my mind was put at ease, knowing that I wasn't just making up mysteries where there were none. The tale he told me, however, has turned me into what I am today but can't be for much longer. You see, dear, I am old not just old, I am ancient. Whatever age you thought when I asked you that question, I am suré you would need to add quite some years. This year I will turn 350 years old." I almost choked on my coffee and started to cough to get it out of my lungs, how old did she say she was? She seems lucid, but I guess she's still crazy as a bat.

"Please, hear me out, child. I lived to be this old because I was like you are, a chosen one. Chosen to be a guardian of this town and its people." "Wait a minute? Are you seriously trying to tell me that you are 350 years old, and you are some kind of guardian protecting this town? Do you get any superpowers? Oh no wait, don't tell me, your superpower is bird magnet and you get to feed pigeons all the time!" Mrs. McHenry shook her head. "Mock me all you like, child, but hear me out and you will understand." Not like I had anything better to do, so I decided to hear her out.

"This town is built on top of another world, the underworld. Right underneath the center of this town, lies a gate, and behind that gate, there is a doorway that leads to another world. This world is made of fire, the air is filled with screams of pain and agony, it's a place demons call home and where evil reigns supreme. This world thrives on misery and always hungers for more. What 'lives' behind the doorway can't wait to get out and spread its evil wings into our world. Destroy all that is, was and could be. They will consume the world as it is and no human, animal, or any kind of soul, will survive. Children will be born into a world of agony, and slowly, we will all cease to exist. The old man wasn't a guardian, he was the keeper of the book, and together with the gatekeeper, he was looking for a new guardian. Every day, he was out on the town square, feeding pigeons. At almost every hour of every day, you could find him there. He was looking for a new guardian, anyone that would pique their interest was worthy of a closer look. I was the lucky one, or an unlucky one depending on your view. He explained to me that the book was written to warn for the danger of opening the gates. If the population count of this town would reach 3000, the monsters below would have a chance to open the gate and pass through the doorway straight into our world. 3000 people would die instantly, 3000 souls to counter the ones that are keeping the gate closed.

Long ago, long before there even was a town here, the gate lied exposed. Sometimes a demon would pass through and wreak havoc on the towns and people nearby. Many wise and strong men ventured forth to investigate what was going on. An ancient incantation was found, it required six people to recite it and 3000 people to sacrifice their lives. They had to be willingly giving up their lives. Seeing the havoc, some of those demons already caused, it was overwhelming to see how many people turned up to give their lives for a brighter future, a demon-free life for their children and grandchildren. 3000 people were chosen, and sh made sure that they were all sacrificed in the exact same wa' She gutted them, from their throat to their groin, removed the intestines because that would give their souls the easiest a fastest way to leave their vessels. By the edge of the pit lead up to the gate, a group of six people, men, and women stood

As soon as the last sacrifice was made, they started chanting something in a foreign language. The 3000 souls made their way to the gate and started to form an eternal, ever-moving, shackle. The only thing that could ever break this chain was an attack, with 3000 souls at exactly the same time. The chanting continued, and the ground closed up. There was no hint of the underworld left. Nothing but a small hole in the center of the town.

At first, a statue was placed over it, and centuries later a fountain was set to mask the hole. The fiery world below remained to shine through the hole, so the illusion of lights was created. Plexiglas buried in the ground around the structure to feed the illusion that they light up the fountain. Sometimes if you look closely at the fountain in the dark, you can see the dancing flames of the underworld." I had to admit that at times I have looked at the fountain in the dark thinking the water could pass or flames, but a fiery underworld? I didn't know what to think it. This story was getting stranger by the second, but in an way, it also started to make sense. I poured Mrs. McHenry myself a fresh cup of coffee while trying to digest all she had so far. I was pretty sure she still had more to say.

Henry took a sip of her coffee. "Thank you, dear, just eeded." She put her cup down and continued. "The old duced me to the current guardian. This guardian was er man, and he appeared to be very ill. If anyone ever t in the grave, it was this man. The grave is what he ut he couldn't pass on. The town needs a guardian, kept alive through all means possible. They a guardian, in essence, is eternal until they decide ardian will only be able to do his or her task if edly believe in their cause, and are willing to

r
d
ıg
ɔy.

fight for it. In the end, we are only human, no human will want to live for all eternity, and we wouldn't be able to cope. For every guardian, there comes a day when they will say, and mean, that they want to give up. From that day on, the search for a new guardian will begin. The guardian will not be able to perish until a new one has been chosen. If the chosen one chooses to not accept the task at hand, the old guardian is left with a choice. Leave things as they are and continue to search for a new guardian or state that the contract has been fulfilled and a new guardian was chosen. In other words, opt to die and leave the town, the world actually, in utter despair.

With their departure, the town is left with an ever-growing population count, and 3000 is a number that will soon be reached. If at that point the earth cracks open to reveal the gate, it's too late. The original incantation was lost centuries ago. Bits and pieces have been recovered through the dreams guardians have had over the years, but it's far from complete or confirmed. The actual demise of a guardian is not pretty. They will suffer until their last moment. See it as retribution for all the pain and suffering their actions have caused others, it also works as a threshold. Knowing how you will eventually die, knowing the pain and suffering involved, is a guarantee that you won't give up being a guardian on a whim or just because you had a bad day. The first task of a new guardian is to watch and fully take in, how the former guardian meets their end. Let me assure you, it's not pretty to look at. The primary task of the guardian is to keep the population count below 3000, by any means possible, and I do mean, any means possible.

With this being a little town in the middle of nowhere, that never was a hard task, but with the earth's population growing, big cities were, and are, built nearby. This makes our little town more attractive for others to move to. Over the years, I have caused buildings to collapse, accidents to happen, got people killed and killed people. The first few times made me feel like a really bad person, and I truly hated myself, but then in the early 1800s the town reached 3000 citizens, the earth started shaking, and the ground started to tear. This is a slow process, it will take at least a day for the pit to be exposed, after that, all is lost. I knew I had 24 hours to get rid of souls, I influenced one of the townspeople to start killing others in the same way the sacrifices were made. These weren't willing sacrifices, however, but the plan worked. A lot of people were murdered in those years, which caused a lot of others to move away. Population count stopped rising, it only lowered for the next decades, even after the killer stopped killing. The town was safe once again. That day, when the earth started shaking, and the ground started tearing, I realized that sacrificing a few for the many, though still feeling bad, was a necessary evil. It was the weight I had to carry on my shoulders. And I have done, for a good portion of almost 350 years."

She let out a long-drawn sigh and continued, "I can't do it anymore, I am tired, so tired, I long for my eternal sleep. Today the choice is yours. You are the one we chose, if you accept, you will become the next guardian of this town, and it will be your task to keep its population low. If you do not accept, however, hell will be unleashed upon the world. I can't be here for another hundred years looking for a new guardian, and you are perfect for the task. We have tested your endurance, your emotions, your understanding, your resilience, and your stamina. You are the one. I had guidance from the old man throughout my guardianship. He will be your guide too." Mrs. McHenry looked at me while she took another sip of her coffee as if she was waiting for me to give her an answer. I had no idea how to respond to this story. I was staring at her in disbelief, I couldn't think of anything to say. The old man would guide me? If he was an old man when she was young, how could he still be around to guide me? This all had to be some joke, none of it made sense. I was getting ready to leave when Adam walked into the kitchen.

Adam sat down with us at the kitchen table. He smiled at me and said, "Quite a story, isn't it? I can imagine it is a lot to take in right now," Wait what? Adam knows about this too? Is this an elaborate prank? If so its timing is far less than perfect. "You must be pulling my leg or something. Our little town built on a gate to another world filled with demons? Mrs. McHenry, our noble guardian, keeping us safe for over hundreds of years, a frail old woman, warding off the demons' tricks for years." As I uttered those words, the lights went out. "I might be old, and I might look frail, but I've got some tricks up my sleeve dear. You asked if you get any superpowers in jest when I started to tell you my story, but in a way, you do. You will gain the power of manipulation. With it, you can manipulate people, animals, and objects to do your bidding. Notice how the lights went off? Look out the window dear, do you see any lights on? I looked outside over the town square. All bars and restaurants were filled with darkness as if it was way past closing time. The only light I saw was the light of the fountain. "So we had a power surge, they happen," Mrs. McHenry shook her head. "That wasn't a power surge, the lights went off because I wanted them to turn off, here, let me turn them on again" Within a second all lights turned on again. I was so lost in my thoughts. Everything rational inside me told me none of this could be real, but I saw this with my own eyes. It could be a coincidence that the lights turned back on at the exact same second she claimed to turn them on again, but that wasn't likely.

"Don't worry kiddo, I'll be here to guide you every step of the way" I looked at Adam in wonder. "I guess she didn't get round to tell you yet, huh? I am the old man in her story. I am the bookkeeper and the one that guides the guardians" I looked at Adam, from head to toe. He didn't look like an old man to me, he couldn't be older than 25, maybe 26. Adam started laughing. "Oh dear, I am sorry to add to the confusion. If you are around for as long as we are, you can't just grow old and stay old. It will seem rather suspicious to the people around you, that are much younger, start dying of old age and you outlive the entire town, time and time again. That's where we meet the gatekeeper. She will transform our looks into someone younger at a time we please. I have always been here, and I've always owned this antique shop from the day it was built. I have retired so many times over the years, only to come back as a new, younger, owner.

I am the one the guardians call if they have questions or need to get at peace with what they had to do. I am here to clear their conscience and lighten their burden. Normally I do have quite a few years to get a new guardian ready for the task at hand, unfortunately, this time, there is haste. Do you know how many citizens this town currently holds?" I looked at Adam, and without even thinking about it, I said "2985" Adam looked pleased with my answer. "That's right, which means only 15 more people are needed to open the gate. Tomorrow afternoon, a bus filled with seniors will arrive at the newly opened retirement home. This bus will hold more than 15 people, 43 are scheduled to arrive. If they make it, we are doomed. We would only have 24 hours to bring the total population below 3000. That bus should not make it to the monastery." I really had no idea how to react. Should I laugh? Cry? Call them crazy? They sure seemed to believe it. What is it they wanted from me? Who and where is this gatekeeper? It felt as if my head was spinning.

Mrs. McHenry got up and poured us some more coffee. "I am sorry dear, that we are flooding you with this information, but you are the only hope. Not only for this town but for this world. I truly hope you will accept the offer to become our next guardian. I can imagine you have a lot of questions, please don't hesitate to ask them," I only had one question that was burning in my mind. I knew she was responsible for the freak accidents, and the killer that was on the prowl. I could have asked her why any of them had to die, but those answers didn't matter, it wouldn't bring any of them back. No, I had a question about someone that could still be saved. "I will give you an answer on becoming the next guardian or not if you give me a truthful and acceptable answer to this one question I have." Both looked at me in anticipation of my question. "Why, Paul?" Mrs. McHenry choked on her coffee. "You figured that out, you'd make a good detective. I went for Paul because he was the easiest to manipulate. It was easy to make him think he had nothing to live for and that his sister would want him to avenge her. Don't worry dear, Paul will be released from the grip of my manipulation as soon as I perish and he will remember none of what he did, you will be the only one who knows that secret, unless you have shared it with your friends already" I hadn't shared it with anyone just yet, I first wanted to be very sure. "I have answered your question, now it's time you answer mine. Will you accept the role of guardian?" Both Adam and Mrs. McHenry were staring at me. What should I do? It's not like they gave me much of choice. If I were to say no, the gates would open, and the world would come to an end. "I accept" As soon as I spoke those words the kitchen window burst open and a white dove flew in, followed by about thirty pigeons. "Allow me to introduce you to the gatekeeper" This was the gatekeeper? A dove? If anything, it made even less sense than before. The pigeons started to fly in a small circle, as the white dove looked at me as if it was inspecting me. After it looked at me from head to toe, it flew to the top of this little whirlwind of pigeons. They started to fly so fast you couldn't make out what they were anymore and when the flying stopped there were no more birds, instead, there was a young woman.

She had long brown hair that reached to her waist and a childlike innocence in her face. She was wearing a long white summer dress. "I am happy you chose to accept" Her voice was light and calming but almost seemed to have an echo. "I am Navina, the keeper of the gate, but without a guardian, I am nothing. I will be the one, that turns you into a guardian, but before I do, I will claim the current guardian." Mrs. McHenry got up from her chair and walked up to Navina. She looked at me and spoke her last words. "Don't worry dear, what you will see happen to me, I deserve, and one day, when you give up, it will happen to you too" She kneeled and closed her eyes. Navina stepped in front of her and started spinning. Navina disappeared, and the pigeons and dove reappeared. If I didn't see this with my own eyes, I would never believe it. The pigeons started to peck away at Mrs. McHenry. They went for her eyes, her nose, and her flesh. She was torn apart bit by bit. It looked horrendous, but she just sat there and let it happen. She didn't even make a sound. It didn't take longer than 5 minutes for there to be nothing left of Mrs. McHenry but some brittle old bones. The whirlwind of pigeons turned back into Navina, and I felt lightheaded, ready to faint. "You can still walk away from it all and decline, but you will doom us all if you do" Navina looked at me waiting for a response. Seeing the end of Mrs. McHenry did leave me shocked, especially knowing that this would be my fate too, if I were to go through with it. I let out a deep sigh. "I gave her my word, she wouldn't have given up if she knew I would still say no. I am going through with this!" Navina smiled, "Come, we need to complete the ceremony."

I followed her into the store. The dining set was lit up with candles. She told me to sit at one end, as she sat down at the other. This was the first time I had ever seen anyone sit at this table. These chairs were every bit as comfortable as they looked. Navina started to chant something in a language I didn't understand. After that, she handed me a small diamond-shaped stone. "Consume this, this is the essence of the guardian, this is what makes you a guardian" Without thinking twice I grabbed the stone from her hand and ate it. I don't know what I expected to happen, maybe lightning to shoot from my eyes, sparkles, and rainbows to cover us, but nothing did. I ate the stone, and nothing happened. "Congratulations, you are now the new guardian, and Adam will be your trusted guide and servant. If you need anything, Adam will make sure you'll get it" And with those words, Navina disappeared. Adam walked up to me and asked if he could get me anything. "A double shot of whiskey and a package of cigarettes!" Adam laughed "Now is not the time to take up smoking and drinking, we have a mission. We have to figure out how to stop that bus" I forgot about that bus. "Adam? How am I supposed to survive? Am I to start a shop as well and pretend to retire from time to time? Where should I live? How do I get money?" Adam gave me a serious look and cleared his throat. "Mrs. McHenry might have seemed cruel in choosing her victims, but she didn't choose them all at random. Take your father for instance, not only did he have quite some money to his name, but he also owned a big mansion, pretty secluded from the rest of the town, not to mention all the antiques he has gathered over the years. If you invest it all wisely you can live there forever" Hmm, take up residence in Dennis' house. Knowing why he died made it a little less creepy, I suppose that's where I had to go and live then. Maybe get in touch with his lawyer to help me maintain the dwelling until I am old enough to go and live there. "Adam? Can we figure out what to do about this bus tomorrow? I really want to go home now, this has been quite a lot to take in for one evening" Adam escorted me to the door. "Of course you can go home now, just be here bright and early tomorrow morning, let's say 9 am?" I told him I'd be back at 9 am the next day and left on my way home. I had spent all afternoon and the better part of the evening at the antique shop. When I got home, Mom was already in bed, I decided to do the same and went to bed. Surprisingly I fell asleep straight away.

When I woke up the next morning, Mom was still asleep. I took a shower and got dressed all the while thinking I wanted some nice fresh hot coffee. When I entered our kitchen, a nice cup of steaming hot coffee was waiting for me at the table. The power of manipulation, hmm, I might like this power. I wrote Mom a note saying that I would be at the antique shop today, helping Adam do inventory. Adam looked worried when I arrived at the antique shop. "They changed their schedule, the bus is already on route" He pointed to a little monitor that showed a bus, images from traffic cams. "It will take about an hour to reach the monastery, we have to figure out how to stop it fast" I looked at the screen, at the bus. What if I would make the bus driver turn around and drive elsewhere? No, that would not be a solution, they would just be driving back again at a later time. I knew what had to be done, I just really didn't want to do it. Adam was thinking of ways too, friendly ways, have the bus break down, make the seniors sick and have them stay in the hospital for a while, but none of those solutions would be permanent. "I know what I have to do" I stood up and stared at the screen for a few moments and then I closed my eyes. I knew what I had to do, but I didn't need to witness it. After I closed my eyes, the bus driver apparently seemed to lose control of his bus, it drove through the guardrail and tumbled down the steep cliff, at the bottom it exploded. A single tear escaped from my eye. I had just killed 44 people with a single thought. A lot of noise emitted from the town square, the monastery had collapsed. Killing it one residence and 2 of its nurses. 47 people dead at my hands. Now I knew what Mrs. McHenry meant when she said she deserved it. I felt awful. I didn't know any of these people, but they were innocent, their only crime was to take up residence in our town. Population count went down to 2982 and still had to be lowered. Adam came up to me and gave me a hug. "I would tell you that it gets easier with time, but it never does, living in a close-knit community means you will always know someone that is affected by your deeds. You did good kiddo, and together we will get through this" I stared at Adam. "So this is my life now, I can kill people with a single thought and tell myself it's all for the greater good, this is who I will be for all eternity, or until I give up" I felt dirty, but not the kind of dirty a shower could fix. This was going to take time to get used to.

At least now, my Mom and Sean would be safe. I would make sure nothing would ever happen to them. Same goes for my friends, nothing bad would ever happen to them as long as I was around. "Paul!" I yelled out. "Where is Paul, and what is going to happen to him now?" Adam answered my question calm as could be. "Paul is back in the psychiatric hospital and will remember nothing of what he did" Lucky bastard, he gets to live a happy, normal life as to where I am to carry this burden. I am supposed to pretend to live a happy, normal life. "There is one thing we haven't told you about." What happened to full disclosure before making a choice? I looked at Adam a bit annoyed and waiting for what was to come. "This isn't the only town that's built on top of a gate, and you aren't the only guardian in the world. In total there are 13 gates and 13 guardians. There are 12 other towns all over the world just like this one." great, 12 other people carrying the same burden. I know my journey as a guardian is just about to start. It is not one to be taken lightly. I will have to overcome many obstacles and make many choices others would condemn me for if they knew, but this is now my path and my burden to bear. I will keep this town safe even if that is at the expense of a few.

I had to write down my story, all of it to keep my mind at ease. If you are reading this now and you live in a town that is about to celebrate a new population milestone, be wary. If a lot of accidents and deaths occur, be very wary. Be on the lookout for a man or a woman at your town's square that seems to always be feeding the pigeons. Try to have a conversation with him or her. Maybe you live on top of a gate as well, without knowing it. But be aware, if you talk to this person you have a chance to end up in my shoes. They might give you the same choice I had gotten. If this is not something you want to consider, don't start a conversation but move out of town. Move away, and convince as many others as possible to do the same. Don't let your town hit that number, for it could release hell on earth. Adam now has two books to keep. He received a copy of this one as well as the one he handed me in the beginning. We are now a few years ahead, and I took up residence in Dennis' house. The room that cost him his life, I had destroyed and turned it into a greenhouse, where I now grow my own vegetables.

Sean is turning into a nice young man, and Mom found love again with uncle Artie. My friends all went to college in different towns, I took up journalism at the college one town over, so I could remain in town. Over the years, a few more buildings collapsed, and some were deemed unsafe to live in which caused quite a few families to leave town. Population count has been reduced to below 2500. 3000 citizens is a number we won't be seeing anytime soon. Even though quite some years have passed since the beginning of this story, I am still relatively new at being a guardian. Adam has been a great help to me, and I still have my weekend "job" at the antique shop. I hope to keep my town safe for all eternity, but if there comes a time that I have to give up, I hope it will be made clear by reading my story. The story of a guardian.

ABOUT THE AUTHOR

I'm just an individual with a rich imagination. I have a fondness of horror and thriller stories. I decided to write this book as a result of a discussion I had with a friend. We were disappointed by the lack of good scary stories and movies these days. They all seem to center around a group of teens that venture into some abandoned place, preferably in the woods. The group always seems to contain a jock a nerd a slut a virgin and one kid of ethnic origin. The ethnic kid dies first, then the jock followed by the slut leaving the nerd and the virgin. Nerd dies next, virgin somehow survives. I wanted to write a different story and I hope I succeeded. Who I am, where I'm from, what I do, has nothing to do with my writing and is in no way, shape, or form an addition to this book.